Diamonds, Diesel & Doom

Mary Seifert

Books by Mary Seifert

Maverick, Movies, & Murder
Rescue, Rogues, & Renegade
Tinsel, Trials, & Traitors
Santa, Snowflakes, & Strychinine
Fishing, Festivities, & Fatalities
Diamonds, Diesel, & Doom

Visit Mary's website and get a free recipe collection!
Scan the QR code

Diamonds, Diesel & Doom

Katie & Maverick Cozy Mysteries, Book 6

Mary Seifert

Secret Staircase Books

Diamonds, Diesel, & Doom
Published by Secret Staircase Books, an imprint of
Columbine Publishing Group, LLC
PO Box 416, Angel Fire, NM 87710

Book layout and design by Secret Staircase Books
Cover images © Cynoclub, Cheeese, Avagyanlovon, Supachai,
Magenta10, Marcel Pelz
First trade paperback edition: August, 2023
First e-book edition: August, 2023
* * *

Publisher's Cataloging-in-Publication Data
Seifert, Mary
Diamonds, Diesel, & Doom / by Mary Seifert.
p. cm.
ISBN 978-1649141460 (paperback)
ISBN 978-1649141477 (e-book)

1. Katie Wilk (Fictitious character). 2. Minnesota—Fiction. 3.
Amateur sleuths—Fiction. 4. Women sleuths—Fiction. 5. Dogs in
fiction. I. Title

Katie & Maverick Cozy Mystery Series : Book 6.
Siefert, Mary, Katie & Maverick cozy mysteries.

BISAC : FICTION / Mystery & Detective.

813/.54

This one's for you, Dad.

Acknowledgements

Although the jeweler in *Diamonds, Diesel & Doom* is nothing like any jeweler I've ever met, this book is written in honor of my dad, John Gehlen, a jeweler for over fifty years, and his jeweler friends Don Jensen, Ray Brink, Richard Inlow, Pat Chappuis, and so many more. Helen Fox is loosely based on my friend Helen Wolf who has known the ins and outs of the jewelry business for decades. This book wouldn't have happened without the help of my fine jeweler friends — salesmen and artisans par excellence: Mike Noonan and Chrissy Forsell from Elmquist Jewelers, and Al Marquardt and Jenny Turek from Marquardt Jewelers. The real Ramona Steinke substituted in my classroom many times and still has a chocolate a day. I had phenomenal help choosing names from Sophie Pederson, Margaret Sullivan, and Lara and Chris Duininck. And a special note of thanks to Dan Merrill, Dave Opsahl, and Randy Baker for answering author electrical questions.

Note, the mistakes made under the guise of artistic license are all mine.

The words were corrected, polished, and ordered correctly with the help of Evy Hatjistilianos, Dennis Okland, Colleen Okland, Lisa Donner, Margaret Sullivan, Michael Gehlen, Deborah Peterson, and the fabulous team of beta readers, Marcia Koopman, Georgia Ryle, and Isobel Tamney.

Stephanie Dewey and Lee Ellison, as always, gave wisdom, guidance, encouragement, and help whenever necessary.

Thank you to my family for your terrific insight, comfort, support, and unconditional love. I couldn't do this without you.

Whoever said that diamonds are a girl's best friend
never had a dog.
—*Anonymous*

ONE

I'd unfolded and reread the letter Maverick found under the Christmas tree skirt so many times in the last few weeks the paper came apart at the creases. Reading through tears, the words blurred again. Maverick closed his big brown doggie eyes and leaned into my hand, begging for a scratch, almost like an apology.

A tear rolled down my cheek. "I don't know what to think anymore," I said.

"Think about what, darlin'." I hadn't heard my dad's footsteps as he padded to the coffee machine and emptied the contents into his mug. He took a noisy slurp, giving me time to swipe the tip of my nose.

"I knew so little about Charles."

"You loved him, Katie, and he loved you. What more

did you need to know?"

"You're quite a romantic, Harry Wilk."

I rubbed the smooth wedding band hanging from the chain around my neck, polishing the calming talisman. We'd only been married seventeen days when Charles died in my arms. His last words were, "Promise me you'll be happy." A year and a half later, my chaotic life had at long last settled into a more satisfying routine and I was getting there.

Dad glanced at his wrist. "Aren't you meeting Dr. Erickson for dinner tonight?"

The clock read four-thirty. I slid my chair from the table, rose, and wrapped my arms around him. "Thanks, Dad."

"Careful." He held his fragrant steaming cup to one side and returned my hug with his free arm, searching my face. "Are you going to tell him?"

I smiled, shrugged my shoulders, and prepared for the onslaught of winter weather.

The temperature had dropped ten degrees in the last hour, and unimpeded by anything on the Minnesota prairie, the wind stretched the tree limbs across the sky. Bundled in my quilted coat, I hustled to the car. All week I'd looked forward to seeing Pete, but I chewed on my lip. He wanted a chance to talk, and we had a lot to discuss.

I parked at the front, studied the façade for a sign of affirmation, and the 'Welcome' sign flashed on. I took a deep breath, marched to the entry, and pushed through the double doors of Santino's, the best Italian dining establishment in town—the only Italian dining establishment in town. It was also the site of our first date almost six months ago.

Pete rose from the bench near the door. "Am I late?"

I asked. His chocolate-colored eyes took my breath away.

"Not at all. I'm glad you're here."

I met Dr. Pete Erickson in the ER when I had my head examined. I'd fallen against a metal sign and my injury wasn't severe, but he'd given me seven stitches. At first, he'd shown interest, but I hadn't been quite ready to invest in a new relationship and had guarded my heart. The busyness of life had taken us in different directions. He'd been accepted into a specialized training program, and I'd begun my teaching career. Now our lives entwined again, and the way my heart pounded looking up at him, the peaceful orderly existence I'd almost achieved might have encountered a slight hitch, but one I embraced.

"I purposely made an early reservation to ensure a quiet dinner before the supper rush, but…" He hesitated. That charming dimple appeared. He straightened the black jacket he wore over his fitted black t-shirt and jeans.

"But …" I prompted and tried to read his face.

"Hey, you two," a voice called. I turned and caught Drew and Jane cruising through the doors, stomping snow from their boots.

Serious talk was off the table tonight.

"Dinner at Santino's is always a great idea, Pete," said Drew. He removed his fogged-up horn-rimmed glasses and his bright blue eyes sparkled. Then he whipped off a Cougar blue-and-gold stocking cap and his staticky hair crackled. Even in high-heeled boots, Jane stood on her tiptoes in order to reach the top of his head and tamp down his short-cropped blond tangle.

Pete stared at his shoes in feigned embarrassment. "You grilled me mercilessly and I gave in to your exceptional interrogation skills." He tipped his head my way. "He has ways to ferret out the most—"

"All I did was ask what you were doing tonight, and you caved." Drew's eyes gleamed with impishness. "Are we interrupting something?" He waggled his eyebrows. "Not that it'll change our plans."

Jane's brown eyes went wide. She drew her puffy white coat around her, and looked ready to bolt, so I threaded my arm through hers and patted my best friend's hand. Mr. Santino steered us through an obstacle course of off-white damask-topped tables of varying sizes, covered with glinting place settings and flickering candles, to a table in the back.

"How's the fellowship going, Pete?" Drew asked, dropping into his chair.

"Susie and I finished the off-site program just in time. The new equipment arrived a week ago and our tech people are setting it up now. We'll be joining the ranks of the outstate hospitals with the capability to connect virtually with providers anywhere. We still have some paperwork to complete our telemedicine credentialing, but then we'll be ready to roll."

A server in black pants and a white tuxedo shirt materialized next to our table and delivered huge menus. He plucked at his black bowtie. "Do you have any questions?"

I relaxed to the sounds of a beautiful solo clarinet drifting from the overhead speakers preceding the unmistakable voice of Pavarotti and held up my hand like a student in my classroom. "Is that Puccini?" The server looked surprised at my query and nodded.

Jane closed her eyes and inhaled the air redolent with garlic, tomatoes, and onions. She squeezed my hand and raised it in triumph. "Katie and I are celebrating the completion of our first semester of teaching tomorrow. What would you recommend?"

Without a pause, the server said, "The Fabulous Feast for Four. It comes with a bottle of cab, Caesar salad, an unending supply of breadsticks, the house special—lasagna, and crème brûlée."

"Pete, you're the expert at this dining establishment." Jane flipped her wavy locks over her shoulder, rested her elbows on the table, and set her chin on the backs of her hands.

"Santino's lasagna is my go-to order and it's the absolute best."

"Fantastic," Jane said, unbuttoning the fuchsia jacket she wore over her jeans. Grateful I wouldn't have to choose one from the considerable list of mouthwatering offerings, I gladly surrendered my menu.

Drew tilted his head and Jane looked puzzled. It took a moment to realize the buzzing I heard was the annoying sound of a mosquito I used for the ring tone of one particular contact. I read the name and paused.

Drew peeked at the screen. "Why's she calling you? You'd think she'd be a little more circumspect." He winced and reached under the table. Rubbing his shin, he turned to Jane. "What was that for?"

She rolled her eyes. I imagined she was looking out for me.

I inhaled and punched the button. "Susie. What's up?"

"Is Pete with you? In one of my less intelligent moments, I purchased a new phone, and his was among the numbers deleted from my contacts."

"Yes, he is."

"My first shift is starting out so well." Sarcasm riddled her sing-song voice. "Can you put me on speaker? I don't want you to misconstrue our conversation."

I punched the button and set my phone on the table

between Pete and me. "You're on, Susie."

"Pete, I picked up a vehicle from the off-campus motor pool just like I was told and it's already out of gas, so I'm filling it up, using my own credit card, and it's taking like a gazillion gallons. I'm going to be late. I don't have contact information for my new supervisor, my phone is almost out of juice, and my charger is in my car. Can you call him for me?"

"No problem," he said. "You're filling it with diesel, right?"

"No." She hesitated. "Why?"

Pete sat up straighter and spoke clearly. "All the hospital SUVs are diesel and if you fill the tank with something else …" His voice rose. "You'll wreck the engine."

"How am I supposed to know that?" she whined.

"There's a label on the fuel tank door and—"

"No, there's not."

"There should be." Pete's brow furrowed. "Can you take a photo and send it?"

He picked up my phone and scrutinized the screen.

"Was I right?" she said. "Am I good to go?"

Pete spoke over the six noisy patrons Mr. Santino seated near the front door. "Can you take a photo of the entire vehicle?" He examined the screen again, zooming in. "Where did you get that SUV?"

Clinking glasses and the raucous voices of the new diners muffled her answer.

"Would you repeat that?" Pete asked.

"I said from the hospital garage." Sirens wailed in the background.

"Susie, that's not a company car."

"What? I can't hear you. A bunch of police cars are flying by. I've got to go." She clicked off and we stared at the silent phone lying on the table.

Jane broke the quiet. "At least you don't have to work with her all the time."

"The nursing supervisor wisely suggested time apart would be beneficial to both of us, and one of her new duties is Outreach ER in Ortonville." When Susie found out she was expecting and couldn't connect with the baby's father, Pete stepped in to marry her. He'd witnessed the difficulties his best friend had growing up in a single parent home and had wanted to help. Susie returned Pete's ring when the baby's father reappeared, and she was no longer Pete's responsibility, but not everyone always understood the dynamic between them, including me.

Pete rubbed the stubble on his chin. "I can't figure out what she's driving. All the hospital vehicles have a big red parking sticker in the windshield, and I didn't see it on this one. I suppose it could be a new addition." He excused himself to place a call to the supervisor and returned to the table as the server delivered our wine.

The waiter poured a small test taste. "I've got this." Jane lifted the glass and peered through the intense garnet liquid. After twirling the contents, she watched the wine drip down the sides of the bowl. Her eyes closed as she inhaled. She took a small taste and her eyes opened as if awakening from a lovely dream. "Seen, swirled, sniffed, and sipped. Delicious. Now savor." The server filled our glasses and disappeared.

Jane looked around and leaned forward. "I want to know about …" she whispered. "… the envelope."

My heart thumped against my chest. I'd shunted the envelope from drawer to drawer in my apartment afraid the contents would conjure up painful memories, but promised Dad I'd open it at Christmas. I almost succeeded in losing it, but Maverick's superior retrieving skills found the envelope before it was tossed out. I was still mulling over what to do with what was inside. My fingers brushed the ring hanging from my neck again.

"Not much to tell really." My knee jostled up and down under the table. Jane laid her hand on it, and I felt her support. "The vet was told to deliver the envelope only if I kept the dog." I sniggered. "Had the vet come a few days earlier, I'd have given Maverick back in a heartbeat. I didn't know how to take care of a dog then, but he certainly took care of me." I sighed.

"What did it say?"

"Even though we'd met only once, Charles' sister considered me family. Charles and I planned to return to England for a formal introduction to the rest of his clan after our honeymoon, but …" My breath caught. "He died before we made it."

In my mind, as if it were yesterday instead of a year and a half ago, I felt the breeze on my face as we pedaled down the bike path and heard my dad yell, "Gun." A bullet creased Dad's brain, and he still suffered some of the effects of his traumatic brain injury.

Charles crashed his bicycle into mine, knocking me off the path, and two bullets struck him. They never found the shooter. I blinked back tears.

"I'm sorry, hon," said Jane, her eyes full of concern. "Let's change the subject."

Pete took my hand, and lightly squeezed my fingers. My heart warmed. Charles would've liked Pete.

"It's okay. I want to talk about it." What could I say? The pleasant recall brought a smile to my lips. "It seems Charles wasn't just a cryptanalyst of the finest order, working for New Scotland Yard. He was an English feudal baron."

"Oooohhh," Jane sang. Until she took a teaching job, Jane had worked for her dad's company, Sapphire Skies, which flew the rich and famous. She'd run in high-class circles and knew the ins and outs of a less provincial life. I hoped she could help me navigate the muddy waters of my new role, if necessary.

I picked up my wine glass, mimicking Jane, and finally took a sip. "The envelope contained the results of a pet DNA test. Maverick is a pure-bred British Labrador retriever, son of Charles' dog, Bonnie Star. It also contained a letter." I lowered the glass and raised my chin. "I'm Lady Katherine Jean now."

TWO

Thankfully I'd swallowed my mouthful of wine, or it would have exploded all over the table accompanying my hoot. "If you could only see your faces."

Before anyone could respond, the front door crashed open, and the short, stout owner, Mr. Santino, hustled to intercept the intruder. A huge man bulldozed through the restaurant and shoved the empty chairs aside as if they were toys. The table of six diners seated near the entrance froze.

"Stop. Please." Mr. Santino attempted to grab the immense forearm. "Sir, you can't just—"

The huge man shrugged off Pete's beloved Italian restauranteur and cleared a path to our table. He loomed over us.

"I'm sorry, Doctor Pete," Mr. Santino said, tugging ineffectively on the canvas shirtsleeve.

The dimple on Pete's face deepened. "It's fine, Romano. I know this man."

"If you're sure." Mr. Santino held up his hands and nodded, backing away.

"Doc, she's got to say yes." The man heaved, sucking mouthfuls of air in a face surrounded by russet-colored curly hair. His hazel eyes blazed.

I leaned back. I'd seen this man only once before and from the stunned look on Jane's face, she didn't know him well either.

The man glanced around our table. "Oh, man." He rubbed his palm over his grizzled face. "Sorry for interrupting. I'm Gregory Teasdale, but everyone calls me Tiny."

Pete held back a grin, maybe because Gregory was anything but tiny, and made introductions.

After tugging his fingers out of the massive grip, Drew sat back, massaging his knuckles. Oblivious, Tiny yanked a chair from a nearby table. It scraped the floor with a loud squeak as he spun it around and plopped into it.

"I've heard about you." Tiny tilted his head and squinted to get a better look at me. His head moved from side to side. He pointed a finger and grinned. "You're the snoopy dog-whisperer."

"You've got that right," Drew said, chortling. "She and Maverick stick their noses in all the wrong places."

"I resent that." I crossed my arms over my chest and blew a wisp of my light brown hair from my face. "Isn't there something about being innocent until proven guilty?" Jane and Pete laughed, ignoring my discomfort.

"Susie talks about you all the time," said Tiny.

I stiffened. Susie Kelton wasn't my biggest fan.

"Haven't you solved a couple murders?"

My chin dropped. Sometimes my curiosity put me in precarious situations and maybe Maverick and I had assisted the police, but I hadn't thought about how we contributed to solving the crimes. I had to admit, he might be right.

Mr. Santino returned, balancing five goblets and a pitcher of ice water. He set them on our table, drawing my attention back to the conversation.

Pete filled the glasses, and I watched a series of emotions drift over Tiny's face.

He drummed his fingers on the tabletop, unzipped his quilted down vest, and fumbled with a pocket in his jeans, hitching his belt to wedge his fingers into the tight space. Out came a forest-green velvet box. Jane and I craned our necks to get a better look at what he cradled in his skillet-sized hands.

"I'm sweating bullets. What if she doesn't want to take me on? I don't know what I'll do." He juggled the box back and forth.

"You've talked about getting married, haven't you? It won't come as a complete surprise," said Pete.

Tiny nodded. He held the box for a moment and lifted the lid. I sucked in a breath.

Jane's eyes popped and her jaw dropped. She shook her head and collected herself. "My goodness. What scintillation. It looks like it's on fire."

"Do you think she'll like it? My grandfather made it, and my grandmother gave it to me before she passed away."

An emerald cut diamond on a narrow gold band glistened from the white satin interior.

Pete leaned in to take a closer look. "Tiny, if she

doesn't, she's—"

"Absolutely stark raving mad," Jane finished. "What girl wouldn't want an heirloom the size of … How big is it?"

Drew fiddled with his blinking hot pink bowtie. "That's not very tactful, Jane."

Tiny smiled. "I don't know if it'll fit." He cleared his throat. "Do you know Susie's size, Doc? I only ask because …"

I used mathematical gymnastics as my go-to coping mechanism. It soothed my nerves and helped me focus. At that moment, my head computed the entire length of Pete and Susie's past engagement as just under two and a half million seconds. Pete had good intentions when he offered to marry her, and they were no longer together, but Susie had used my initial hesitancy to sabotage my fledgling relationship with Pete from the moment we'd met in August. Tiny's welcome return signaled a change for the better. I concentrated on taking a long drink of water.

Tiny drained his glass, stared at it, and rotated it in his hand. "I needed that," he said. The glass came down, caught the edge of the tray, and tipped over in my direction. It shattered into hundreds of tiny pieces and showered me with splinters.

"Oh, man." Tiny cupped his fingers and extended his arm over the table. His hand hovered over the shards, but Pete steered him clear. "I'm so sorry."

Mr. Santino dashed in and carefully brushed the glinting slivers onto a dustpan. "Things happen all the time. Let me move you to another table." We were still ahead of the rush and there were plenty from which to choose.

"That would be great," Pete said. He looked at me and his gorgeous brown eyes went wide. "Katie, hold still."

I slowly glanced down at the glittering bits sprinkled

across the front of my sweater and my gaze locked on the blood pooling around a narrow fragment sticking out of the back of my left hand.

"Oh, man," Tiny said again.

Jane wrapped her fingers in a thick linen napkin and swept the minute pieces from my sweater and pants. She teased a few from the ends of my long hair as well. Pete cradled my elbow and led me to a new chair.

"Romano," Pete said. "I could use a first aid kit."

"Sì, sì." Mr. Santino called over his shoulder and one of the servers disappeared. She returned with a white plastic box emblazoned with a big red plus sign.

Pete opened the case filled with all types and sizes of bandages, bottles, salves, and ointments. He let out a low whistle.

Mr. Santino shrugged and said, "Many types of accidents occur in the kitchen."

Pete lifted a pincer from the case and knelt in front of me. He gave me a curious smile as he took my hand. "This might hurt." He gently teased out the splinter and examined it. It clinked as he dropped it onto a saucer at the edge of the table. He pressed a piece of gauze over the slice. "I'll just brush on the Liquid Skin and—"

I caught sight of Tiny's face turning ashen and he dropped with a thud onto the floor behind Pete.

Jane rushed to his aid. She and Mr. Santino pulled, Drew pushed, and they succeeded in getting Tiny upright. Watching the spectacle, I thankfully missed the sting of the wound glue.

"How are you feeling, Tiny?" said Pete.

"Oh, man," Tiny said a third time, and he shook off what remained of his cloud of wooziness.

"Tiny, I find your limited word choice sorely lacking,"

Drew said.

"Don't do it, Drew," I cautioned, shaking my head.

"You must intumesce your vocabulary."

Jane's tiny but pointy elbow poked Drew, and he faked a grunt. He often annoyed us, replacing any number of respectable words with much larger ones. I'd have to research today's addition.

Tiny cocked his head. "Why?"

Drew rubbed his side. "Why what?"

"Why do I need to expand my already Brobdingnagian vocabulary?" Tiny latched onto the seat from the chair in front of him and hauled himself to standing. "What would you do in the Canadian backcountry during off-peak hunting and fishing hours amid well-intentioned but self-centered, prosperous dendrologist-wannabes?"

"He's got you there, oh sage one. Serves you right," I said, and a snort escaped from Jane. "You have no filter."

Pete assessed Tiny's eyes. "Are you hurt?"

"No. I have the constitution of a …" Tiny looked beyond Pete and gave Drew a sly smile. "… a <u>Perissodactyla</u>."

Drew blinked a few times, and a grin grew across his face. "Just the man I've been looking for. Join us for dinner. I'd love to spar with a fellow logophile."

"Thanks, but I'm going to Donaldson's to have the prongs checked and my ring cleaned and polished. I'd like to give it to her as soon as possible."

"Tiny." Pete looked down at his hands and said quietly, "She wears a size seven."

"Thanks, bro." Tiny sucked in a chest full of air. "Do you think she'll say yes?"

Pete grinned. "I do."

Tiny bounded out of the restaurant looking fifty pounds lighter, and still not very tiny.

"Susie will say yes, won't she?" I asked.

"She's been with Tiny—she's the only one who can get away with calling him Gregory, by the way—on and off since middle-school," said Pete. "Circumstances got in their way, but I think they're finally on the same track. I'm happy for them."

I was happy for them too. I understood how circumstances could get in the way. I took a greedy sip of wine and conjured up good thoughts.

Drew ordered a second bottle and the mood lightened.

The serving dishes emptied amid friendly 'persiflage.' I fondly remembered Drew's first sesquipedalian attempt to score points with Jane at the new teacher orientation. We'd begun the year together, but Drew had been sent on to other, more pressing assignments.

"Flowers or chocolates?" Drew dropped the question without preamble.

"Flowers or chocolates what?" Jane said, batting her eyelashes. "Whatever are you talking about?"

Drew glanced down and fiddled with his tie. When he looked up, his face burned and he stammered, "If you were to select a gift for Valentine's Day, would you choose flowers or chocolates?"

"Flowers can cost a pretty penny and there are more practical gifts that don't wither and die or add inches to an already bulging waistline."

"Let me rephrase. If you had the option, what would you like to receive on February 14th?"

"So you think I have a bulging waistline?"

Drew stammered and turned crimson.

"Jewelry, tools, clothes, or a gift card would be great." One eyebrow rose as she watched him squirm. "But I'd be happy with flowers or chocolates."

Drew exhaled. "Why don't you give me a few ideas?" He hesitated. "Then *if* I decide I want to get you something, I'll have a list and you won't know what it might be."

Jane's eyes grew wide.

I melted at the sight of Pete's dimple, and he added. "You should both make a list, just in case." His phone rang again. He excused himself and stepped away from our table.

Even after filling up on salad, breadsticks, and lasagna, I didn't leave a smidgeon of the creamy dessert in the ramekin.

Jane's spoon clattered in her empty dish. "Well, Lady Katherine. What do you have to say for yourself?"

"Someone's going to have to roll me out of here." I moaned and patted my stomach.

Pete returned to the table with a frown. "That was Susie's supervisor. She still hasn't arrived for her shift and her phone goes to voicemail."

THREE

Light from the streetlamp crept in around my window shade, and I slammed my eyelids shut, hoping for a few more minutes of warm slumber until a warm damp tongue tickled my ear. I peeled my eyes open and giggled, a good way to start the day.

"It's dark-thirty but I guess we'll take our walk now." I pulled on comfortable, warm clothes and my stocking cap with the built-in flashlight. Maverick romped through the wonderland encrusted in three feet of snow, dragging me across the ice rink covering the avenues and streets. I skidded along behind him, trying to keep from landing on my backside.

At the end of our walk, Maverick tugged me through my kitchen door to enticing aromas as my landlady, Ida

Clemashevski, flipped the last steaming lemon-blueberry pancake onto a serving dish. Ida occupied the front half of her Victorian home, and we rented the back. She was the better cook by far and often shared her delicious comestibles with my dad and me.

"I always say, start your day with a good breakfast." Ida waddled across the narrow space and delivered a stack of sausage links on a small plate and a bowl of grapefruit sections to the table. "And it's a big day. You've successfully made it through the entire first semester and they are lucky to have you." Her mischievous green eyes sparkled.

"Ida, you're spoiling Katie," Dad said, sipping from a cup of something hot.

"And I'm loving every minute," I said, spooning a liberal helping of homemade blueberry jelly on top of my pancakes. "What are you up to today, Dad?"

"Shopping for a Valentine's gift for Elizabeth."

My fork stopped on the way to my mouth. "Have you heard from her? How's her new job going?"

Dad shook his head. "I haven't heard from her exactly. She's busy. But I still would like to find something to send her for Valentine's Day. It was the day we met." The wistful look on his face melted my resolve to put Elizabeth out of my mind. She married my dad when I was ten and had treated me as one of her own. "She's earned her dream job. She put her career on hold for me."

"I know, Dad." Her new position required she travel, and after his convalescence, she didn't want to leave Dad alone, so he'd been staying with me. But I'm not at all certain she missed him as much as he missed her.

"Good luck with your quest," I said, and turned my thoughts to more food. "Ida, would you like to join us for dinner?" I scraped the last of the pancake off my plate.

She clamped her hand over her heart. "You're not cooking, are you? You know that never turns out well."

"No." I put on what I considered an insulted face. "Friday is still pizza night."

She let out a breath. "Okay, then."

The clock chimed.

"Thanks for a lovely breakfast, but I've got to get going. Wish me luck!"

* * *

Jane stepped into my classroom before the first bell rang. "Any news about Susie?"

I shook my head while putting the final touches on my prep for the day, listing salutations, assignment pages, and homework answers.

"It's not like her. She probably got lost and checked in late, right?"

"I suppose." I stopped rearranging my papers. "You do think she's all right? I'm not her biggest fan, but the night she guarded Lorelei in the ICU I could've hugged her. Almost."

Jane scrunched up her face. "She's probably fine. Let me know when you hear something."

I spent the rest of the day calming students either anxious about exams or ill-prepared for them and correcting late assignments necessary to finalize semester grades. I even provided a puzzle for students to complete over the weekend if returning second semester: The day before two days after the day before tomorrow is Saturday. What day is it today?

I thought no more about Susie until Jane dropped by for our science club meeting at the end of the day.

"Still no word?" she said.

"No news is good news, right?"

Polar opposites, Lorelei Calder and Carlee Parks-Bluestone rounded the corner of my classroom, whispering and twittering, followed by Galen Tonlenson and Brock Isaacson.

"My DNA results came back. Anyone else get theirs?" The pile of books Lorelei carried thumped onto the table in the commons, and her backpack slid from her shoulders. "When my dad found out we're Italian, he started speaking like Vito Corleone."

"Who's Vito Corleone?" asked Carlee.

"Da Godfadder." Galen's attempt to mimic Marlon Brando fell short, but Carlee slowly nodded her head anyway.

"That was faster than I expected. I haven't checked for mine. Anyone else have results?"

"Not me," said Brock. "But you know Lorelei. She always has to be the first and had her sample turned in before we could work up enough spit to fill the saliva tube."

Lorelei nudged him and he snickered.

"Especially when trying to make weight." Galen patted his flat wrestling stomach.

"The test links to possible relations. Maybe I'll turn out to be royalty." Little did she know—not too far-fetched, I thought. Lorelei lifted her chin, sniffed, and said in a poor British accent, "We are always amused."

"Remember, we talked about safety. Don't ever accept a contact without checking with your parents first. You never know."

"Too right." Carlee's hard voice pierced the room. She knew from firsthand experience online so-called relatives weren't always who they said they were.

The students mumbled. "Safety first." So far, we'd studied blood typing, the characteristics of polymers, the magic of heat, geocaching, DNA testing, and every week one of my students came up with a new idea.

"We found the best next experiment," Carlee said.

"I've got the alligator clips and the cans, but we need a few pieces of PVC, plywood, tubing, Styrofoam cups, and paint. What's our petty cash balance?" Lorelei wound her wavy blond hair in a roll and secured it with a pencil. She pulled her laptop from her backpack and opened it. Squinting, she concentrated on her spreadsheet. Her organizational skills drove some of her friends up a wall, but when it came to logistics, she never let them down.

"I've already gotten the okay to use the tools in the industrial ed shop," Brock said. "As long as Mr. Simonson is in attendance, hovering."

Galen shrugged. "He knows his stuff and he'll make it safe and easy for us to use."

Carlee laid the blueprint flat on a desktop, and we circled around to read the guide and look at the instructions.

"A Kelvin Electrostatic Generator. This is great," I said. "And it doesn't look too difficult. Who found this?"

"I had to return my mom's stack to the library and pick up her reserved books, and while I waited, I thought I'd …" Galen hedged, searching for the right word.

"Be honest. You wanted to play a game." Carlee swung her long black hair away from her face and her steel gray eyes gleamed in a challenge.

"You know me too well," Galen said, chuckling. "Anyway, there was a video clip from a movie I like, on screen and ready to play. It ended with a link and since we'd already talked about experimenting with electricity, I thought it looked cool. This one creates sparks and stuff."

Lorelei handed me a spreadsheet, itemizing the cost of materials, and all eyes turned my way. "I'll check with Mrs. McEntee."

"Just keep using the funds she has available to you," said Jane. "My dad is really into experiments so if we run low, I'm certain he'll subsidize our science club plans. Besides, then he'd have an even better reason to visit me." It'd be nice to have an unlimited source of funds.

"Hey, we're building our own K.E.G." Brock threw back his head and the hank of dark hair flew from his face, revealing a huge grin and impish eyes.

They divvied up the remaining list of required materials and assigned tasks to accomplish. The Kelvin Generator would come together on Monday, a federal holiday, and the day off to the rest of the students.

"Are we still doing a mock trial read through Sunday?" Lorelei said, gathering her jacket and backpack. "I know we've been besting the competition, but we decided we'd feel more confident if we could just take one more look at it."

"Let's meet at one o'clock. It'll take less than an hour, I'm sure." I was proud of the work they'd done. They knew the case and had not only won their trials, but they'd annihilated the competition with their preparedness and intensity.

Jane trudged from the math office with the last student in tow. As I was preparing to leave, our long-term math substitute, Ramona, handed me a small box wrapped in sparkly gold paper.

"What's this for?" I asked.

"I'm good at math, but when my students had any kind of real problem, you always helped. This is a very small token of my appreciation."

"You didn't have to do that."

"Yes, I did. I'm finishing up today."

"What do you mean?"

"I'm off to Florida."

"Oh, no." I'd be the lone female in the department again. I'd miss her bad math jokes, witty comments, and lively camaraderie.

"There haven't been many qualified mid-year applicants, but they've finally been able to hire a full-time teacher, and my husband and I are hightailing it south for eight weeks. He likes his snowbird status, and we won't be back until spring is underway." She packed up her few personal belongings and tossed the strap of her briefcase over her shoulder.

"You will be missed. They'll never be able to replace you."

After several failed attempts to fill the position of a colleague who was fired in the fall, the administration had stumbled upon Ramona Stine, a talented retiree who had a major in communications and a minor in math, and she'd been subbing since October. Her students lucked out and so did I. But she never signed on for a full-time job.

"Go ahead. Open it." She encouraged me with a winding motion.

Inside the box were seven miniature chocolate candy bars. "You're allowed one a day, just like a vitamin," Ramona said. "These'll get you through the first week without me, but you'll be fine. I've met my replacement."

"Have a warm winter," I said, shivering at the thought of our recent brutal below zero temperatures.

The overhead speaker crackled. "Ms. Wilk, please report to Mr. Ganka's office."

"And there's your introduction." She gave me a big hug

and disappeared.

I took jaunty steps down the hall, wondering what the new teacher would be like. We had a great department. My associates loved teaching kids and did everything they could to make the study of mathematics as entertaining and educational as possible. All performed duties beyond teaching: coaching girls' and boys' basketball, tennis, football, swimming, softball, baseball, and volleyball or advising extracurricular activities. I was learning from pros and loving it.

I walked into the main office and Mrs. McEntee, the principal's administrative secretary, smiled broadly, her dark eyes shining bright with insider information. She stood and adjusted her wool plaid skirt. "Mr. Ganka will see you now."

I knocked on his door and a deep voice said, "Enter."

I opened the door a crack and stuck in my head. "You wanted to see me?"

"I did." One eyebrow rose over the grim set of his lips. He glared for a moment but couldn't contain his enthusiasm. His mischievous eyes glanced to his right and alighted on a curvy brunette standing in the corner. "Surprise."

Exotic amber eyes gleamed. Bright red lips smiled around straight white teeth in a perfect, porcelain face. She rushed me, and wrapped me in a huge hug, pinning my arms to my sides.

"My dearest friend, Katie. How I've missed you," she said with the lilt of French noticeable in her throaty alto voice. "You haven't changed a bit. The cat got your tongue, has it? Or has it been so long you don't remember me? No, not that. Isn't it exciting? Working together again." Her fingers clutched my shoulders, and she held me at arm's length, searching my face with her penetrating gaze. "You haven't forgotten your old friend, have you?"

"Hello, Isabelle." Noting her trademark Chloé outfit made me conscious of my efficient pulled-back hair and practical, monochromatic clothing, but I couldn't afford a button on her sleeve. My hand ran through my flyaway hair in a failed attempt to tame it. I threw back my shoulders and elevated my chin, bracing for the inevitable air buss on each cheek.

"Come now. It is ZaZa." Her effervescence lit the room.

Mr. Ganka tented his fingers in front of his face and looked pleased with himself. He slapped his hands on his desktop. "This calls for a celebration. What do you think, Katie? Isn't she a great find? Two marvelous math professionals with credentials from the Royal Holloway in London, teaching at the same high school in outstate Minnesota." His hands rose in delight. "What are the odds of that happening?"

"I'd calculate two million seven hundred ninety-two thousand to one," ZaZa said.

Mr. Ganka let out a guffaw. "You're a hoot, ZaZa. We're going to get along famously." He pushed himself to stand. "Katie, do you have a minute?"

"Certainly. What do you need?"

"Please take ZaZa to the math office and show her around. She's had the official tour, but maybe you can get her set up for Tuesday?" He raised one eyebrow to his flat top and winked.

"She doesn't have to do that," ZaZa said.

"Of course, she does. Don't you, Katie?" His tone brooked no argument.

The school district hit the jackpot with ZaZa. She was

smart as a whip. I knew from personal experience how lucky we were she was here. "Of course."

"If you're sure, let's pop over then, shall we," ZaZa said.

Mrs. McEntee stood on the other side of the door, holding a huge basket filled with an assortment of office supplies, individual bags of snacks, and classroom niceties. "We're so happy you're here," she said and shoved the heavy container into my arms before giving ZaZa a hug.

I realigned my grip and balanced the basket on my hip, realizing I hadn't received a basket of goodies when I'd been hired. It must have been a mid-year-hire gift, a signing bonus.

Mrs. McEntee grabbed ZaZa's elbow and ushered us toward the door. "If you need any help at all, I'm here for you, dear." She patted ZaZa's arm. "And you were afraid Katie might have forgotten you."

We walked toward the math office.

I tried to make my voice carefree. "What made you decide to take a job here?"

"Oh, *ma chérie*." She stopped and put her hand on my arm. "I heard about Charles, and I want to offer my sincerest condolences. I'm so sorry."

Sudden memories slammed into my heart, and everything blurred around me. In the blink of an eye, I recalled the three of us sitting around a table drinking ale at the local pub, scratching solutions onto notebook pages, laughing at a shared joke, hiking the campus, or researching encryptions. I saw the merry twinkle as Charles rolled his eyes at another of ZaZa's antics, and I shook my head.

When I could finally take a breath, I whispered, "Thank you." We continued down the hall. I hesitated because no matter how I posed the question, it sounded intrusive.

"But why are you here?"

"I tired of government work and couldn't think what else my skills would be good for until I remembered *ma bonne amie*, Katie. I followed your career, you know." She looked at me. "You are happy in your work?"

"Yes. I love it."

"That is what I want."

I'd heard those words before. She wanted what I had.

"I'm so glad you haven't forgotten me," ZaZa said.

How could I have forgotten the woman who had wanted to marry Charles?

FOUR

ZaZa played with her phone while I fumbled for the doorknob. Before I could get a good grip on it, the door crashed into me, upending the basket, and the contents scattered everywhere.

Jane's head came around the door and she looked aghast. "Katie!" She bent down, grabbed two bags of pretzels, and caught sight of ZaZa. "Where did you get those Louboutins?" she said, admiring the multicolored patent leather stilettos. She handed me the pretzels and stood. Fortunately, my easy-walking shoes flexed with my maneuvers to retrieve the rest.

"Are you a friend of Katie? I'm ZaZa." Her smile gleamed and she gave Jane a hug. "And I brought my shoes with me from Paris."

"You're French," Jane cooed.

I have to admit, while they exchanged their bubbling babble in a language I couldn't understand, I might have pulverized two or three of the pretzels.

I collected the remaining welcome items and hobbled to standing. The weight shift knocked me to one side, but I wrapped one hand around the handle and opened the door. Jane and ZaZa waltzed through, oblivious to the juggling act I performed in their wake.

Jane switched to English. "You're teaching here? Katie, why didn't you tell me your friend was coming? We'd have planned a welcome party."

"I didn't know."

"We love parties and can still have a meet and greet tomorrow." I should have thought of it. "I'll gather the guests. Six o'clock at your apartment, okay?" I nodded.

"That is so kind of you both. Thank you. Moving to a new place can be difficult."

"Any friend of Katie's is a friend of mine."

I heaved the basket onto the table in the commons. "I thought you were on your way out, Jane. What brought you back?"

Her eyes darkened with concern. "I almost forgot. I came to tell you the police picked up Susie for grand theft auto."

I thought she was kidding and almost laughed, but she was deadly serious. "What happened?"

"The police cars we heard in the background last night were coming for her. Pete was right. The SUV didn't belong to the hospital fleet and had been reported stolen. The vehicle belonged to Liselle Donaldson. Lucky for Susie, Mrs. Donaldson wouldn't let her husband press charges even though he was adamant about the theft. She said the

SUV should never have been parked in the hospital garage, and it was his fault it was borrowed." Jane's fingers ticked air quotes around the word 'borrowed.' "Mr. Donaldson left the keys in the ignition, tempting anyone to take it. She told the arresting officer it was her SUV and if she needed to, she'd say she gave Susie permission to drive it."

"All the way to Ortonville?"

"I think Mrs. Donaldson was angry with her husband and would say anything contrary."

"Is Susie okay?" I asked. "Even I know she wouldn't steal a car."

Jane looked at me and said carefully, "Susie called Tiny who called Pete who explained the situation to Chief West and got her released. It was all a misunderstanding after all, but she could've been in real trouble."

"Oooh," said ZaZa. "Intrigue."

"There's a lot of that around," said Jane.

"And I thought I was moving to a quiet little town."

Jane gave me a wink and said, "I'll put Drew and Pete on wine duty, and I'll bring my famous bean dip. You can ask Ida if she can whip up some of her fabulous finger food. *Au revoir.*" She disappeared out the door, leaving me staring after her.

"What a delightful friend you have. She's been to Paris and speaks fluently. Does she teach French?"

"She's great, all right. And no. Jane teaches history."

I led ZaZa into the office and through the bank of cluttered desks. "This one is yours."

She ran an elegant hand over the top, circled around the desk, and dropped into the comfy, padded, ergonomic chair. Her perfectly manicured nails, sporting bright red polish, tapped the armrests as she rocked. I glanced at my chair and noticed the worn, discolored seat on rickety wheels and had a tiny moment of 'why does she get the nicer chair?'

"The teacher manuals are on the shelf behind you. Supplies should be in the desk. The closet has more textbooks, markers, erasers, and copies of most of the school forms. If you need anything else, talk to Mrs. McEntee. She knows where everything is and helped me get through my first semester."

ZaZa opened the drawers and hummed in satisfaction. She rose and perused the contents of the closet, nodding.

"Let me take you to your classroom. You'll have quite a view." I felt another twinge of jealousy. The teacher she replaced had taught at Columbia High School for his entire career and had earned his spot, complete with all its perks. She would be taking over one of the rooms coveted for its windows to the outside world, one with real sunlight.

I flipped the switch, and the light shined on a bouquet of a dozen yellow roses and baby's breath on top of the teacher's desk. ZaZa glided to the front of the room and extracted a card from the blossoms. A cattier person might've said slithered.

"They're from human resources. It says, 'We're so happy we could find someone to take over in the middle of the year.' How sweet. I'm going to like it here."

The math department door banged open behind us, and I glanced over my shoulder to catch sight of the offending entrant.

"Hey, Miss Wilk, I forgot to ask. Are you coming to our wrestling match tonight? My opponent went to state last year." Galen took long strides across the commons. "I need all the support I can—" He jolted to a stop when he saw ZaZa.

"Galen Tonlenson, meet Ms. Lavigne. She's our new math teacher."

"Pleased to make your acquaintance, Ms. Lavigne," he stammered. "You're going to love it here." He kept his eyes on ZaZa but said to me, "Hope to see you tonight, Ms. Wilk." He turned and fled.

"What a nice young man. Is he a student of yours?"

"No, but when he has time, he participates in the extracurricular activities I supervise."

"Teaching is not enough? What else do you do?"

When I applied to teach at Columbia, in order to sway the hiring balance in my favor, I consented to work with students in after school activities. "I work with the science club and the mock trial team."

"Maybe I can assist?"

The ZaZa I knew never volunteered for anything. My skepticism radar on alert, I said with a chipperness even I thought sounded forced, "It isn't all that much work, and Jane is already helping, but I'm sure there are other opportunities for you. Maybe French club?"

I grabbed my briefcase and puffy blue jacket and escorted her back to the main office where she donned a long camel-hair coat. She hauled her hair from under the collar and shook long dark tresses into perfect waves over her shoulders. I sighed. How on earth had Charles ended up with me?

I zoned out for a moment and didn't track the conversation until Mrs. McEntee said, "She can meet you there, right Katie?"

Wary, I said, "I'm sorry. I was thinking of something else. Where?"

"At the wrestling match tonight. Varsity starts at seven-thirty. Ms. Lavigne, the ticket price is reduced if you use your employee's pass. I'm sure they'll be happy to see you both."

"My cab driver insisted I take his card, but I don't believe he runs in the evening," said ZaZa. "An auto purchase is on my to-do list, but I haven't gotten around to it."

I wondered how she planned on getting to school every day.

Mrs. McEntee said, "There's only one cab in town, and he works seven to seven. We have no other rideshare service yet. Could you give her a ride, Katie?" She glanced at the wall clock. "Time is fleeting. Maybe you should just take her home with you and then on to the match? Would you like that, ZaZa?"

Please say no.

"I would love that," ZaZa said.

"Have a great weekend you two," said Mrs. McEntee.

Zaza followed me down the hall toward the exit, the red soles of her shoes clattering on the terrazzo floor. "I don't think I can make it across the slippery parking lot. Would you mind driving around to pick me up?"

I stomped out to my car, wondering how I could be pleased they hired a qualified mathematician and yet have such uncharitable feelings about ZaZa. When I pulled up to the door, ZaZa sashayed from the nice warm building in the company of Jane.

"Hey, girlfriend." Jane stuck her head in the passenger door. "Drew has some prep work to complete for his next assignment and I don't have anything to do. It's pizza night, right? I'll pick up the pies and meet you at your apartment. We can go to the match together."

Lucky Drew. He'd worked undercover as a psych

instructor last fall until they'd caught the teacher facilitating the sale of drugs in school. As an agent with the Minnesota Bureau of Criminal Apprehension, his assignments took him away from Columbia and, at the moment, I wished I could be with him.

"Good plan," I said as brightly as possible.

After a long quiet drive, I pulled into my garage stall and let ZaZa hang onto my shoulder as we made our way up the sidewalk. "Those aren't very practical winter footwear," I said. "You have boots, don't you?"

"Sadly, Katie, I have come with only a few suitcases. Perhaps you and Jane will be able to help me choose the items I'll need in this tundra."

FIVE

Ida and Dad helped us demolish the three large pizzas, refrigerating the two skimpy leftover slices. Jane invited them to ZaZa's party and talked Ida into making her special seafood dip and a few choice delectables for the meet and greet. Against my better judgement, I allowed ZaZa to feed scraps of cheese to Maverick. He stuck to her side like glue, nuzzling her hand, and she scratched behind his ears.

Et tu, Brute? I gave Maverick the new cue we'd practiced, raising my thumb, pointing my forefinger, and curling my other fingers into my palm. He plopped on his side and played dead—for two seconds. His head popped up, checking for approval, but before I could hand him the treat in my hand, he darted to ZaZa for more mozzarella.

ZaZa enchanted Dad, Ida, and Jane with stories of

London and Paris. I chided myself, sagging at the sink while I washed the dishes.

Of course, gorgeous, intelligent ZaZa made friends easily and that was all there was to that. She couldn't help being who she was. Everyone would embrace her. Even my dog had taken kindly to her, and I didn't need to worry about … My shoulders slumped. Did I worry they'd like her more than they liked me?

I remembered one of the first conversations I had with ZaZa when we met at the campus housing for foreign graduate students. Our mathematical cryptanalyst program provided practical opportunities to study the art of problem solving, and we talked at length about our future contributions to cybersecurity. We'd quizzed each other on all the greats, striking studious poses memorialized in the scarce photos of trailblazers like Wilma Zimmerman Davis, who had her path to teaching sidetracked, captivated by the work of codebreaker Elizebeth Friedman. We reviewed strategies we might implement to become the next irreplaceable member of our respective national security administrations, and ZaZa bet she'd make it to the top. It looked like we each took a different path.

ZaZa had already been in the program for six months and had fallen hard for an Englishman, but he didn't reciprocate her affection. Yet. She was going to act strictly professional and politically correct until such time as she could win him over. Not wanting to spoil her chance at true love, she'd kept the particulars close.

As the slightly more seasoned student, ZaZa took over as one group's leader and I was assigned to Charles' team. He fell for me. But I didn't know he was the man ZaZa had her heart set on until we finished the program. Charles and I had a falling out, and as I packed to return to the States, she told me how relieved she was Charles and I were going our separate ways. But that didn't last long. Charles loved me and followed me home. I loved him too and we married.

I blinked away tears. If ZaZa had been the one to win his heart, would he be alive today?

I exhaled slowly, folding a dishtowel. "We'd better go, or we won't see Galen wrestle."

"Jane bought supper. If you drive, Katie, I'll purchase the admission tickets."

How else was she planning on getting to the school?

"And if you don't mind, Jane, I'd like to sit in front, the easier to see the sights."

"I'll be your tour guide." On our short drive, Jane pointed out more highlights to Columbia than I knew existed.

I let ZaZa and Jane off as close to the front entrance as I could so ZaZa wouldn't slip and fall. I expected by the time I parked the car they'd be ready to hit the stands, but they still stood next to the ticket booth.

"Sorry. All I have are euros." She patted her tan suede hobo handbag, making sure I noticed the YSL insignia at the end of the shoulder strap.

I counted out the necessary bills in exchange for our admission tickets. "Do you need some cash? I don't know where you'll find a currency exchange."

"The banks can communicate. I'll go on Monday."

I shook my head. "Monday's a federal holiday and the banks are closed."

She pursed her lips. "Don't worry. My credit card will get me through."

The rest of her words were drowned out by the crowd's ecstatic roar as the first Columbia Cougar took the mat. We cheered until we were hoarse, yelling along with Galen's groupies: Brock, Lorelei, and Carlee. He won his match. ZaZa read the crowd with an uncanny ability, and she correctly congratulated Carlee on her excellent taste in boyfriends.

Carlee beamed. "I know, right?"

I did, however, notice sparks in Lorelei's eyes when ZaZa tapped Brock's arm and asked, "And in what sport do you participate?"

After the match, Jane, ZaZa, and I opted for one glass of wine at Santino's, and we ran into Tiny and Susie.

"Look," Susie said excitedly, dropping into the extra chair at our table and flashing her left hand. "Isn't it gorgeous? I have the best guy on the planet. Even after I spend a night in the slammer and a long day of work from Hades, he asks me to marry him." She looked at him with adoring eyes and coyly tugged at the end of the chestnut ponytail dangling over her shoulder.

Tiny turned three shades of pink.

"We're officially engaged," she squealed. "I'm telling the world. You're all invited to the wedding." Susie glowed. She stared at ZaZa, and her brow furrowed. "Who are you?"

"This is our new math teacher, ZaZa Lavigne," I said.

"Then you're invited too. I'm so happy, I'd even invite the little green people from Mars."

"And you must come to our party tomorrow night." Those words started a pleasant repartee between ZaZa and Susie who raved about the wonders of Columbia.

I looked closely at the ring. "Tiny, did you trade in your grandmother's ring?" I said softly.

Tiny chuckled. "No. Why?"

I rose from the table. "Can you help me with our order."

Jane looked at me curiously. She followed because the three glasses of wine we'd ordered were already on the table.

"How would you describe your grandmother's ring?"

"I've insured a .97 carat, emerald cut, GH color, VS1." He recited as if it were on a list.

"That specific, huh? I'm no expert, but this stone looks different from the one you showed us last night. This one's icy white but doesn't have the fire we saw." I searched his face. "I'm pretty good with geometric figures too. It looks slightly more square, and I think you should check out the inclusion with some kind of magnification."

His shoulder sagged. "I was afraid of that. It looked a tiny bit different to me, but I asked the jeweler when I picked it up, and he told me that was because he cleaned the diamond, and straightened and polished the band. I guess I'd better go back and talk to them again."

"Bring the appraisal for your grandmother's diamond. Maybe there was a mix-up."

"But what will I say to Susie?"

"Honesty is always the best policy."

"I guess I'll go to Donaldson's tomorrow and—"

"And what?" said Susie brightly, sliding her arm through his.

"Susie." His intake of breath took forever. Jane nodded, encouragingly. "I think I've been fleeced."

We excused ourselves when Susie pulled her arm from Tiny's and asked him to explain.

"Where to?" I said, as we climbed into the car.

"The Monongalia Bed and Breakfast," said ZaZa. "It'll suffice until I can find alternate housing."

"I have three bedrooms," Jane said. "My boyfriend will be busy for the next two weeks and I'd love to have the company while you search for something more suitable. You have to say yes as long as it isn't permanent," she teased.

ZaZa's six massive suitcases filled my trunk and half the rear seat. Jane picked up her car on Maple Street and we caravanned to her apartment. While Jane played ZaZa's guide through the small house, I reached my exercise goal for the week hauling the luggage up the single flight of stairs, thankful she hadn't brought a seventh suitcase filled with appropriate winter footwear.

Jane joined me in the living room, and she held her finger to her lips.

"ZaZa's exhausted, and she's gone down for the night. Poor thing. She said she could sleep for days. Would you like another glass of wine?"

"No, thanks. It's been a long week." The thought of a soft, warm bed pulled a yawn from me. "Would you like to go window shopping tomorrow? If we're to receive gifts of our choosing, we should come up with a few ideas. I scoured the newspaper insert and, so far, picked out a popcorn popper, a shovel, and a pair of thermal snow pants."

"Those don't sound like valentine gifts."

"I've covered different levels of commitment—inside the house, outside the house, on the person."

"I'm thinking we could hint at a sweater, watch, earrings, or necklace—something a bit more personal. I'll pick you up at nine."

As I made my way to the front door, my thoughts wandered to her new roommate who I hoped slept in—late.

My car bounced through the ruts in the driveway at 3141 North Maple Street, and I shook off the feeling of inadequacy I seemed to get when ZaZa was around. I spotted Maverick through the kitchen window as he jumped from my dining table, anxiously awaiting my arrival, and I chuckled. He had room in his heart for everyone. Lucky for him, he was happy to see me, or his sojourn to the tabletop would've required a reprimand.

SIX

Maverick and I took a short walk in the blustery, early morning hour. I squinted against the blinding sunrise glinting off the white, white snow. He usually fought to keep us outside walking as far as possible, but this morning he was more than happy to return home and curl up on his mat in front of the fire Dad had blazing. I sat with him, correcting and recording exam scores, until Jane knocked on the door ten minutes early.

"Do you have time for a cup of coffee?" Dad asked. Before I went away to college, Dad had been the major meal maker in our house, always trying new recipes, inventing scrumptious comestibles that would rival Ida's. After his accident, his charred grilled cheese sandwiches and gelatinous macaroni resembled my feeble attempts at cooking. But he could make a mean cup of joe.

"I'll take one to go, if I may," said Jane, briskly rubbing her hands together. "We've got serious work to do."

He brought out a thermal mug and said, chortling as he poured, "Shopping, right?"

I grabbed my own mug, and we hustled through the icy wind to her forest-green Ford Edge.

"Where to first?" she said, donning a pair of sunglasses fit for a movie star.

"Donaldson's." I sipped my dark brown aromatic liquid.

"I've heard that name three times in the last two days. Didn't Tiny take his grandmother's ring to that store?"

"Yes, and it's also the name of the family who owned the car Susie … borrowed." Goosebumps crawled up my neck.

"Are you sure that's where you want to go? Or do you have an ulterior motive."

I shrugged. "I'm sure the dimensions of the ring Susie showed us last night differed from the ring Tiny showed us at Santino's. I'm curious and want to check it out. Besides, I like Tiny."

"You want to see them hitched."

"That, and I could maybe use a new pair of earrings."

Construction vehicles crowded Main Street, and Jane maneuvered her SUV into one of the few spaces remaining, showing off her prowess, parallel parking in front of a yellow brick building.

We skirted the four-foot-high mound of dirt and ice surrounding a gaping hole fifteen feet deep and stepped next door to Donaldson's.

Susie's jarring voice carried all the way across the shop. "We won't press charges if you return it immediately."

"Oh, boy," I whispered to Jane.

She shook her head.

"I know you stole it," Susie said.

"I assure you, Miss Kelton; we didn't steal anything. You've been misled." The cadaverous-looking man tugged at the hem of his blue jacket, straightening it over his vest. The patch of fuzz above his lip resembled a Giant Leopard Moth caterpillar, and as he twitched his lips, I half expected the rippling splotch to crawl across his face. He ran his fingers lightly over his head, arranging sparse, black hairs into a not-very-successful comb-over.

Susie pulled a page from her satchel and waved it in front of his face. "Mr. Donaldson, this is the appraisal for the ring we gave you Thursday. It doesn't read anything like the description of the stone we got back."

"It's not uncommon for a diamond to get a slightly different grading from alternate sources. That doesn't mean anything. Your ring was a mess. The ultrasonic cleaner takes gemstones to the next level and the realignment and polishing done on the band would have given that antique ring an entirely new look."

Susie's voice rose and she turned a deep shade of red. "Nothing is the same, Mr. Donaldson. We would like to have our ring returned. Wouldn't we, Gregory? It's a family treasure." She opened a small box and said, "This. Is. Not. It. Don't you have a policy about the customer always being right?"

"Until she isn't," he sneered.

Not wanting to appear eavesdropping, I looked down at the jewelry display in front of me and Jane followed suit.

A tall, sturdy woman gave a final swipe on the glass surface and stowed a can of cleaner and a cloth beneath a fingerprint-free case. She tucked a wisp of ash-colored hair behind her ear and adjusted a gold stud earring. "Good morning. I'm Helen. How may I help you?" She attempted to draw attention away from the fractious verbal exchange near the jeweler's bench.

"We're looking for gifts for Valentine's Day," Jane said. "From our boyfriends."

My heart tingled and I sighed. I snuck a glance at Mr. Donaldson. He held a ring up to his loupe, rotating it under the vivid light.

Tiny dwarfed Susie, but he said in a soft voice. "I'm sure there was a mix-up. But I don't think this is the ring I brought in to have cleaned."

"Let me show you what I have," Helen said, in a slightly louder voice, her straight bob sliding in front of her face as she turned and came out from behind the cabinet.

We breezed by the watches and landed in front of a case of precious gems. My eyes locked onto the necklaces in front of me, but my ears tuned to the discussion at the back of the store.

Jane pointed into the case. "Could I see that one?" She sounded like a little girl at Christmas.

Helen pulled out a sapphire pendant on a gold serpentine chain and retrieved a portable mirror. "Would you like to try it on?"

Jane lifted her blond curls and Helen clasped the chain around her neck. Jane shuddered as the cold wind whipped around a man entering through the front door, snaking its way inside, and I pulled my jacket closer. He removed his black fedora, uncovering a head of wavy red hair. He dusted the sleeves of his long leather coat and scuffed his boots across the carpet. He unbuttoned the coat and unleashed a bulging stomach. A salesman popped in from the backroom. Taking long strides to the front, he said,

"May I help you, sir?"

"I'd like to look at engagement rings." The man stepped forward and held out a pudgy hand that didn't quite reach the salesman, as if he was taking stock of what was in front of him.

"I'm William." William reached out and grabbed the offered hand.

A clear angry voice said, "How do I know you haven't switched the rings yourself? This could be payback for being accused of stealing my SUV."

The door opened again with another blast of frigid air, and a tall young woman entered. She made one circuit, looked for assistance, and when it didn't appear, left the way she'd come.

Tiny leaned forward, but before he could say anything, Susie said through gritted teeth, "I didn't steal your wife's crummy SUV and how do I know you didn't steal our diamond to get back at *me*? If you don't return my ring, I can't be held responsible for what I might do."

"So, sue me," the jeweler said, and handed the box back to Susie.

I caught the tail end of Susie's muttering about getting an attorney. "We'll be back." She turned, stormed from the front of the store, and ran right into the customer, jostling him as she skirted by. "Excuse me." She looked up. "Oh. Hi, Lenny." She exited and never noticed us.

Lenny smiled indulgently and shrugged. A photo lapel pin glinted at his collar. He wrapped his fingers around it and took a deep breath.

"Yours?" I asked.

Lenny tipped the photo of a smiling young girl wearing the colors of our local gymnastics club so he could get a better look and smiled wistfully "Maybe one day. She's my girlfriend's daughter." He turned back to William.

The phone rang. "Donaldson's Fine Jewelry and Diamonds. Pat speaking … Oh, it's you." Mr. Donaldson said sweetly, "How's your friend getting along?"

"… Sorry about that. I should have told you. They're issuing new cards which should be here early next week."

"… I'll *bet* you did." He said with saccharine sweetness. "Love you too."

Donaldson dropped the receiver into the cradle and huffed.

He put on a fake smile and meandered to the engagement ring cabinet. "May I be of assistance, William?" He stuck out his hand and Lenny shook it. "Pat Donaldson."

"I've got this, Pat," said William.

"All righty then." Donaldson marched to the workbench, snatched a notebook, and stalked into the back room.

In the ensuing quiet, Helen carefully arranged the contents of the jewelry boxes and lined them up in neat rows. I selected a pair of earrings and a ruby pendant, and Helen recorded them on a notecard. Jane tried on three more necklaces, two bracelets, and Helen noted Jane's contact information and the descriptions of the items she'd chosen with Drew's name written in bold letters across the top. "I'm sorry about that dust up. We usually get very good reviews," she whispered. "Is there anything else I can show you?"

Jane's focus drifted to the engagement ring case where Lenny was busy admiring a countertop full of rings.

As if she could read Jane's mind, Helen beamed. "I can show you my two favorites. It's always fun to look, isn't it?"

Jane returned the smile.

With a stern voice, Donaldson called from the doorway,

"Helen."

She gave us an apologetic look. "I'll be right back."

Donaldson shook a fob dangling on a gold chain at Helen. "This is not the name on the work order," he hissed. "Are you blind? Can't you read? You'll have to redo the engraving during your lunch break. The customer is scheduled to pick it up this afternoon. It's E-N, not O-N."

"Sorry, Pat. One mistake in twenty-two years isn't too bad," she said in a cheerful voice. "It's the first time you weren't here to check my solution—"

"Now it's my fault," he hissed.

"No, of course not. I just meant …" She shrunk a bit. "It won't happen again."

"I'm docking your pay for the screwup."

Donaldson grabbed the ringing phone from the wall. "Donaldson's Fine Jewelry and Diamonds." He listened and shouted, "You busted the water main, and I've got water seeping into my basement. I won't have it. The construction site is a mess. There's no parking and it's tearing into my profits. You need to finish your project this week." He slammed the receiver.

Helen scurried across the store and held a short conversation with her associate. She returned with two gorgeous rings. "Try this on." She tilted her head as she put one on Jane's finger and looked at me. "You too?"

I shook my head and said wistfully. "Not this time." *I'm not ready yet.* I leaned away and reached for the ring around my neck.

When she slid the second ring onto her finger, Jane emitted a delighted sigh. She asked for the carat weight, the color, and the clarity of the marquis cut stone like a seasoned diamond shopper, which she probably was.

"I love this—"

We heard a thunk and turned. Lenny said, "Sorry, it slipped."

The salesman bent down to pick up something from behind the counter.

"I can't decide. I'll come back closer to Valentine's Day. You wrote all the information on the registry, right?" Lenny said, securing his hat and buttoning his coat.

"Yes, and remember to ask for William."

Lenny walked past us and tipped his hat. "Ladies."

Jane removed the ring from her finger, admired it once more, and returned it to Helen. She looked longingly at the engagement ring showcase, watching the salesman align the rings in their proper places.

"Would you like me to write this down with the others?"

Jane took a moment and inhaled. "No, but thank you, Helen. You've been a big help."

Helen tucked the cards in a file. "When you decide, have him come see me."

Helen joined William, straightening the boxes in the display case. William said, "I've got this. You don't need to help."

"It's no bother."

Helen reached for one of the last boxes, stood upright, and stared at it open-mouthed. "There's a ring missing."

Mr. Donaldson muttered from the front, "You imbeciles."

SEVEN

When crawling on our hands and knees proved fruitless, Helen called the police, and Chief West arrived within minutes. Her tone was serious. "Not you two again."

Chief of Police Amanda West had been in Columbia for almost two months, and we'd become well-acquainted, both personally and professionally. Only weeks ago, I assisted with her second case in Columbia.

"Wrong place, wrong time," Jane said with a grin on her face.

"What are you doing here?"

"Drew and Pete wanted us to come up with some ideas for Valentine's gifts, and Helen kindly prepared a list of items for them to look at."

"You're lucky. Helen Fox corroborates your version of events. You couldn't have stolen the diamond."

"Are we free to leave?" Jane said.

"Before you go, do you have any idea what happened, who might have had an opportunity to steal the ring? Did you see anything suspicious?"

Her dark astute eyes jabbed at my certainty. Before I opened my mouth, a fresh-faced officer interrupted us. "Chief? Mr. Donaldson claims there've been only five customers in this morning." He read from an iPad. "Jane Mackey—"

"That's me," said Jane, wagging two fingers.

"Katie Wilk—"

"Present." When nerves got in the way, I guess I acted out. "Sorry."

"That leaves Gregory Teasdale, Susie Kelton, and a guy named Lenny Capsner."

"Kelton was here?" Amanda's eyebrow rose. "We'll have to talk to all three of them. I'll take Susie and Gregory. You find Capsner and get his story."

"And that girl." I said and gazed into questioning eyes.

"What girl?" asked Amanda.

"The tall one. You saw her, Jane. She came in after Mr. Capsner, looked around and left."

Helen heard just enough to add, "That's right, Chief West, but she darted out so quickly I didn't get a look at her."

"Chief." The officer lowered his voice. "It might be nothing. But this guy, William, never checked all the display boxes. Now he thinks he may have put out an empty ring box. They keep extras on hand to display old jewelry brought in by a customer who wants to have a ring redone or maybe trade it in." He leaned closer. "Or this could be the third jewelry heist this week."

Both Jane and I turned our attention to the young officer to see if he might drop more juicy tidbits.

Amanda looked at Jane and me and shook her head. "You two can go now."

We left the store and picked our way around the hump of dirt on the sidewalk out front. "Four more stops," said Jane. I thought we'd finish shopping, but even after the possible theft, Jane had other ideas.

The next three stops were, thankfully, not as thrilling, but she found a cute, pink cashmere sweater and pants set at Bella's Boutique, an abstract art piece for her living room at Studio Nine, and I found an ice chipper to match my shovel at Carlson's Hardware.

Our hunger pangs attacked at noon, and we steered through the Sip and Savor. One of my students greeted us at the window. "And what can I get you ladies? A donut perhaps?"

"The only donuts to pass these lips are homemade by Ida, thank you very much."

After we placed our order, I leaned across the seat. "Do you have to work all weekend, Kindra?"

"Oh no, Patricia and I are going cross country skiing later today and snowmobiling tomorrow. I'm sure glad she's back." Patricia lost her hearing a few years ago and had attended a school for the deaf but hadn't gotten along well there. She recently returned to Columbia and her sister was ecstatic. "Look at me. I'm practicing communicating better." Kindra's hands danced the two sentences in beautiful American Sign Language.

Kindra delivered two white deli bags and two cups. "Two croissant chicken salad sandwiches, vinegar and sea salt chips, and hot chocolates," she announced. "What are you up to today?" Her blue eyes shined with mischievous thoughts.

"Window shopping," said Jane. "And party planning." She glanced at the clock on her dash. "We'd better get a move on. We've got things to do."

The smile on my face froze. I'd forgotten about the party. My heart rate picked up and my palms itched. I took slow breaths, as Jane handed over the cash.

"Keep the change, Kindra."

"Gee, thanks, Ms. Mackey." She signed again.

Jane shifted her vehicle into gear and said, "Have you heard anything about these other jewelry robberies?"

I shook my head. "It hasn't been in the news, and I haven't heard Ida talk about it. She's usually in on everything that happens in Columbia."

"Chief West keeps information close to the vest." Jane put the pedal to the floor, and I latched onto my seatbelt. We careened around the corner, and I tried to keep the terror off my face, but she eyed my white-knuckled grip and said, "I've never been in an accident."

"Jane," I shrieked as we stormed down Maple Street. "That's because everyone sees you coming, and they get out of your way."

It took a beat, but she let loose a howl. "That's a good one. ZaZa and I will be here around five thirty, and …" She felt the top of her head, then banged her hand on the steering wheel and moaned. "I must've left my sunglasses somewhere. They're new designer Dior's from Dad. I don't have time for this now."

"I've got time." She didn't trust my culinary skills, so Jane hadn't given me any assignment. "I can take Maverick out. We'll walk down Main Street and call on the stores we visited to see if they've found them. If they don't want

Maverick to enter, they can surely send someone out with your glasses."

Relief flooded her face. "Thanks."

She slammed on the brakes, and I jumped from the car with my white paper bag in hand. The door had barely closed, and she stomped on the accelerator. As she soared down the street, barking interrupted my fascination. I spun around to see Maverick bounding through the snow and Dad holding the door.

Maverick shortened my lunchtime by inhaling a quarter of the sandwich I left on the table while searching for some carrot sticks, trying to be health conscious.

"Okay. Let's get going, my furry friend."

He ripped the polyester restraint out of my hand and leaped back and forth, just out of reach. I said, "Sit." Twice. When that didn't work, I pulled up our new cue and he flopped onto his side, playing dead long enough for me to curtail his antics. Practice makes perfect. I grasped the leash, and we headed out of the yard.

The snow crunched beneath my boots and although the frightfully cold wind cut through my gloves and froze my fingertips, the brilliant sun brought a smile to my face. Somewhere a neighbor had a fire burning; I caught a whiff of smoke.

We have four distinct seasons in Minnesota. Granted, when in the throes of January, winter seems to last more than half the year and if you blinked you might miss spring, but each season had its defining characteristics. Today checked all the right boxes for a lovely winter day until I remembered the party for ZaZa.

We hastened our pace. Kindra waved as we trotted past the coffee emporium. I came to Bella's Boutique first and punched in the phone number.

"Hi Bella, this is Katie Wilk. Did you happen to find a pair of sunglasses anywhere? Jane lost hers, and Maverick and I are right outside …"

Bella hung up mid-sentence and the pixie-like owner bounded out her front door, billowed her long skirt to the sides, knelt on the cement, and nuzzled Maverick. "Kissie, kissie, Maverick, my pal. Are we having a good walk? Are we?" She scratched that hard-to-reach spot on his lower back, and he moved closer to get as much out of it as he could. She truly loved my dog, probably all animals. When enough cold seeped through her chunky purple sweater, she shivered and stood. Rubbing heat back into her arms, she said, "I'm so glad you stopped by. With the construction, you and Jane have been our only customers all day. It's so boring without my clientele. But, no, I haven't found the errant sunglasses." Her eyes danced in the sunlight. "I do know where you can purchase some new ones."

"I'll tell Jane," I said, chuckling, and headed to Carlson's. They hadn't found the sunglasses in the hardware store either. Our stop at the art gallery proved fruitless even though they allowed me to bring Maverick inside to help look. One of the owners had heard about his great nose and hoped to see it in action.

Although next door to Bella's, Donaldson's had been the last place I wanted to visit, but I was out of options. I stepped over the mound of snow and dirt and skidded to the front of the store. According to the hours posted in the window, someone should be on site. I called the number listed on the webpage, but no one picked up. I knocked on the glass door and hoped Helen would see me so I wouldn't have to speak to anyone else. No one acknowledged my presence. I cupped my mittened hand, shielding my eyes, and peered inside. I hadn't noticed before, but lacy pink and red hearts hung from curling ribbons in the windows, and each bore the words like those found on hard heart candies. I opened the door a crack and was just about to call out when Maverick tore the leash from my hand and bolted through the narrow gap. I took a deep breath and chased him, with a ready apology on my lips.

"Hello?" I didn't hear a sound. "Maverick. Here boy."

Nobody.

I took careful steps through the store toward the back room, and repeated, "Hello. Anybody here?"

I heard a bark and hurried toward the sound, navigating a back room crowded with a cluttered desk and two rolling chairs, a carton of colorful bows, rolls of shiny gold and silver giftwrapping paper, shelves of chemical supplies, a bright lamp hanging over a workbench covered with fine tools, filing cabinets, a refrigerator, and piles of boxes.

Three more yelps wound their way through the passageway at the rear of the storeroom. Maverick's trainer, CJ Bluestone, had taken an inordinate amount of time teaching me to differentiate my dog's varied ability to communicate, and this combination signaled a find. A door at the top of a set of steps hung open. I felt warm, humid air, and my nose crinkled at the tang of something charred. I peered down the dark stairs and whispered, "Maverick?"

A tiny pulse of red illuminated the silhouette of a dog standing in front of a person at the bottom of the stairs. "Maverick."

He barked again. The person turned toward me, and I looked into the ashen face of Susie Kelton. I tramped down the treacherous stairs in the dim light, nearly tumbling, and stared across the expansive room, covered with an inch of water. Between flashes from a flickering white light, I glimpsed tiny bits of paper and a weird yellow-orange fuel can bobbing up and down. An oily residue created an undulating rippling rainbow-like effect on the surface of the water. On the right loomed a six-foot-high metal safe. Storage shelves, filled to capacity, lined the back wall next to an industrial sink, and to the left, crumpled under a workbench, was a body.

Susie held out her arm to block me from entering the basement.

"He needs our help," I said.

"He's beyond help."

Before I could ask what she meant, an angry voice sounded from behind me.

"What are you doing down there? I've called the police. Where's Pat?"

"Maverick." I snapped my fingers. Maverick barked once, turned, and bounded up the steps in front of me. A slow-moving Susie followed.

She staggered through the doorway with heavy footsteps. "Donaldson's dead."

EIGHT

Chief Amanda West took a small notepad and pen from her inside jacket pocket and pulled me aside. "Katie, you're a magnet for disaster." She sighed. "What are you doing here? Again," she said quietly.

"Looking for Jane's sunglasses." Amanda glanced at the shafts of light streaming in the front windows and raised an eyebrow, prompting me to continue. "She left them someplace while we were shopping this morning. You can check. We visited Bella's Boutique and—"

"But what brought you here?"

"I'd already checked the other shops. I stood outside and phoned but no one answered, so I opened the door to call inside but before I could close it, Maverick disappeared through the gap." Maverick raised his head at the sound of his name, looked to Amanda and back to me, then curled up again around my ankles. If only he hadn't raced inside, we'd be home, prepping for ZaZa's party, and I couldn't decide how that made me feel. "It's part of his training when he knows something's amiss." I was going to pay for stretching the truth. CJ would easily determine I momentarily lost control of my dog. His training helped us get this far, but I think we had a long way to go before Maverick and I would be as good a team as CJ and Renegade, and she was only a puppy.

Amanda turned her attention to William. He juggled a pair of large sunglasses, studded with crystals, between his hands. "Are those the glasses you were looking for?"

"I think so. Can I take a photo and send it to Jane?"

"Take the photo, but don't send it yet. William, place the glasses on the counter and tell me where you've been for the last hour or so?"

His fingers fumbled, and the glasses fell from his hand and bounced on the carpet. "Sorry," he said, scooping them up. "I just can't believe he's gone. I-I took my customary lunch break at eleven thirty—"

"It's nearly two o'clock."

"I had errands to run. Unless it's the week before Christmas or Valentine's Day, Saturdays are never busy, and this January is especially slow due to the roadwork." His Adam's apple bobbed up and down. "During the afternoons lately, what with the street all torn up, we're lucky if we see one customer. I checked our neighbors, to see how badly the construction is affecting their bottom lines."

I felt sorry for him until I remembered the last hostile word Donaldson had to say about him. Imbecile.

"Where's Helen?" I asked. Amanda gave me a side

glance. I might have overstepped my bounds, but I liked Helen, and she might have more answers.

William looked out the window. He almost smiled when he said, "She should be here by now. She took her break thirty minutes before me, and I know she had her engraving to redo. Poor Helen." I picked up on the change in his demeanor. He relaxed. It felt like he was happily diverting the spotlight by bringing in a new player.

"Poor Helen? Tell me about that." Amanda turned on the full force of her charm.

"Donaldson and Helen have worked together for years. They played this engraving game. He had the habit of spelling words using a system his wife called Phonic Infographics and required Helen to decipher the correct spelling. Of course, she nearly always verified it with Donaldson before she engraved anything, but this morning, he wasn't available. She made a mess of it and had to correct her mistake before the customer comes in …" He glanced at a fancy watch on his wrist. "In about an hour."

"Do you have an example of a Phonic Infographic?"

"Sure. Imagine all the times words in English sound like they are spelled one of two or three different ways." He scribbled some letters across a white work envelope. "Here. Read this." He handed the envelope to Amanda, and she in turn passed it to me. 'Ghoti.'

"Do you have a guess?"

Amanda tossed out something that sounded like goatee and William shook his head. "That's not even close."

I'd seen the word before, but it took me a moment to pull together my scattered memories. "Fish."

Amanda's eyes went wide, and she gave me a double take. "How is that fish?"

A smile crept across William's face. "Go ahead. Explain it to her."

"The 'gh' is an 'f' sound as in rough," I said. "The 'o' has a short 'i' as in women, and the 'ti' is pronounced 'sh' as in detection."

"That's just weird. And you say he did this all the time, and Helen was given the odious task of deciphering the sounds? For fun?"

"Donaldson thought the irregularities and inconsistencies were funny, and I think Helen liked being the only one who could figure out his strange spelling. She'd always get it correct in the end but every once in a while, he'd give her a really hard time." William looked to me for confirmation. "Today was the first time she'd completed the engraving with a mistake and had to redo the work."

"Do you have another example of a Phonic Infographic?"

William snorted. "Are you kidding? The only reason I remember 'ghoti' is because I've heard it often enough. Helen knows plenty more."

"Can you tell me where Helen might be?"

William shook his head but held up his phone. "Here's her contact info."

Amanda read the display and copied the data. She turned the page on her notebook. "Susie, you must've come here soon after we had our little talk."

Susie's face paled, and I thought she might faint. I grabbed a folding chair and slid it behind her so she could sit. "Thanks," she said. She looked up at Amanda and her eyes flashed rebelliously. "I came to complain about my ring again. I brought indisputable proof Donaldson replaced the stone in the ring Gregory brought in to have cleaned."

She lifted her chin and held up a computer printout. "After I left you this morning, I visited the jewelry store in the mall and had a preliminary appraisal done by a respected competitor. It doesn't list any of the same characteristics as our original appraisal. I know those traits can be subject to interpretation but …" Her eyes took on a pleading look. "Back me up here, Katie. Numbers don't lie." She had me where she wanted me. "The dimensions of the stones are decidedly different, and they are measured with a caliper. There's no ambiguity."

Amanda flipped a page on her notebook. "Why didn't you check Mr. Donaldson? He could've still been alive down there."

"Chief, I'm an ER nurse. I know dead, even from across the room, although if Maverick hadn't stopped me, I might have considered stepping through the water to check. When I took a careful look, I could see his unblinking eyes, and the rictus in the surprised look cemented on his face. If you sniff, you can catch the trace of char. An iridescent sheen floated on top of the water, and I wasn't sure the noxious fumes wouldn't have been lethal to someone going farther into the basement." She lowered her eyes. "And I'm pregnant, and I didn't want to put my baby at risk." She looked up defiantly. "Although it makes the least noise I've ever heard, there's a generator plugging away down there, and with the water, I think he might have been electrocuted."

"And how do you know about generators?"

"The ER has a backup generator we all had to learn how to use in case power goes out—which it has."

The front door blasted open, and Pete blew in on a gust of arctic wind, stomping his boots and removing his gloves and hat. My heart skipped a beat, and a smile inched its way onto my lips, momentarily redirecting my focus away from the tragedy. I frowned when I understood why he'd been summoned.

"Hi, Katie," he said with a nod. He must have been briefed because he didn't look surprised to see me. "Chief, what do you have for me? I have double duty today. I'm in the ER, and it's slow but—" He cocked his head to one side. "Susie?"

Susie waved two fingers. A bit of pink returned to her cheeks.

"Katie, you can send that photo to Jane, but only the photo, and then you three wait here." Maverick barked. "You four wait here. I'll be right back. Follow me, Dr. Erickson."

Our community had benefitted when the mayor appointed Pete as county coroner even if he was the only one who wanted the job. He went at everything he did with the same intensity and thoroughness, whether as an emergency room physician or an avid biker. He thrived on problem solving, and the intellectual pursuits of his second profession provided another dimension to his medical practice. He'd figure out what had happened.

William took a seat behind the workbench.

I didn't want to dislodge Maverick, so I leaned against the showcase and watched for Jane's reply. In the quiet, I discerned more than one analog clock ticking and searched for the annoying offenders. An ornate pendulum swung from a decorative cuckoo clock affixed to one wall at the back of the room and, by the location of the hands, it would be chirping soon. Another oversized disk with visible, moving gears and Roman numerals fit in an alcove behind the watch counter, and across the sales floor, the slim, red second-hand of an industrial clock lurched all the way around the three hundred sixty degrees. The ticking seemed to intensify.

Although I was sure Dad and Ida had everything under control, I wanted to go home and help get ready for the guests. Watching the time pass second by second, I had the urge to pace, but Maverick lay heavily on my feet, staring up at me, his tail thumping a nerve-wracking contrapuntal rhythm.

Jane responded to my text at the same moment the birdsong of the cuckoo clock heralded the return of Amanda and Pete.

Amanda waited until the final coo. "It appears Mr. Donaldson knelt in the water accumulating on the basement floor in order to plug in a piece of equipment on his desk. He was unable to dislodge his hand and a loose connection short-circuited, sending the current through the path of least resistance. We're ruling Mr. Donaldson's death a tragic accident, but there will be an inquiry." She looked directly at William. "The safe is hardwired to the generator, but the other cords hooking up various appliances to the generator have been disconnected. However, a fuel can tipped over during the accident and spilled diesel on top of the water on the floor. There's a distinct odor. It too will need to be cleaned up, but it's safe now."

The door flew open again. The wind whooshed and pitched Helen in with it, carrying boxes and bags piled up to the tip of her nose. She peeked around the top box with a startled look, and set the stack on the nearest counter, aligning the teetering boxes. "Who died?" she said in a lighthearted tone.

"Where've you been?" William said and furrowed his brow.

"Pat sent me out to pick up goodies to celebrate. I

figured out one of his toughest infographics." Her words slowed as she gazed at each of us in turn. Her eyes darted around the room, and she said, "Pat. Pat?" Her voice sounded panicky. "Where's Pat?"

"I'm sorry to inform you Pat Donaldson is dead."

Helen paled. She crumpled in a heap on the floor and tears streaked down her face.

NINE

I sailed into the kitchen, gasping, and all eyes turned to me.

Jane stood with her arms akimbo. "Where've you been? ZaZa and I have been here for a half hour already. Drew took time off for our party, and he's in the living room playing the perfect host."

"Sorry, but you'll never believe what happened," I said, peeling off my cap and jacket and hanging Maverick's leash on the hook by the door. "Susie called Maverick a hero. He stopped her from stepping into the basement. The spilled diesel wouldn't have been as bad as stepping in the water with the electricity running through." I hopped on one foot, trying to remove my boot. "And Helen Fox fell apart when Amanda made the announcement Donaldson was electrocuted."

"Slow down, darlin'," Dad said. "Could you repeat all that?"

I did, in a more chronological order, adding details while I tugged off my other boot. "Power to the store had been intermittent because of downtown construction, and the store alarms were going off at all hours. Donaldson wanted to protect the contents of his safe, so he hooked the alarm up to a generator. However, he also liked to save money, so he did the work himself. He even installed a refrigerator compartment in the safe where he kept his lunch. Helen said he was notoriously punctual, eating at precisely noon every day. Following lunch, he would sit at his jeweler's bench and complete pending work orders. Downtown construction caused a leak, and the businesses are still trying to get rid of all the water accumulating in their basements. Donaldson must have finished his lunch and started work on the orders. The electrician Pete brought in to check the apparatus reported some stripped wires connected with the water on the floor. Amanda is ruling it an accidental death." I took a breath. "Poor man. He tried to plug in one of the machines he needed, and the appliance short-circuited. His hand was crammed in the tight space, and he couldn't get it out of there. The electricity took the path of least resistance, and it ran right through him. Pete said he probably died from either cardiac dysrhythmia or ventricular fibrillation."

Ida stopped fussing with garnishes for her meat and cheese tray. "How awful. What about his dear wife? How's she taking it?"

I blinked. "I don't know. No one mentioned his family."

"There are just the two of them. Liselle Anne is such a sweetheart. I'll have to take her my hotdish." With Ida, it was always the same. She brought comfort food in the form of her baked bean casserole for celebrations, memorials, weddings, divorces, funerals, births, and deaths.

"How do you know Mrs. Donaldson?"

"She is a gifted silversmith and was one of my most talented art students from a lifetime ago."

Jane cleared her throat. "I'm sorry to ask, but did you bring my sunglasses?"

I looked around and smacked my forehead with my palm. "They're still on the counter at the jewelry store. I'm sorry, Jane. But at least they know they belong to you."

Ida placed an artful charcuterie board on the dining table amid plates and bowls of sweets and savories, and I reached out to steal a taste. She tapped the back of my hand and shook her head. "You'd better get changed."

I thought what I had on looked fine but glancing at Jane's form-fitting pantsuit and remembering I'd be in the company of another fashionista, ZaZa, I took Ida's suggestion. I raced up the stairs to find something suitable to up my game.

I didn't have much to choose from, so it didn't take long. By the time I reappeared at the top of the steps, however, more of our guests had arrived.

Drew regaled a small entourage with one of his latest exploits, fiddling with his sparkly yellow bow tie. ZaZa leaned forward in rapt attention. Pete looked long and lean in his customary black ensemble. Damp tendrils curled around his collar. He rested against the wall, listening to the story, watchful. When his dreamy eyes met mine, I almost missed a step. He stood and just before he brought the full force of his glorious dimple to bear, ZaZa laid her hand on his arm, and he bent to hear her.

Jane scurried from person to person, prepared to pour from a bottle of bubbly. Ida's knitting needles clacked rhythmically, and she kept watch for additional guests. Her adjoining door stood open and helped accommodate the number of friends who had come to meet ZaZa.

When my eyes met Dad's, he waved me over. I plopped on the couch next to him. He wrapped his arm around me and kissed the top of my head. "How're you doing, darlin'?"

I leaned into him. I didn't know how I was doing, and he could see it in my face. "Fine, I guess." I looked Dad in the eye. "Did you ever meet Mr. Donaldson?"

"Can't say I have, but I heard he could be a difficult man." He searched my face. "Don't go getting any ideas. Accidents do happen, although you've found yourself involved in your fair share of undesirable situations," he teased.

"Thanks, Dad." I'd come face to face with more than one murderer since I'd begun teaching last fall.

"You've built a rather storied reputation."

Maverick wriggled his way to the doorway. Ida secured her stitches and rose, answering a knock only she and Maverick heard. She returned, escorting Tiny and Susie into the mix. Maverick weaved between them, wagging his tail, nuzzling for a scratch which Tiny gave. Susie hung their coats and dragged Tiny to the food table before making the rounds. A little color had returned to her cheeks. She wasn't showing yet, but she wore a long pastel shirt dress over black leggings, and it seemed pregnancy suited her.

I expected Tiny's plate to be full, but it was Susie who hid behind a mountain of goodies, gobbling the tasty treats as she sat in the chair opposite Dad and me. Tiny sat on the arm of the chair and held his plate close enough for her to pluck a few grapes. In fact, I didn't see Tiny take even a nibble.

"What a day," Susie said between mouthfuls. "I'm starving. I don't think I've ever been this hungry."

Tiny gave an indulgent chuckle. "Well, hon. You're eating for two now."

She slowed for a moment. "I'm so glad you came home." They both glowed. The plateful of apple slices and cheese disappeared as did the Reuben dip and rye crackers. She leaned back in the chair. "The only foods I can't tolerate are sweets," she said as she plucked a piece of creamy fudge off Tiny's plate.

She rubbed her tummy. Tiny shook his head and inhaled two pink macarons.

"Ready to mingle," said Susie, handing over her plate.

Tiny searched right and left, and Ida swooped in as the proper hostess, rescuing the paper plates on her way to answer the door again.

This time she returned with Amanda and Officer Ronnie Christianson, both out of uniform. Jane made a welcome overture and Amanda nabbed a champagne flute before she ever removed her coat. She drained the contents and returned the glass to Jane's tray. She finally handed her coat to Ronnie, and he hung both garments as if they were offensive in some way.

I stood. "Hi, Amanda. Glad you could make it. Long day?"

"That isn't the half of it." She blew a few loose hairs away from her face. "We're thoroughly investigating Mr. Donaldson's death. I want to make sure we check all the boxes."

My brow furrowed of its own accord. I whispered, "Are you thinking someone else may have cut the wires and rigged the switch?"

She pasted on a smile. "Katie, we came to meet your friend."

She had me at a loss for a moment until I realized she meant ZaZa. While I was packing to come home from England, ZaZa had explained the relationship she'd dreamed of with Charles and said she never wanted us to be rivals. ZaZa was my friend. Maybe.

I led Amanda to the circle where ZaZa was holding court, telling stories to the entire assembly. As I waited for a break to introduce them, my phone rang. The screen read Donaldson's Jewelry. It unnerved me enough I tilted the screen to show Amanda. She indicated I take the call where it wasn't so noisy. She accompanied me to the unoccupied kitchen. I put my phone on speaker. "Hello."

"This is William Dix. We met earlier today."

"I know who you are, Mr. Dix." What I thought was, how could I forget? "I'm so sorry for your loss. What can I do for you?"

"I have those sunglasses."

"Thank you. I forgot them after …"

"We open at one tomorrow if you'd like to stop by. I'll have them sitting by the cash register." He hemmed and hawed. "You seem to know that little diva who accused Pat of stealing her diamond."

"Susie Kelton? Yes, I do."

"Can you tell her I'm helping Mrs. Donaldson figure out what might have happened. I assure you her ring was not stolen, but it could have been misfiled. I plan to go through all the work orders. Kelton seems a bit high-strung, but you seem level-headed enough, and she listened to you. Could you bring her to the store tomorrow afternoon?" Before I could say no, Amanda nodded vehemently.

"Of course, I'll ask her. I'm sure she'd like to get everything sorted out as well."

"I'd like to get that problem taken care of before it

causes Mrs. Donaldson any more trouble than she already has."

Amanda mouthed the words, and I repeated, "What trouble does Mrs. Donaldson have?"

"She has to put together a memorial. Not fun under any circumstances, but Pat hasn't been on his best behavior as of late."

If Amanda were surprised by the revelation, I couldn't tell. At her urging, I promised to bring Susie in at one and pick up Jane's sunglasses, and he hung up.

"Amanda, why do you want me to take Susie to the jewelry store?"

"I'd like you to listen to what Mr. Dix has to say to her. He's the one who reported the other supposedly stolen ring." She eyed me carefully. "Susie isn't off the hook yet. We haven't been able to nail down her timeline. She's cautious with what she shares. Maybe she'll let something slip when she's with you."

"She and I haven't always seen eye to eye so it's rare indeed that she'd let her guard down around me." I snickered. "She may not be guilty, you know."

"Would you keep your eyes and ears open? See what you can pick up. I think Susie's hiding something." Amanda massaged her forehead. "Speaking of hiding, we haven't found Lenny Capsner yet."

"Did you ask Susie? I think she knows him."

Amanda tilted her head. "Really. Huh."

I groaned as I remembered another promise for one o'clock. "I have mock trial at one tomorrow. I can't take Susie to Donaldson's."

"Please, Katie. Ask her. Maybe she won't go, but using information about the ring as a lure might give her incentive. It won't take long, and it'll help my investigation.

Something is not quite right. I'll be along after a few minutes. I have one or two more questions for all of them."

I gave an exasperated sigh. It was an odd request. "So, Donaldson's death wasn't an accident."

Before Amanda answered, the kitchen door banged open and Jane and ZaZa fell in laughing. They stopped when they saw my face. "What's wrong, *ma chérie*? You look dreadful."

"It seems I've overcommitted for tomorrow." I plastered a grin on my face. "Jane, I might need you to supervise the students by yourself tomorrow for mock trial practice."

Jane screwed up her face. "I was just going to ask you if you wouldn't mind me skipping to spend the afternoon with Drew. He's only around until three and then he goes back on the road."

"Go right ahead. I'll message the kids and ask if we can meet later, or simply skip rehearsal,"

"Glad we have that settled." Amanda reached out and took ZaZa's hand. "I'm Amanda. You must be Katie's friend. Welcome to Columbia."

"Thank you. I'm going to like it here. Katie and Jane have so many wonderful friends."

"I'm sure you will. And now I'd like another glass of that superior bubbly," Amanda said.

She and Jane headed out of the kitchen, heads bent together, and I turned to follow when ZaZa said, "You are still a bit frazzled."

"I hate to renege on a promise with the kids. They've worked so hard, and I'm sure some of them will have changed work schedules to be available."

She wrapped her forefinger around her chin and looked up to the ceiling for inspiration. Both hands flew into the air as if she'd been struck by an unforeseen revelation, and she gave two thumbs up. "I'll stand in for you." A big grin filled her face. "I would love to work with the students and get to know a few of them before Tuesday."

"Would you? I mean, they just need an adult to unlock the door and be on the premises. They're well prepared and wanted a run through. You have your key, right?"

A puzzled look came over her face. "No, I don't think so."

I grabbed my set, spiraled off the math department key, and handed it to her. "It's a holiday, but different athletic teams are scheduled to practice on and off all day and the building will be open. It shouldn't take me long."

"No problem. What are friends for?" ZaZa pocketed the key and coasted after Jane and Amanda. I exchanged messages with my team members so they would know what to expect.

The kitchen door opened again, and Dad stumbled in. My heart raced. "Dad, are you okay?" I led him to a chair.

"Just a bit dizzy. Don't know what happened for an instant."

"Does anything hurt?" He shook his head. "Are you hungry?"

"How can anyone be hungry here?"

I poured a glass of water and handed it to him. My hands shook more than his.

"I just got light-headed." He downed the entire glass. "I'm fine darlin'. Let's go back to the party," he said, beaming.

"Dad, has this happened before?" His eyes darkened, a sure sign he would try to avoid answering directly. "Dad?"

"I think I'm a little anxious about Elizabeth and the kids, and I'm a little run down, not sleeping too well."

"Let's make an appointment and get you seen by a doctor here. We can get some names from Pete."

"I don't think that's necessary."

"I do." Dad needed to have a primary care physician in Columbia he could call on, and now would be a good time to make the arrangements. He nodded slowly, but the pout indicated his displeasure.

The mood had changed by the time we returned to the living room. Ronnie and Amanda had disappeared. The evening rapidly drew to a close. Drew yawned and frowned as he held ZaZa's coat. Jane hugged Ida, and the three of them fled without a backward glance. The quiet was disheartening.

Pete's dad, Lance Erickson, continued telling a story to my dad as he shoved his arms into the coat Pete held out to him. Pete slid on his black leather jacket and sauntered my way. He put his arm around me and rested his chin on my head for a moment before he said, "Have a good night, Katie."

Tiny and Susie navigated the furniture, picking up glasses, bottles, napkins, and plates. I retrieved a towel and traipsed after them, wiping the surfaces. "You don't need to do that," I said and shook my head at Susie's continued nibbling.

"Susie, William Dix called about Jane's glasses and asked me to give you a message. If you could visit the store tomorrow around one, he'll try to figure out what might have happened to your ring."

"I can't make it," Tiny said." I have a fishing tournament in Mille Lacs, but you should go Susie."

Susie's eyes grew round and misty. "Did they find it?"

"I don't think so, but I'll go with you, and then I can

pick up the sunglasses."

"I know the diamond in the ring Donaldson gave us is not the same stone Tiny had insured. He could make a claim, but we'd rather have his grandma's ring."

We ended up in the kitchen. I glanced at the clock and said, "That was a short night."

"Long week for everyone, I think," said Tiny.

"Gregory, you know it's because of what ZaZa said." Susie scooped what remained of the baked brie onto a piece of toast. It oozed from the crusty bread as she bit down. "She's something else, that one," she said, wiping her lips.

I stopped what I was doing. "What did ZaZa say, Susie?"

Susie nabbed another piece of fudge and popped it in her mouth. Her eyes closed as she chewed and swallowed. When she opened them, she said, "It wasn't so much what she said as how she said it. She fluttered her eyelashes and tittered, kidding, but indicating she was letting you take advantage of her. Again. It came with a positive spin, like she didn't mind doing your work for you, hinting it had happened in the past. She said you pawned off the rehearsal with your students, but there was an undercurrent of 'poor me' in the mix."

"That doesn't sound like ZaZa. You must have heard wrong. ZaZa told me she *wanted* to supervise my students and meet the kids. It was her idea." My head spun. Could I have mixed up our messages?

"I don't think ZaZa is happy unless the world revolves around her." Susie nailed it. Of course, she understood. Any other time, I'd say it sounded like something Susie might have done. I stared at her, and Tiny did the same.

Susie popped a shrimp into her mouth and swiped away the cocktail sauce dripping down her chin before it landed on her shirt. Her eyebrows rose. "What?"

TEN

Susie pounded on the glass door until William finally unlocked it and held it open for her. He raised an eyebrow at Maverick but opened it wider and didn't say a word as he dropped Jane's glasses in my hand and led us to the counter at the rear of the store.

"Did you bring your ring?"

Susie pulled the box from deep within her quilted over-the-shoulder bag. "It's not my ring," she said through clenched teeth. She held it out with some reluctance, and he snatched it from her open palm. William plopped into a chair and wheeled himself behind the work bench, put a loupe to his eye, and turned on a bright lamp. He removed the ring and rotated it in his long fingers. "This looks like the right stone to me. I can't imagine what you hope to accomplish by accusing us of replacing it. Mrs. Donaldson has to take on the business, and you're just going to stir up trouble for her."

Susie squinted, and I could see the ire rising.

A bell dinged, announcing a new arrival, and we all turned. A tall young man strode in. "I need to see Pat. He here?" He wore dirty blue coveralls with the name Ricky embroidered in a fancy scroll over the left front pocket. His heavy Red Wing work boots made a clunking noise as he tromped across the floor.

"What can I do for you?"

"Pat hired me to tune-up his wife's car. He said he'd leave it out front, but I don't see it," he said in a pleasant voice.

"I'm sorry, but you'll have to talk to Mrs. Donaldson."

"Just tell Pat I'm here," he said, his voice rising. He gnawed on his bottom lip.

"Sorry, I can't do that," William said dully, examining Susie's ring. "Pat's dead."

I missed the man's reaction because the door dinged again, and Helen trudged in. Her hair stuck out in all directions, framing her pale face. She rubbed her slate gray eyes and sniffed. The long black coat flopped open over gray wool pants and a bulky sweater. She stopped in the middle of the store, eyeing something over my shoulder. I followed her gaze to the industrial clock on the wall. I'd already missed ten minutes of the mock trial run-through.

"Helen, Pat's wife is coming in today to take over the operation," William said.

"If Mrs. Donaldson's coming here, I'm going to wait for her too," said the young man. He removed a grimy STP cap and loosened a nest of light brown curls down his back, and upon closer inspection, I determined Ricky wasn't a Richard.

Surprised by another voice in the room, Helen looked up, her brows knitted in puzzlement. "Fredericka, what are you doing here?"

"Helen," William said, a little patronizingly, "Lock the door. We can't have customers traipsing around in here while we're trying to organize for reopening. I want to make this as easy for Liselle, Mrs. Donaldson, as we can. We'll have to help her out. She hasn't worked anywhere since she married Pat."

Ricky scratched her brow and muttered. "I ain't leaving 'til I pick up that car." She slid her boots back and forth in an arc across the carpet. "The job's already paid for." She lifted a grimy thumb to her lips and examined her hand. She lowered it to her side, keeping her distance from the sparkling cases, and stuffed her hand into her pocket. Out came a cell phone.

Susie cocked her head. "Aren't you the manager of the hospital carpool?"

"Who wants to know?" Ricky swiped through something on her phone.

"You were supposed to take care of Mrs. Donaldson's car on Thursday, right?" Ricky looked at Susie suspiciously, as if she had a magic power. "I happened to be the one to find it."

"And you stole it." Ricky gritted her teeth. She dusted the cap against her thigh and fitted it over her curls, yanking it down on her head.

"At least part of the mystery is solved," Susie said.

William returned Susie's ring and shook his head. "I don't know what you expect, but you can talk to the boss when she gets here." He headed toward the storeroom.

Susie turned blazing eyes to me. "I thought you said he

was trying to help me find my ring."

"That's what he told me."

William called out from the back room. "What do you think we do about the caution tape, Helen? Can we get the merchandise out of the safe?"

The cuckoo clock struck the quarter hour and peeped. *Where was Amanda?*

"What do I do now, Helen?" Susie asked.

"I don't know how it will be processed with Pat gone, but you could turn in an insurance claim."

"That's just it. It's not that the money isn't important, but it's a family heirloom, and I'd rather have the ring." Susie squinted. "Or are you afraid you'll find more problems than you bargained for."

Ricky's phone fell to the floor with a thud and bounced out of her reach. She bent to retrieve it.

The clock read one twenty. Unable to think of a way to hurry Susie along, I sighed.

"I guess we'll wait for Mrs. Donaldson too," said Susie. *Oh great.*

Ten minutes later, the door opened, and a tall woman wearing sunglasses and bundled in a long black fur coat strode in, gawking behind the showcases. "Where's William?"

"William," Helen called. "Liselle is here."

Rolling wheels bumped over the tile in the back room and stopped with a small collision. William grunted. Maverick raised his head, looked at the woman, and rose to all four. He stretched with his paws forward, rocked back, a true downward facing dog, and stood tall, wagging his tail expectantly. I thought her frown would be followed by a reprimand, but her face softened, and she removed her sunglasses. Even though gray bags encircled her shiny eyes, her high cheek bones and long neck gave her a regal bearing. "Good doggie. Is she yours?"

"He. And yes, Maverick's mine."

"You found Patrick?" She reached out. "May I?" I didn't have time to nod. Maverick moved in close. She let him sniff her hand before she scratched behind his ears. Her Nordic blue eyes glistened. "I'm so grateful. I don't know what I would have done if I'd have been the one to find him." Her voice hitched. "I'm Liselle Donaldson."

"Katie Wilk."

"Are you being helped?" Her perplexed eyes looked from me to Susie.

Susie stepped forward at the same moment William made his appearance and an awkward silence ensued. Finally, she glared at him, turned to Mrs. Donaldson, and said, "Katie's here with me. I'm Susie Kelton and I'm here to lodge a complaint."

Mrs. Donaldson inhaled and lifted her chin. Her eyes shifted from Susie to me. "Let me hang my coat." William followed her into the backroom, and their voices rumbled with quiet words.

Mrs. Donaldson returned without William. She tugged on the jacket of her three-piece winter-white suit and straightened the bow on her emerald-green blouse. The color matched the large stone nestled among a circle of diamonds glimmering on her right hand. Emeralds also winked from her lobes as she tucked her curly blond hair behind her ears. With her perfect makeup and stylish attire, she was a walking billboard.

I cleared my throat. "Mrs. Donaldson, we're sorry for your loss. If you'd prefer, we'd be happy to postpone our conversation until a later time." Susie's disbelieving eyes widened at the mere suggestion we wait to find her ring.

"Thank you. But if Donaldson's is going to survive, we have to be open for customers because it's so near Valentine's Day, one of our biggest sales times of the year. And I know Patrick would have wanted the store to be successful. But I also need to get back on the job. I've been away for too long." She gazed out the window. "Working here was my first and only job. I've missed it." Her eyes lost focus until she shook off her nostalgia and looked at Susie. "What can I help you with?"

The door dinged, prompting William to reappear and mutter, "Grand Central Station." In contrast to Mrs. Donaldson's desire to make use of the time for jewelry sales, his words sounded like a protest to the intrusions.

ELEVEN

"hief West. Officer Rodgers. What brings you out on this brutally cold afternoon? Shopping for that special someone perhaps?" William said, with a little too much jolly in his tone.

Amanda acknowledged me, and her left eyebrow rose. When she saw Ricky, she tilted her head, and when she registered Susie's presence, her head fell back. I heard her neck crack from across the room, and I cringed. Amanda eased her shoulders up, rolled them one at a time, and said, "I have a few questions, and Mrs. Donaldson agreed to meet me here."

Mrs. Donaldson stepped closer to Susie. "We'll pursue your complaint with as much rigor as possible. Patrick Donaldson believed in good customer service." She turned to Amanda. "Now, what can I do for you, Chief? I'm not very conversant in the day-to-day workings of the business, but Helen has been here since Patrick opened, and William was his right-hand man. We'll try to help you."

Amanda took a long look at the new owner. "Again, my condolences."

"Thank you. He was …" She searched for the next words. "… quite an entrepreneur. He will be missed."

"How's business?" Amanda said casually, perusing the showcases.

Liselle glanced at William who rhapsodized about how well they were doing, but Helen seemed to temper his enthusiasm. "I do the books. We're holding our own, but we really need these next few weeks to be successful. I hope we can get everything on an even keel, with the construction, and, of course …" Her words caught in her throat. "The loss of Mr. Donaldson."

"Mrs. Donaldson—"

"Please call me Liselle."

"We've been told Mr. Donaldson liked to do things for himself."

"He sometimes had a misplaced sense of frugality," Helen said, deferentially.

William snorted. "Be honest. He was cheap. He wore his shoes until the soles had holes."

"We've been investigating your husband's death as accidental. Wires, electricity, and water don't mix, and this time they lined up like the perfect storm. There was nothing he could have done once his hand got wedged in next to the outlet."

"That can't be right," Helen said. "The outlet is in a very difficult to reach space so the equipment always, and the operative word here is *always*, remained plugged in.

If Pat ever needed to do anything, he flipped the power switch off for the outlets on that wall."

"Good to know. At any rate, we now have reason to believe his death may have come at the hands of another."

I swallowed hard, and Susie's respiration rate increased. Liselle's brow furrowed so slowly I watched the words coalesce into a message that made sense to her. "Someone killed him. Who? Why?"

"I wondered," said Helen. "He was so careful with electricity."

"Anal," William said, and, noticing the strange looks on our faces, amended, "In a good way."

"The insulation around the wire on the floor touching the water had been scraped away rather than worn away as we initially thought. In addition, we found the heating element and the entire length of wire in question, which we thought might have been tampered with accidentally by a do-it-yourselfer, had been wiped clean, as well as that power switch. When the line went hot, he didn't have a chance. We examined the rest of the basement, and it's inundated with prints and that, in turn, leads us to believe Donaldson might not have done this to himself." She searched our faces.

"We expect to find prints belonging to Mr. and Mrs. Donaldson, Ms. Fox, and Mr. Dix. We'd like to take your prints to narrow the field of possibilities." Liselle slowly nodded. As if on cue, Officer Rodgers opened a black leather case and removed a scanner. He took Liselle's limp hand and applied her fingertips to the screen, then waited for Helen and William. "Susie and Katie, we'd like to have your prints as well. You were both in the basement."

Amanda turned to Ricky. "Ricky Lattimore, correct? You've been to the store before?" She almost nodded.

"Do you have any objections to giving us your prints?" She blinked and held out her hand. When Officer Rodgers finished, Amanda continued with her questions. "We're hoping one of you can help us. What do any of you know about Lenny Capsner?"

Liselle's eyes shifted back and forth, hunting for an answer. "I recognize the name. Why? What does he have to do with any of this?"

"We've discovered he visited the other jewelry stores in town, and after those visits, a piece of jewelry was missing."

"He was in here yesterday looking at engagement rings. He might have taken one of ours," said William.

"The ring you can't quite describe?"

Big red circles appeared on his cheeks, and he cleared his throat. "Do you suspect him of killing Pat?"

Susie looked at her boots. "He wouldn't do that."

"What can you tell us about Capsner, Ms. Kelton?"

"I knew him a long time ago. I just don't think he has the chutzpah to kill anyone."

"We haven't been able to find him, so he remains a person of interest. We need to talk to him. Do you know where he is?" Susie shook her head. Amanda continued as if William hadn't asked an important question. "May I go on?"

"Yes," said Liselle. "But before I forget, I want to ask if we are able to remove the caution tape. We have inventory in the safe."

"I'll get it out of your way before I leave. Is there somewhere we can talk with a little privacy?"

Susie and I headed to the door, and Amanda said, "I'd like a few words with you too, Ms. Kelton. Could you wait a bit?"

We stopped next to the necklace case. If all had gone

well with the students and ZaZa, enough time had passed the students would've finished, and I'd missed the entire mock trial practice.

Liselle led Amanda into the back room. Amanda pulled the pocket door closed, and, although it was much quieter, I could still make out some of the words. I tried to block out the voices, but I clearly heard Amanda ask, "Mrs. Donaldson, Liselle, were you and your husband having marital problems?"

Liselle gasped. Maverick responded with a bark. I ignored the rest of their conversation and concentrated on rubbing his tummy. I found three treats in my jacket pocket, and I used them to practice the 'play dead' cue. I checked to see if anyone caught how spectacularly Maverick responded, but all eyes were otherwise engaged.

Liselle's voice rose. "I can't tell you exactly where I was yesterday around noon. I wasn't paying attention. I didn't know I'd be required to remember." She sniffed. "I loved my husband. I wouldn't hurt him."

The green color creeping up Susie's face didn't look good, so I grabbed a chair from behind the counter, and, under William's eagle-eyes, I rolled it closer to her. "Sit." She sat, and so did Maverick. I was getting better at giving cues.

Amanda and Liselle stepped from the storeroom, and Amanda re-slotted the door.

"We're just doing our due diligence, Mrs. Donaldson. If you remember anything, here's my card."

William moved next to Liselle. "We have to tell her." He squeezed her shoulder, and she winced. Liselle reached up to touch his fingers. "We were together for almost a full ninety minutes yesterday around noon until I returned and found these two." He jabbed a long finger at Susie and me.

"They were hiding in the basement."

The stones in the bulky gold ring on his pointer finger splashed like white lightning and distracted me. I almost didn't catch the accusatory tone in his voice.

Amanda lowered her chin and glared at William. "You said you were running errands. Why change your story?"

"You didn't ask what those specific errands were, and I didn't offer. But you can't attack Liselle like this. We were together the whole time."

"Liselle?" She snuffled and nodded. "What were you doing those ninety minutes?"

Liselle turned to William, and he said, "Looking for an appropriate Valentine's gift for Pat."

"Did you find one?"

William's arm dropped away. "We got a few ideas but hadn't decided on anything, and after the church bell chimed one thirty, I didn't think I had enough time to wait around for a salesclerk."

Amanda scribbled some notes and turned. "Ricky, you reported the theft of Donaldson's SUV from the hospital carpool. What business do you have here today?"

"Mr. Donaldson hired me to do a job. Tuning up the SUV."

"How well did you know him?"

"I didn't know him."

Susie took a breath and cleared her throat. I put my hand on her arm, willing her to keep quiet and let the hospital carpool manager tell her story.

"I was hired to change the oil and tune-up his wife's car that *she* took on Thursday night." She glared at Susie, and Susie swallowed hard. "But I didn't know anything about his death. I can give the money back," she said, without much conviction.

"My car? Patrick was always thinking of me." Liselle teared up. "He followed a regular maintenance schedule. Can you take my SUV now? I'd hate to mess up the timeline."

"Sure, but I won't get to it today. You got transportation?"

"I'll get her home." William pointed at himself.

Liselle dug in her purse and fished out a set of keys. She unhooked a black-and-silver fob and handed it to Ricky who pocketed it.

"Okay if I go now?"

Amanda handed her a card and gave her the go ahead. Ricky glanced over her shoulder and headed out the door.

Amanda took a deep breath. "Ms. Kelton, can you and Ms. Wilk join me while I remove the caution tape from the top of the stairs."

Susie slogged into the backroom where we watched and waited. As she spooled the yellow barrier, Amanda said, "Susie, you also visited the jewelry stores that are claiming to be robbed."

Susie transferred her weight from one foot to the other. I didn't want to stare, but I had to see what was written on her face.

"I never looked at any jewelry. I wanted to find evidence Gregory had been swindled. The first jeweler couldn't complete even a rudimentary appraisal in the time I had available." She lifted her chin, defiantly. "But when I approached the owner of Sam's Stones in the mall, he said he'd do what he could. There seemed to be no love lost between them. He said it served Donaldson right for trying to cheat his customers and besmirch the honest, hardworking jewelers of Columbia."

"Between the time we talked, and when you found the body, you were searching for someone to appraise the ring in your possession."

Susie stammered. "I-I told you. Gregory and I had brunch—it seems I'm always hungry—and he dropped me at home. I picked up my car and drove to the two jewelry stores. The first guy blew me off—'no time,' he said—but Sam took the ring and told me to return in an hour. I did some window shopping, picked up the paperwork, and came here. I called out, and when no one answered I followed a weird noise to the top of the basement stairs. Halfway down I smelled diesel fuel." Her voice reached a higher pitch, and she sped up her words. "That's when Katie's dog rushed in front of me, blocking my path. Without him …" She sniffed and looked at Maverick appreciatively. "I could have met the same fate as Donaldson."

Despite the seriousness of Donaldson's death, my cheeks hurt, keeping my pride in check.

"Did anyone see you at the mall?"

"I don't know. I didn't know I'd need an alibi." Her voice cracked on the word alibi, and she blinked rapidly.

"Susie, please don't leave town."

"I have my shifts at the ER in Ortonville."

"Call the station and let someone know how they can contact you." Amanda stood very tall. Her intense dark eyes searched Susie's face. "It's important."

Susie seemed to shrink. She bowed her head, and her shoulders fell forward. "Do I need an attorney?"

Amanda took a breath and said softly, "It wouldn't hurt."

TWELVE

Susie stared out the passenger window for the entire ride home and didn't say a word until I put the car in park. "What am I going to do?" Her eyes met mine. "Katie, can you …" Her words stopped in midsentence. She slipped out of the car and slammed the door.

I watched her jog up the steps. Her shoulders quaked, and I thought she might be crying. I waited until she closed the front door before edging away from the curb.

I dropped off Maverick and drove the quiet streets to school, hoping to catch my students and find out how they fared with ZaZa at practice.

I found the last parking space in the high school lot and hopped out of my car. As I neared the building, the gym doors opened with foot traffic from varied athletic practices. I walked briskly through the halls and rounded the corner to the math department, jolting to a stop when Lorelei jumped to her feet.

"What took you so long?" she said, with the hint of impatience.

"My little chore was more involved than expected. I'm sorry. Where is everyone?"

"We finished fifteen minutes ago." She rubbed the back of her neck. "You won't miss any more practices, will you? I'm not sure your friend knows what she's doing."

A little laugh escaped. "No, but you do. All you needed was an adult to supervise. She got you in the room without a problem, right?"

Lorelei scuffed the carpet with her boot. "I don't want her to help us again. She gets on my nerves."

"I remember when *I* got on your nerves."

"It's not the same." She folded her arms across her chest. Her intelligent eyes pleaded, but I couldn't read her mind.

"I'll try not to miss any more rehearsals. We have a short but busy week coming up—our experiment in electricity tomorrow and a mock trial meet on Thursday. Ms. Lavigne is new and trying to find her way. She'll be getting accustomed to her school schedule, so she won't have any time for us. Ms. Mackey is free for the next two weeks, and we won't need additional help." I watched her eyes darken. "Did something happen?"

"She's too …"

I smiled and filled in the blank. "Smart? French? Stylish? Beautiful?" Hopeful she wasn't perfect, I said, "Cocky?"

"Untrustworthy."

My eyebrows jumped to my hairline. That was not the word I anticipated.

"Lorelei?"

"I can't put my finger on it, but I don't like her, and I thought I should tell you how I felt."

"I appreciate your honesty." How could I tell my student I was beginning to feel the same way. "That wasn't so hard, was it?"

She plastered a smile on her face. "My mom says I'm overly sensitive, so thanks for not belittling my feelings. See you tomorrow."

She bounded out of sight before I could respond.

I jiggled the door to the math office. It remained locked, so I made my way back through the school, peeking into the gym to catch a glimpse of the action. Wiry, sequin-clad, elementary-sized athletes from various city clubs leapt and soared and bounced and flipped and balanced on bars and mats and beams and vaults all over the gym. Fans filled the stands, quietly watching the amazing, completed skills and lightly applauding the posted scores.

I scanned the bleachers, searching for a familiar face, and on the topmost corner bench, closest to the exit, wearing his black leather coat and a fedora, sat Lenny Capsner. I reached for my phone, but before I connected with Amanda, he stood. Afraid I'd lose him, I rushed around the mezzanine, whispering into my phone, "Pick up, pick up." Amanda answered as I reached the far side of the gym.

"He was just here."

"Katie, who was just where?"

"I just saw Capsner at the gymnastics meet at the high school, but I lost him. I think he was watching his girlfriend's daughter."

"What girlfriend?" I took a breath to give her the scoop, but she continued. "Never mind. I'll send Ronnie. Katie, be careful. We don't know that he didn't kill Donaldson."

"He might already be gone." I pocketed my phone and wandered among the supporters and athletes who navigated the entry hall and the atrium. I searched the faces of the gymnastics fans who passed the registration desk and lined the concession stand, but no Lenny Capsner.

I sauntered back into the gym and found him reseated, intently focused on a serious, tiny red head with a smattering of freckles across her pug nose. Dressed in a sparkly gold leotard, she flipped and spun on the balance beam. She stuck her landing and raised her arms straight above her head, and he jumped to his feet, clapping, whistling, hollering, and waving his hat. When he caught her eye, her resolute expression melted like wax and an effervescent smile beamed. She waved and ran into a pack of similar bundles of energy herded by a tall blond woman to a corner across the gym.

He smashed his hat back on his head, and his eyes grew round as he tuned into the whine of the siren increasing in volume at the same moment he saw me. He bolted, and I gave chase. With so many big and little people going in every direction, I felt like a salmon traveling up stream. I stormed the stairs, reached the mezzanine level, and slammed into Officer Ronnie Christianson. He scowled.

"Where's Capsner?" He did not use his happy voice.

"He ran up these steps just a minute ago. Didn't you see him?" I glanced right and left.

"Do you enjoy sending me on wild goose chases?"

"Capsner was here."

"Why'd he run?"

"The siren … and he recognized me. I'm sure it was him. He wore the same black hat and coat he had on Saturday."

Realization dawned on Ronnie's face. He spun around and spoke into a device that crackled in response. I chased him to the entryway and followed him as he crashed through the double doors, sliding into the squad car idling at the curb. He reactivated the siren and drove away.

I stood on the sidewalk, staring after him. He'd done an adequate job as Columbia's temporary chief of police after Lance Erickson had his heart attacks, but he didn't appreciate my friendship with Amanda. And he seemed to like me even less now that the city council hired her, and she'd be the one to replace Pete's dad as the permanent chief of police.

Puffy gray clouds swept across the blue sky and cast moving shadows over the car hoods. One of the shadows broke apart and threw light rays on a familiar dark wavy head of hair.

"ZaZa." She continued strutting across the lot. "ZaZa? Isabelle Lavigne."

She halted as if lassoed and slowly turned to face me. The grin on her face didn't quite reach her eyes. "Katie. You made it."

I ran to catch up to her. "Thanks for taking the practice. Sorry I missed the kids, but good thing I caught you. I need my key. How did it go? Did you have fun? Did they do well?"

"Yes. They did well. We had a grand time. They want me to attend their competition Thursday. I replied I would love to watch them in action."

My throat closed. I swallowed hard and shook my head. "We leave at noon, and I'm not sure they can get you a substitute just to be a spectator."

"But, *mon amie*, I would help coach your team. Coaches are released from duties, yes?"

My heart pounded against my chest. I hoped she couldn't hear it. "Math subs are so hard to get, and our best one just left for Florida. Maybe next time. I'll have to work out the financials." I stopped myself from saying 'with Mr. Ganka' because I was certain she could talk him into finding the funds.

"Jane said her father has many resources. We could tap him for whatever we require."

"Thanks, but you haven't even begun teaching yet. You probably won't want to miss class during your first week, and I won't need any help this time. For future reference, most of the rest of our meets will be held on the weekend, and maybe we can work something out."

"Next time." She tugged at the top edge of her new dark brown suede high-heeled designer boots and pivoted the heel to give me the full effect.

"Better choice in footwear." I searched the lot. "Do you need a ride?"

"No, thank you." Her eyes shifted, and she glanced over her shoulder. "I called a friend."

The freezing air I sucked in caught me off guard, and I coughed as the big, blue Ram truck rolled to a stop next to ZaZa. The passenger window opened, and Pete said, "Hi ladies. Columbia rideshare at your service."

"Thank you, Dr. Erickson." ZaZa yanked open the door and hauled herself into the cab. "See you later, Katie," she said, and pulled the door closed.

I forced a smile, and Pete gave me a look I couldn't interpret, but if ZaZa was looking for great friends, I had them to share.

My hand came up to wave, but I grabbed the window frame before they drove off.

"ZaZa, key, please?"

THIRTEEN

The Focus revved to life. Knowing it would take time for the engine to heat up, I took the longest route home, mulling over the incidents of the last four days. Thursday's dinner had been interesting, good food, great company, and even a bit of romance, though it wasn't mine. On Friday, Jane and I successfully completed our first semester of teaching, and Susie and Tiny got engaged. Saturday's window shopping had been overshadowed by the discovery of Pat Donaldson's body, but we topped off the day with a welcoming party for ZaZa. Today Amanda declared Donaldson's death more than a little suspicious. Capsner was in the wind again, and Amanda considered Susie a person of interest. My mock trial students had found time to practice for their upcoming meet. But when

I thought about ZaZa, I couldn't guess what she was up to.

Susie, Maverick, and I had found Mr. Donaldson, and my thoughts centered around his death. Assuming someone tampered with the wires in the basement, he must have made that someone very unhappy. Who could have had it in for him? A competitor? A rival for his wife's affection? An employee? An old girlfriend? Maybe a new girlfriend? A disgruntled customer? Susie?

Maverick met me at the door with his leash in his mouth, so we walked the neighborhood. I thought about Susie's diamond and the death and decided I'd have to visit the store again.

Ida and Dad were nowhere to be seen when we returned. I fed Maverick, and without Dad and Ida to tend to me, I munched on leftover pizza. Maverick waited patiently for his nibble of cheese, and, not to be outdone by a Frenchwoman, I gave it to him. I cleaned the kitchen and, surprisingly exhausted, retired to the living room where I curled up on the couch. I knew what Liselle could be going through, losing the one you loved. Assailed by thoughts of Charles, I buried my face in Maverick's fur and wept until I heard his last words again, 'Promise me you'll be happy.'

I gained enough willpower to sit up and rubbed my cheeks. Maverick kept his big, brown eyes on my face as I related blissful stories about when Charles and I first met, our decryption assignments, excursions to the countryside, Bonnie's rescue from the steel jaws of a trap the night she escaped the kennel and had a tryst with Maverick's sire, our first big fight and reconciliation, our hasty wedding, and my nephew's kidnapping and subsequent safe return.

"All the belongings I brought with me to Columbia fit in my poor Jetta. I miss that car, but remember its battle with the buck, Maverick? The Jetta couldn't limp away." I stood up and Maverick followed. "I think a few of those boxes of memories have yet to be opened. It's time."

I sorted through the cartons in the closet of the spare bedroom I used as an office. My letter opener slashed the tape on the first box on the bottom shelf, and I carefully unsealed the lid.

I slouched to the floor. Maverick put his head in my lap. Paging through the now-outdated textbooks, I noted Charles' scribbles in the margins and reached for a handful of files containing papers Charles and I had coauthored and codes we'd deciphered. The rubber bands disintegrated under my fingers and the stack of programs and ticket stubs fanned out around us, including the facsimile of a first-class menu from the dining room on the *Titanic*, a meal Charles recreated the night he proposed. When I needed comfort or strength, I smoothed the hairs on Maverick's head or reached for Charles' wedding ring hanging around my neck.

I wiggled free the few mementos tightly packed in the corners, and my hand lightly brushed the burnished cover of a photo album. I stroked the leather and smiled. As I squeezed my fingers around the edges, Maverick rose to all fours and barked before I heard a pounding on my door.

By the time I slid the keepsakes from my lap back into the box and scrambled to stand, Maverick made it down the steps and waited at the back door. I peeked through the curtain, breathed deeply, and turned the knob.

"Come in, ZaZa." I craned my neck to the outside, scanning for her non-existent transportation.

Light flakes floated from the dark sky. She strolled in, dressed head to toe in a Pepto-Bismol pink wool coat and matching fur hat, toting a large, gray fur muff. She looked like Dr. Zhivago's beleaguered wife, Tonya. "Katie." It came out like a sigh.

I closed the door and waited for more, but when it didn't come, I filled the void. "Take a seat. Can I get you a hot tea or cocoa?"

"I need wine."

She stomped her high heeled boots and brushed snow from the fur edging. She pulled off her hat and shook her hair loose. Her fingers fumbled with the big buttons, and she shimmied out of the coat.

"Red or white?"

"Red."

I turned and studied the labels on my limited but alphabetized wine rack, removing one of the less expensive bottles. The battery-operated corkscrew I picked up on sale after Christmas whirred. It came with a pourer that should act as an aerator. I stuck it in the bottle, dispensed the wine and handed her a glass. The pronounced choreography of her swirl, observation, sniff, and taste test rivaled Jane's.

"Don't you have any real wine?"

I filled a glass with water. "Sorry. The wine selection in our local liquor store is limited. We usually get our French fix when we visit the cities. How did you get here?"

She took a large swig and let out a breath. "I walked. Katie, I don't know if I can do this without your help."

I had always seen ZaZa as indestructible, stoic, and tough. This new ZaZa confused me. "Do what?"

She took another large gulp of wine, and I sipped my water.

"I've never taught before. The licensing department waived the student teaching requirement because the need for mathematicians is so great. I foresee failure and don't think I can go through with it."

"ZaZa, you know the math. I've seen you shred

problems, taking equations down to their studs, and recreating entire numerical systems."

"But the language barrier. What if I don't understand the kids?"

"Galileo said, 'Mathematics is the language with which God has written the universe.' And you will find our department extremely helpful. You have Mrs. McEntee, and you have me. You will do great."

She downed the last of her wine. "You are sure?"

"Absolutely."

"I trust you." She smiled and rose from the chair. "Now I will walk back to Jane's—"

"You'll do no such thing. I'll give you a ride. It's important you stay healthy.

She donned the chic costume and twirled. "Do you like it?"

"Yes," I lied.

I'd almost forgotten her droll sense of humor until she shared her wild observations of my students at practice, and we laughed during the entire drive to Jane's.

Maybe she wouldn't drive me crazy, and her presence would work out.

I returned to find a folded note stuck between the doors. I grabbed it as it fluttered to the ground before it blew into the snow and carried it inside. I pressed it flat on the kitchen table and read, 'Hi there beautiful. Just thought I'd stop by on my night off, but I guess you were busy. Call me. We'll make some plans. Pete.'

I punched in his number, and it went to voicemail. I didn't know how she did it, but suddenly ZaZa's appearance seemed less random.

FOURTEEN

Maverick had been welcomed by Liselle when they first met, so we took a chance and walked to the jewelry store. We lucked out, arriving as she unlocked the front door to admit a short line of patrons. She quickly ruffled his ears before helping the first of the customers requesting the return of jewelry, whether or not the work was complete.

The door closed on the last client, and she slumped and said, "They heard about Patrick and don't trust us with their prized personal possessions, although Helen and William are perfectly capable jewelers and have done more than their share of the repairs." She shook her head. "What can I do for you, Katie?" She picked up a bottle and sprayed cleaner on the glass tops. "I hope you don't mind. Business is slow enough at opening, we're usually able to shine the counters, polish the silver, and put out the jewelry. With the roadwork going on, one of us has been enough, so I told Helen and William to come in a little later today. That was probably a mistake."

"Have you found Teasdale's ring?"

"No, but we've been combing through the work envelopes." She swiped the glass. "Come with me. I have a diamond display to arrange."

She unlocked a rectangular chest and lifted prearranged displays of dark brown ring boxes lined up on white satin-covered cushions. In no time, the cases were loaded and secured for the day. She crossed her arms and tilted her head. "That's strange."

"What's strange?" Maverick and I moved closer to the showcase.

She removed a box from the display. "This must be the empty one William found on Saturday. He wasn't sure it had a ring in it because it wasn't one of the rings Capsner asked to see. Pat could have sent the ring back for repair or cleaning, or he may have sold the ring and the box was replaced accidentally."

"I was here when William noticed the empty box, and Patrick didn't confess to having any part of moving the ring."

"Everything was a game to him. Everything except money. He enjoyed setting up little trials for William and Helen. If they found an empty box, it was up to them to discover where the contents had gone. For items sold, there would be a receipt in the till. If the item was sent back to the dealer, there would be a record of the return. He said it kept them honest." She stored the chest behind the counter. "Patrick loved Phonic Infographics. Do you know what they are?" I nodded. "William hated them and wouldn't play that game, but Helen relished solving them, discovering the correct answer." She looked down at her hands. "Patrick became a little short-tempered lately, and some of his challenges showed a vicious side to him."

She lifted her chin. "I have some loose diamonds I'm going to examine—practice appraising them. It that okay with you?"

I followed her to the work bench. "Liselle, is there anyone you think might have had a reason to hurt Patrick?"

"I knew of no one who would've wanted him dead. But why is it important to you?" She sat and unlocked a metal storage unit. She withdrew a glassine envelope and tipped a large stone out onto her palm. A pair of claw-like tweezers grasped the diamond. She examined it beneath a microscope with a high-powered light, turning it, measuring it, and inspecting it.

"I'm here because Susie Kelton looks guilty, but I don't think she killed him."

Liselle nodded, but her forehead scrunched. She read and reread the description on the liner in the compartment housing the envelope. The stone barely made it back to the case, and she took a second gem, making a similar assessment.

When she hastily grabbed a third gem, I asked, "What's wrong?"

"I've been out of circulation for a while, but I used to be pretty good at finessing the specific characteristics of a diamond. These are not matching up. The stones are either mixed up and out of order or …"

I offered my own answer, filling in the blank. "They've been replaced." I called Amanda. Fifteen minutes later she strode into the store.

"What's happening, Mrs. Donaldson … Liselle."

"The diamond cut, color, and carat weight displayed on the liners closely match the itemization description, but the stones don't match the information on the envelopes." She held out papers from their insurance company. "They've been switched. Patrick didn't tell me about any major changes—"

"Would he have told you?"

"I don't know, but something's wrong."

The door dinged and Helen arrived. "Morning," she said. Her smile faded, and I read confusion written on her face. "Chief, to what do we owe this visit?" She unwrapped the scarf around her neck and removed her coat.

Liselle snatched Helen's belongings and stuffed them behind the counter. "I need you to look at some stones. Right now."

Helen took Liselle's place under the light, took measurements, and wrote out her description of the first of three diamond inspections. She finally picked up a loupe and held the third stone up to her eye. When her hand fell away and she removed the loupe, she fell back, and the chair squawked. "They don't match the description and are not the same or at least they were returned to the wrong slot." She worried her lip. "We have a new piece of specialized gemology equipment in the basement. Chief, I'd like to test this diamond."

Amanda and Helen disappeared for a short time. The frown on Helen's face as she reappeared said it all. "Patrick's new machine measured the stones more carefully and magnified an LG on the girdle of the diamond which means these are lab grown diamonds, beautiful, but much less expensive than their natural counterparts. We've got to check the entire inventory, Liselle."

Tears pooled in Liselle's eyes. Maverick stepped closer to her and shoved his nose under her palm. She scratched behind his ear and said, "Patrick, what have you done?"

"Patrick owned the diamonds and if he's the one who made the substitutions, it opens a different can of worms."

"That's a big if," said Liselle. "And I have to consider the possibility someone other than Patrick replaced the stones."

"Robbery?"

Helen gasped. Her hand flew to her mouth. "You don't think I had anything to do with taking them?"

"No, I don't," said Liselle. "But I do need you to help me sort these."

Helen agreed. As they began the tedious process of careful comparison, she said, "I wonder what's keeping William?"

"I think I need to close the store until I make sense of what's happened," said Liselle.

Amanda agreed. Helen hung a handwritten closed sign. They would take whatever time they needed to mourn Patrick and do a complete inventory.

Amanda escorted me to the front door. "Have you spoken to Kelton today?"

"No. Why? You can't still believe Susie had anything to do with the robberies."

"Not necessarily the robberies, but Donaldson's death may not be linked to the robberies."

FIFTEEN

My science club students congregated in Mr. Simonson's neat and tidy shop.

"I told you to be careful," Lorelei said, not looking up. She concentrated on twisting a sharp utility knife to drill a hole in the plastic container, creating a reservoir she filled with water. Not satisfied with the water stream, she set to work again.

Brock and Galen brandished the narrow PVC pipes twice more, swinging them swordlike and clashing at right angles. The play-weapons froze in midair when Mr. Simonson shook his head and said, "Gentlemen, please." They penitently carried the imagined weaponry to the table and marked the cut line to fit the pieces beneath the acrylic shelf. Carlee disentangled her hair and lowered her safety glasses. She drew a hacksaw from the tabletop strewn with tools of all types and picked up the first piece. Mr. Simonson nodded a go ahead, and she cut away the excess.

Kindra stood over the table and traced the pattern with her finger. Using the instructions provided, she lined up the metal cans, blue rubber bands, and the red and yellow wires with alligator clips attached at the ends in the order they would be used.

Galen and Brock joined Mr. Simonson in front of a steel-sided garment locker. After spinning the combination dial, the teacher removed glasses, a tan shirt, pants, thick brown gloves, yellow and black boots, and a heavy green apron. "Do you see this yellow triangular symbol?" I moved closer and checked over Brock's shoulder. "It's used to classify dielectric footwear and EH safe PPE, personal protection equipment, to use around electricity. Some say I overthink my procedures, but electrocution is real. It's best to wear cotton clothing without any metal attached. I've gotten singed wearing jeans with rivets. Sometimes the pain will drive a victim to cry out, or muscles will clench, and they can't let go, but no one who plays by my rules has ever been hurt in my classroom. I stand by the precautions I take."

My heart rate picked up. I wondered about the safety of our experiment.

"We're supposed to get a spark, and that's it. I hope we get enough to flash a neon bulb," said Galen.

"I made one of these in college. You aren't going to get much," said Mr. Simonson. "But be prepared for anything, I always say."

I breathed a sigh of relief. How bad could one little spark be?

Still a little jumpy, my heart skipped a beat when Mr.

Simonson heaved the clunky overshoes to the floor. I imagined the worst possibility when he yanked the work shirt off the hanger and held it up so Brock and Galen could identify the arc rating. A hand crept around me and nabbed one of the gloves from the table. Patricia affirmed its heft by lifting and letting it drop as she laughed at my jitteriness.

Using the specifications on the blueprint, the students cut the remaining pieces to the precise dimensions and constructed a rudimentary Kelvin water dropper spark generator. When the water stream began to flow, we watched and waited, but our first attempt failed.

Galen read from the list of troubleshooting answers. "Brock, try adjusting the placement of the inductors on top."

"Try adjusting the what?"

Galen pointed and said, "Slide those cans closer to the water. Kindra, put the receiver cans in the plastic Cool Whip tubs to insulate them. I'll narrow the gap between the brass balls, and we can try it again."

Lorelei resecured all the components with duct tape and refilled the reservoir. We watched the stream of water bend toward the cans and break into droplets. No one looked away.

After a few seconds, Mr. Simonson applauded. "Congratulations. You did it. Your generator successfully produced a teeny tiny spark." He held his thumb and forefinger a millimeter apart. "Not bad. Now let's see what happens when we add salt to the water."

The salt improved the conductivity, and the kids took a series of photos to memorialize the flash, and high-fived each other in congratulations. It was a major scientific coup for our amateur group.

Mr. Simonson sidled next to me. "You look like a proud mama." My grin grew.

"The beginning of a very positive week. Next stop, the mock trial podium on Thursday," said Kindra. "What else is going on this week?"

"Galen has a match tomorrow." Carlee beamed. "He hasn't lost one yet."

"And we start semester two."

At the mention of a new semester, they extolled the skills of some teachers and warned of what they perceived as the incompetencies of others.

"Be honest. You didn't appreciate your communications teacher because you didn't like the work, Brock." Lorelei was an exemplary student, and I saw their match as healthy for both of them, tempering a zealous, honor student with a laid-back, intelligent jock.

The kids teased him as we dismantled the K.E.G., stowed the components, and wiped off the machinery. The only trace of our passing through the industrial education department was the echo of our chuckles.

On my trek through the building, Susie called. I thought about letting it go to voicemail, but that would have been the easy way out. "Hi, Susie."

"I know you're getting ready for dinner, but do you have time to talk?"

"Sure." I glanced at my wrist. It wasn't even four o'clock. "What can I help you with?"

"Chief West doesn't think I had anything to do with the robberies, but she still considers me a person of interest in Donaldson's death. What would you recommend I do?"

"Did you get an attorney?"

"I talked to Dorene Dvorak."

Relieved, I said, "She's great. She took care of CJ when

he was accused of murder." I was glad I didn't utter the words that came unbidden next, *but he was innocent.*

"I didn't kill him, Katie. I might have wanted to, but I'm a nurse for goodness sake. Talk to Pete tonight. He knows I couldn't kill anyone."

"Where will I find Pete?"

"Aren't you and ZaZa meeting him at Santino's?" Susie caught my delayed reaction. "You didn't know." The silence blossomed. She said in a small voice, "I owe Maverick my life, so I guess I owe you." It sounded as if she'd shifted the phone from one shoulder to the other. "ZaZa told Pete you and she were taking him to dinner. Katie, I know she's your friend, but I wouldn't let her anywhere near Gregory."

"You don't know her, Susie. She's just looking for a friend."

"I wouldn't trust her out of my sight. I know her kind." A one-syllable cluck came through the phone. "I may have even been her kind. But she's a phony. I almost feel sorry for her but watch her. If you don't pay attention, you may lose a game you don't know you're playing." She hung up.

I checked for a missed call and found nothing. What kind of game was ZaZa playing? I started the car and accidentally revved my engine. I had to consciously release the gas pedal as I zipped home; a speeding ticket wouldn't do. I cataloged my best outfits and calculated the time I could take to change clothes, tame my unruly hair, and apply a little makeup before I'd need to appear.

Maverick followed me from room to room as I collected my arsenal. I laid out my three favorite outfits. Maverick jumped on the bed and stretched out on two of them. After careful evaluation, I chose the blue sweater and twill pants, without the wrinkles and dog hair. I scratched the hard-to-reach spot above his tail and said, "Thank you, my friend."

After I ran a brush through my hair, applied mascara to highlight my blue eyes, and smoothed on light-pink lip-gloss, I pirouetted in front of the full-length mirror on the back of the closet door. It would have to do.

I bounded down the stairs and came face to face with Dad and Ida.

"Don't you look nice?" Ida cooed. "Where are you off to?"

"Santino's. Last minute dinner plans." She looked at her watch. It was still early. "Would you like me to bring something home?"

Ida pouted, offended I would consider commercial fare to her delicious recipes, but Dad said, "Lasagna, extra sauce."

"Don't leave yet." Ida disappeared and returned seconds later with a black box. She lifted the lid and nestled inside was a sapphire pendant and matching earrings. "This will complement your outfit … and your eyes. Down."

I bent at the knees, bringing my five-foot six-inch frame closer to her four-foot-eleven inches. She secured the clasp around my neck. One at a time, I fastened the earrings to complete the look. With a Cheshire cat grin, Ida patted my shoulder. "Now you're ready."

"Thanks." I shoved my feet in my Mukluks and grabbed a coat off the hook by the door, patting Maverick's head as I raced out the door.

My fingers drummed the steering wheel, but I maintained a steady speed as I drove across town. I spun into the parking lot and marched to the door. Pausing at the entrance for a few seconds, I debated whether or not this was my best course of action. I checked the time. Pete frequented Santino's early to avoid the recurrent crowds. Looking through the glass, I found the two of them near the back of the room seated at a table for four. There'd be no sneaking up on them.

ZaZa wore a bright red sweater dress accented with hefty gold baubles. Her hair was pulled up off a face which could have graced the cover of a magazine. I rethought my line of attack. She sat languidly, a half-empty flute of bubbly dangling from her hand and laughed. I donned appropriate acting armor. With my sabotage plans ready, I waltzed into Santino's, my boots slapping the floor.

When I neared the table, I heard ZaZa. "Surely it can't hurt to have one."

Pete shook his head.

I marshalled my courage and, to ZaZa's absolute dismay, strode to the table, hugged Pete's broad shoulders, and planted a light kiss on his cheek. He turned, and when I saw the baffled look on his face, I worried I'd read ZaZa's intentions incorrectly, but his dreamy eyes brightened, and he jumped to his feet.

"You made it." He pulled back a chair. I detected a slight glide of the chair nearer his as he shuffled it forward when I sat.

I laughed at his sappy grin. "Of course, but I'm sorry I'm late. The kids and I celebrated the success of our science experiment, and I lost track of time."

"Then we really must have some bubbly." ZaZa raised her glass, requesting another pour.

Pete tilted his head. "No can do. I'm on call."

The server appeared. I ordered a tonic with lime.

"You can't celebrate with tonic." ZaZa smiled, but Pete's eyes widened hearing her petulant voice.

"I'm driving and it's a school night."

I knew how much Pete loved science so while we waited for our dinners, I meticulously described the minutiae of our K.E.G. experiments in all its mundanity. I finished my narration, put my elbows on the table, and set my chin on the backs of my hands. "Are you ready for tomorrow, ZaZa?"

I think I nodded in all the right places but didn't pay attention to anything she said. I didn't really care if she were ready. I'm sure she could see the fire in my eyes. She knew that I knew what she'd done, and I promised myself, it wouldn't happen again.

She hailed Mr. Santino. "Romano," she cooed. "This is marvelous." He blushed and offered us a free dessert. I inhaled to settle my indignation—another man bit the dust.

I could share my school, my town, my students, and my friends, but no matter how much she insinuated herself into my life, there were lines I wouldn't let her cross. I drew one wide imaginary line in front of Pete.

When we finished supper and Mr. Santino delivered Dad's take out order, I said to Pete, "Thanks for bringing ZaZa. I'll get her home." Over Pete's weak protests and ZaZa's pouting, he escorted us to my car. "Dinner was lovely. Santino's is always perfect. And I appreciate you keeping ZaZa company until I could get here. I promise I won't let that happen again. At the very least, I'll give you a heads up." I wanted him to know I meant it. "Always."

"It was no imposition," he said. He leaned in and gave me a sweet kiss on my cheek.

Content with the evening's resolution, I tuned the radio to my favorite classical music station and hummed along. ZaZa sat as still as the night. At that moment, I was afraid that any communication would shatter the quiet between us. I wondered what motivated her and what I needed to do to understand.

We pulled up in front of Jane's apartment. ZaZa threw open the door and hopped out of the car. "Goodnight, Katie." She waited a moment, almost adding something, before she slammed the door and ran up the walk.

The grin I wore driving home faded as I drove into my garage. She'd used her feminine wiles on Pete for the last time. But I knew to expect the unexpected from ZaZa.

SIXTEEN

Maverick pranced at the back door. He'd always take a second walk, so I snapped on his leash and headed down Maple Street. Fat, drifting snowflakes dotted his shoulders and back like a cold, feathery white superhero cape. We stepped lively and I held a hardy conversation with myself.

Susie couldn't kill anyone, even Donaldson. But who would? According to William, Liselle and Pat were working out some difficulties. Maybe if I spoke to Liselle, she'd tell me. If she had a prenup and they split, how would she share in the profits from the store, and would that give her reason to kill him? How lucrative was owning one of three jewelry stores in Columbia? With the value of the diamond inventory decreased, was it even worth the effort?

Helen seemed overwrought by Donaldson's death. Could their relationship have been more than merely employer-employee? But then wouldn't she have wanted Liselle out of the way instead of Donaldson? Unless he didn't reciprocate her feelings.

William had an opinion about everything. Maybe he didn't get along with Donaldson, or … I stopped in my tracks. Any one of the four—Liselle, Pat, William, or Helen—would have had the opportunity to substitute the natural diamonds with lab grown diamonds. Would they also know where to secure the replacements? And to what end? Money? Where was it?

At the high school gym, Capsner acted like he had something to hide and ran. He may have pulled the old distract and grab maneuver, stealing a ring or two, but would that have led to murder? Would he have had the opportunity to swap the stones? Would he have access to a diamond broker?

Ruling Donaldson's death suspicious opened another line of inquiry. Who knew enough about electricity to flip the switch and guarantee Donaldson would die? A do-it-yourselfer installing a generator could have made the error, but the exposed wire might not have succeeded in short circuiting Donaldson without the addition of the water. I circled back to Susie. She and Donaldson weren't the only ones who knew how to hook up a generator. My students successfully watched a video and built their own, so clearly anyone who could follow directions could do it.

I would do anything for Pete. If he believed Susie couldn't kill anyone, and if Donaldson were murdered, I had to find someone else who could.

The snowfall increased. We turned toward home, into a driving wind.

I loved talking to Maverick. "Am I guilty of overreacting to ZaZa? She can't help being gorgeous and smart. She's alone in a new place. I haven't done anything overt to thwart her quest to find new friends, but I should provide more opportunities for her to meet my welcoming Minnesota family. What do you think, Mav?" A gust of freezing air caused me to stumble. "She never accused me of stealing Charles, but perhaps she harbors some ill will. Maybe we can bridge the uncomfortable gap and find common ground with our memories."

Maverick pulled through the furiously falling flakes blotting out all but a faint glow from the homes on both sides of the street. The snow silenced my hurried footfalls and muffled the city sounds. For a moment I imagined the silence in Patricia's life. I said a quick prayer.

The amber lights illuminating the first floor of Ida's postcard-perfect Queen Anne style home acted like a welcoming beacon. We ran up the back stairs and shook off the snow. As I hung my coat and his leash on the hook by the door, Maverick raced into the living room and barked.

"Dad." No one answered. An enticing box of cocoa stood in wait of hot milk. I poured a cup and set the microwave to beverages. Maverick barked again, and I rounded the corner to join him. Something on the floor caught my foot. I flipped the light switch. Dad sprawled face forward on the carpet behind the couch. Maverick nudged and licked, but Dad remained still. Too still.

"Dad!" I screamed, and fumbled with the buttons on my phone, stammering my address and Dad's condition in answer to the dispatcher.

"Is he breathing?" I choked out a sob. "Stay with me," she said.

The seconds between the rise and fall of his chest

lasted forever. "Very shallow. Yes, he's breathing." I didn't recognize my own panicked voice. "What should I do?"

"Is there evidence of an injury?"

My fingers lightly tap-danced over his body. "I don't see anything."

She talked me through a series of questions and finally asked, "Does he have any pre-existing conditions?"

I gasped, thinking of his recent bout with dizziness. "He almost blacked out the other night."

"The ambulance is just about there. Can you let them in?"

I raced to the door and flashed the light illuminating our back yard. The ambulance roared up the drive. My breath hitched when Pete hopped out and blazed through the yard. His gentle touch opened a conduit to fear and burned my hand.

Oh, Dad.

The door between the apartments opened. "What's going on here?" Ida dried her hands on an apron and took in everything with a glance. In the next moment, she trundled next to me and squeezed my hand as we watched the three work in tandem. They checked Dad's pulse and heart rate, secured an oxygen mask over his face, and loaded him on a gurney. The noise of the rattling wheels grated, and I trembled.

Pete stood in front of me. His hands cupped my shoulders, and he looked directly into my eyes. "Harry's strong. His vitals are good. We have to figure out what happened and deal with it." I nodded, but not vigorously enough. His fingers tightened reassuringly. "We will. I promise. We'll meet you at the hospital." He flew out the door.

It was a good thing I couldn't find my Focus keys. I'd

have made a mess of the drive. Put Ida behind the wheel of her purple Plymouth Barracuda, and it's 'look out, world.' Actually, it's more like 'out of my way, world,' but I couldn't have been in better hands.

The cookies and candies Ida brought to the hospital every Christmas Eve paid off in dividends when least expected. The receptionist greeted Ida warmly and helped me fill out the dreaded paperwork. I stumbled over the questions regarding Dad's physician of record and power of attorney. I reprimanded myself, promising we wouldn't delay the search and realizing we'd have to find a substitute for Elizabeth to make important decisions if Dad could not, while he stayed with me.

When I thought we'd waited long enough, I approached the receptionist. "Have you heard anything?"

She looked at me sympathetically. "We'll let you know as soon as we do. Your dad is in the absolute best hands."

I knew he couldn't have anyone better than Pete looking after him, but it didn't lower my anxiety level.

When Pete finally appeared, I leapt to my feet. Terrified of the prognosis, I shuddered. Pete wrapped his arms around me. "We are going to keep him until we can balance his numbers and give him some rest, but he's going to be just fine."

"What's wrong with him?"

"He's hypotensive. If his blood pressure stays this low, he'll keep blacking out. It can be life threatening. He'll need an infusion. That initial spell before Christmas was a precursor. Do you know how long this has been going on? He doesn't think he has any prescriptions."

"He had another dizzy spell Saturday evening, but I don't know of any diagnoses or medication. I'll contact Elizabeth. I wasn't there when they released him from the facility so I don't know what orders he hasn't followed or what meds he might have stopped taking."

For the first few months of his recuperation, I was with him every day and took care of him the way he'd taken care of me, but eventually his doctor told me he would improve only if I allowed him the luxury of doing things himself. I got a job, moved to Columbia, and by the time he was well enough to go home, Elizabeth's career had taken off, and it required a huge amount of travel. She didn't have the time to watch out for him, and wasn't willing for him to be on his own, so I gladly had him come stay with me. The call to Elizabeth would require careful articulation of Dad's needs without causing her to worry disproportionately. Dad thought she'd earned her dream job, and I didn't want her to think I only called when he needed something.

"Can I see him?"

"He's exhausted. He slept through drawing blood and hooking up the IV. I don't want to wake him. Go home now. I'll make sure we take very good care of your dad." As if he could sense my reservation, he added. "We've had this conversation before. You can't do him any good if you don't take care of yourself."

"Why did *you* show up? How did you know?"

"I've got people," he said gently.

Ida tugged at my sleeve. "Let's go, Katie. Your dad will be getting the red-carpet treatment. All I can give you is pancakes."

My lips turned up because I wanted to make Ida feel good too. "Ok, but they have to be your Swedish pancakes."

"Now you're talking."

The snow had picked up, and the gales ferociously tossed the flakes, like waves roiling on the high seas, splashing onto her Barracuda. We brushed the heavy buildup from the windows and settled into the ice-cold seats.

She revved the engine, and we rolled out of the parking space. Each time she discovered she'd wandered across the center line cloaked in white, Ida blamed the pristine blanket of snow covering everything. We slowly bumped through icy ruts in the streets and skidded into the last intersection before Maple Street.

My feet reacted to our slipping and pressed against the floorboards as if I could assist braking. "How's the road?" I squeaked.

She gripped the steering wheel. "Just like it looks," she said crabbily.

"What are our chances for a late start tomorrow?"

Ida shrugged, crawling away from the intersection.

I punched in numbers, and when Elizabeth didn't pick up, I left a message, saving the mention of his trip to the hospital for our person-to-person discussion. "It's Katie. Dad and I are searching for a local physician to take care of him while he's here. I want to keep him honest, and I have a few questions for you. Do you know if he was given any prescriptions when he left St. Benedict's? Were there verbal instructions I should be aware of?" I swallowed hard. "Would you approve a change in power-of-attorney for Dad? Just in case, while he's here, so I don't have to call you for every little thing. Thanks."

I punched off with sweaty fingers, released a breath, and glanced at Ida.

Her face reflected a ghastly green from the lights on the dash. She sat forward, hands clenched at two and ten on the steering wheel. To ease her tension, I resorted to simple conversation.

"How well do you know Liselle Donaldson?"

"What a sweetheart. Liselle Anne took as many of my

classes as they would allow during high school. Her art graces the walls of the history center next to mine. I guess sometimes opposites do attract because I never did see the allure of Patrick."

The steering wheel jerked in her hands. Startled, she overcompensated, and came close to scraping a car parked on the left side of the street.

She tugged herself closer to the windshield, hugging the steering wheel, peering into the living snow globe. "Four blocks remaining. We'll make it."

Ida knew everything in Columbia. "What have you heard about Patrick's death?"

She slowed the car even more. "Word has it he was killed for his quite substantial collection of loose diamonds." *Diamonds.* "That man had a good head for deals. He bought old jewelry at auctions, removed the stones, and fashioned new settings. He wasn't a poor silversmith, but Liselle Anne was much better. I never understood why he didn't keep her working in the store."

"Maybe it was her choice." *Or maybe he didn't want to be shown up by a woman.*

"Could be, but I don't know how she could bottle up all that creativity."

In the silence that followed, I wondered if she'd used her creativity to find a way to get rid of Patrick and have a stash of diamonds to use in her own designs.

SEVENTEEN

We pulled into the drive, and the snow stopped falling. Before she turned off the car, Ida turned her bright green eyes to me and said, "The snow has let up and it looks like we have a moment's respite. Liselle Anne lives on Lakeside Drive. As long as we're out and about, would you accompany me while I deliver my hotdish? We can still get around now, but we won't know what tomorrow will bring, and I'm certain grocery shopping is way down on her to-do list."

The roads were only barely passable, but how could I refuse. "Sure. Where's the hotdish?"

"It's in my fridge."

I tightened my collar, fought the wind, and slogged up the sidewalk. If Maverick hadn't raised his head and begged for supper, the quiet of my apartment would have unnerved me. "Dad's going to be fine," I told him. He inhaled his kibble.

Ida's Wolf Sub-Zero opened with a whisper. The shelves held four casserole dishes enclosed in quilted fabric, colorfully wrapped for the recipients. I chose the container covered in a black material with bold, primary colors spiraling throughout. Maybe Liselle would appreciate it.

Every once in a while, Maverick treated an open door as a game, a chance to employ his unusual powers of speed and agility against my slow and clumsy plodding while wending figure eights around my ankles. He followed me out to the car and hurdled into the front seat when I opened the door. I urged him into the back seat where he sat, eyes forward, attentive to a new adventure.

"I couldn't get out of the house without him."

"He'll be fine. Liselle loves dogs. You know he's mostly well-behaved." I snickered at the 'mostly.' "How did you know that black one was for Liselle Anne?"

"Good taste?" I said as she put the car in gear. Ida navigated the empty streets and within a few minutes, we pulled into the drive at the front of a two-story brick home. "Good taste." I repeated.

Thick piles of snow weighed down the branches on the fir trees next to the entry and blanketed everything else in the yard in a white plane. The only sign of life came from the faint yellow light escaping through the cracks around the window treatments on the first floor. Maverick frolicked in front of us, bulldozing his way through snow up to his shoulders. Ida gripped my arm as she waddled across the snow-covered walkway. She pushed a button. The pealing gong of the doorbell brought images of a behemoth, tuxedoed butler answering with, "You rang."

Seconds ticked away. The wind shrieked, and fresh white flakes swirled into mounds on the stoop, creating a stopper of snow at the base of the door. Ida rang the bell again. A soft light flipped on above our heads, illuminating a shovel standing in the corner—a slim silent sentry against the snow. Liselle pushed the door, moving the snow like a grader against the winter elements.

"Ida. Katie," she said, without the enthusiasm exhibited earlier in the day.

"I brought a hotdish. It's your favorite." Ida lifted the carrier.

"Hamburger and baked beans." Liselle took a moment before acknowledging Ida's thoughtful meal. "Thank you. I suppose you'd better come in." She backed into the foyer. "Just shove my boots out of your way while I put this in the fridge."

I kicked off my snow-caked footwear and lined them up next to another pair dripping onto a black plastic tray. Ida did the same. Liselle returned, shepherded us into the living room, and motioned for us to take a seat. Maverick sniffed the air and curled around Ida's feet.

Liselle turned her back to us and gripped the mantel above her head, staring into the yellow and orange flames licking the crackling logs in the firebox. She reached for a glass of red wine and took a long swig. She exchanged the glass for a folder on the end table and fed it into the conflagration. The corners flared and blackened. In a poof, the entire scorched packet curled and, reduced to ashes, drifted up the flue.

"Chief West scanned these nonsense notes and even Helen couldn't figure out what Patrick wrote."

Ida cleared her throat. "We can't stay long. The snow, you know."

The blank expression on Liselle's face led me to believe she'd already forgotten we were there. She took another sip of wine.

"How are you doing, Liselle Anne? What's going to happen?"

Liselle took a deep breath and exhaled slowly. "I'd like to keep the store open, but everything is in flux. Helen and I are cataloguing our loose diamonds but so far, all stones larger than a half carat are lab grown substitutions. I'll have to check and update our insurance policy. If Patrick's death is ruled a homicide, the store might be closed for who knows how long, and without the Valentine sales, I don't know if we can make it." She rubbed her hands together. "I know Patrick wasn't happy. We weren't happy, but he loved the store and so did I. It's where we met. It's where we did our finest work."

"Donaldson's was my first job after high school. Do you remember, Ida?" She clutched a beautiful silver bauble on a chain around her neck and I mirrored her actions, my hand instinctively traveling to the wedding ring around mine.

"I do. You were a natural jewelry designer." She hummed. "I had a difficult time finding enough resources to keep you in silver for all your creations."

"I loved those classes." Liselle took a long swallow and reached for another file.

"What do you have there?" I asked.

"Patrick had his own little lexicon." She dropped into a chair. "He thought he'd invented clever ways to spell words using phonetic variations. I hated it." She scowled. "Helen thrived on being the only one able to translate most of his weird spellings into words. He spelled her last name 'G-h-o-c-k-s.'" Her voice took on a sharp edge and she snorted. "I sometimes wonder what would've happened if I'd been able to read these." Red hot coals scattered when she tossed in the last folder.

I sighed. No answer there.

She threw back the last of her wine and wiped her mouth with the back of her hand. She looked ready to say something, but the doorbell rang. Her wine glass missed the table and crashed to the floor.

"Who could be here now?" she said, flustered, stooping to pick up the pieces.

"I'll take care of this," Ida said. She knelt on the carpet and swept Liselle away with a wave of her hand.

I accompanied Liselle to the front door. Ricky stood on the stoop, her hands shoved deep into the pockets of her heavy jacket, hunching her back to the wicked weather. "I finished your car tune-up, but I'll need a ride back to the shop." In answer to Liselle's flummoxed look, she said, "The hospital motor pool garage."

Liselle grabbed a coat and her pocketbook. Her legs wobbled. She blinked and when she opened her eyes, her head fell toward me. "You'd better drive." An embarrassed smile graced her face as she dug in her purse and fished out her keys. The toss was more or less in my direction.

"Let me tell Ida we'll be right back."

"I heard you," she called from the living room. "I'll be fine."

We climbed into a long, white SUV, idling on the driveway next to Ida's purple muscle car, rumbling, spewing exhaust whisked into the night by Mother Nature's mighty hand. The weighty clunk of the doors shut out the groaning gale and provided protection from the elements—if only in my mind—and we backed onto Lakeside.

"Take a left at the next intersection to the industrial

park," Ricky said, clutching the seatbelt hugging her chest.

Swirling flakes sparkled in the high beams and momentarily obliterated the world around us. The wind picked up and I gripped the steering wheel with such intensity, my fingers numbed. I flicked between the high and low beams, trying to glimpse the outline of the stop sign at the crossroads when a figure bundled in black darted in front of us. I slammed on the brakes and shimmied to a stop, shedding all our light on the wan, horrified face of William Dix.

EIGHTEEN

He stomped to the driver's window and was momentarily dazed to find me at the helm. His brow furrowed, and he said, "What are you doing driving Liselle's car?"

"I'm right here." She sang from the back seat. Her slow and deliberate words didn't hide the fact that she was slightly intoxicated. "Want a ride?"

He pulled on the rear handle and Maverick raised a ruckus. "Back, Maverick."

The door hadn't opened. While Maverick jumped over the rear seat and found space in the cargo area, I fumbled with the buttons on the panel and the locks clicked. William tugged on the door. It still didn't open. I pushed another button. He yanked again. A gust of wind snatched the door from his hands, creaking and moaning. I shivered as the blast forced the heat out of the car, replacing it with icy air. Ricky drew her parka close, wrapped up like a cocoon. The face, shaded eerily like a ghoul in the soft green lights on the dash, wore a grimace.

"Hurry. Get in." Liselle giggled.

"What are you doing out in this blizzard?" William asked, sounding as if he knew better, which he obviously did not. He wrenched the door closed behind him.

"Taking Ricky back to work, silly," Liselle said, snickering. Glancing in the rearview mirror, I caught her lightly swatting his shoulder. "She finished my car." Liselle sniffled. "It's the last nice thing Patrick ever did for me." She collapsed and sobbed into William's shoulder.

I glanced at Ricky. She rolled her eyes and pointed to the left, using hand signs to direct me the rest of our slow, tortuous journey through the squalls of white.

Rounding one corner, Liselle commented offhandedly, "Look at the lovely fireworks."

To our right, the craggy black fingers of a falling deciduous tree tore at the feeble electric cables, sending sparks to the ground. I gunned the engine, and we made it to the next intersection before we heard a crash and all the lights in the neighborhood winked out. I slammed on the brakes and took a shaggy breath.

"We made it, Katie," Liselle squealed.

Ricky pulled out her phone and reported the location of the downed power lines.

We continued our slow vigilant crawl to the hospital garage. The oversized door rolled up and lights came on as we made our approach. Ricky noticed my surprise and nodded at the remote control sitting on her palm. "I never leave work without it."

"How come you have lights?"

"Generator, just like all of the other essential departments in the hospital system."

We drove inside, through two straight lines of identical, clean white vehicles arrayed like the Queen's guard standing at attention, and extending to the rear of the garage, and pulled up to the grill of a dented, cream-colored pickup truck. I shifted to park.

"Thanks for the ride," said Ricky. She opened the door. Before she slipped out, she scoffed, "My replacement isn't going to make it into work, scared of the snow, so would you mind waiting for a few minutes while I check the heater? Just want to make sure. We've got state-of-the-art equipment here and refilling the fuel tank is the final task on my list of duties tonight."

I opened the door to a room humming with energy—buzzing lights, whirring fans, and an engine thrumming.

Liselle tumbled out of the backseat after William. "Your SUVs look just like mine." She staggered a bit.

Maverick bounded with ease and grace, landed lightly on his paws, and walked close enough to Liselle to prop her up. "Thank you, furry friend."

Ricky unlocked the door to a cluttered storage room and flipped the light switch. "Your SUV was one of mine first." She yanked a bright yellow can from the floor. "Pat, I mean Mr. Donaldson, bought it at our last auction. Every two years, like clockwork, we sell our vehicles and buy new, so we always have the latest and greatest technology, mean and clean machines for our outreach personnel. Depending on the car, mileage can be relatively low, and he got a good deal."

Liselle pouted. "Patrick and his deals."

Ricky lugged the container to a large thrumming machine against the farthest wall and dispensed the contents.

"That's the new QuiGen," William said, his voice dripping with awe.

Ricky said, "We keep this place at an even sixty-five degrees during the winter, so these cars start right up, and maintenance is easier." She motioned over her shoulder to another big white SUV balanced on a narrow lift at the back of the garage. "The hospital prides itself on maintaining cutting edge equipment. That vehicle is part of a new series. We're just beginning to unlock some of its gadgetry. It has a built-in receptor for voice-activated commands. You can roll down a window or start the seat massage by telling the car what you'd like it to do. We're outfitting the newest addition on the lift with our garage door sensor, owner sticker, and tracking device." She sounded like a proud parent.

William strolled through the garage as Ricky poured the diesel into the generator.

I pointed to the space occupied by Liselle's SUV. "Is that where Susie Kelton picked up the Donaldson's vehicle? I can see how she might have mistaken it for one of yours. How do drivers usually connect with their rides?"

"I park the vehicle, facing the street, and leave the keys in the ignition. That way, I make sure the thing is gassed up and ready for every type of weather. Kelton must have stolen … picked up Donaldson's SUV right after he dropped it off. I never saw it."

"They do all look the same."

Ricky looked around. "They look alike because they are alike."

"Donaldson's vehicle didn't have a garage door sensor and the access sticker. How did he get into the garage?"

"I gave him a door code which I will change now that I've serviced his car."

"You serviced the car here?"

"When the vehicles are sold, the new owner is promised a deal on an oil change and a tune-up. It's a six-month checkup and great public relations. This is a city-owned entity."

My phone buzzed from my pocket. "Ida, are you okay?"

"The electricity is off here. With the fire blazing, I'm plenty warm, and I have my phone flashlight, but I was just checking on you."

"We're in the hospital garage with Ricky."

"I'm not sure I believe them, but, before the electricity went out, the weather channel people were predicting a narrow window when the storm would abate for a few hours. Take your time. The snow may or may not start up again." She paused. "I talked to your dad."

My mouth went dry. "How is he?" Dad's vulnerability gave me insight into what it might be like to be a parent, always worrying.

"He's much better, but he sounds lonely. He wants to play thirty-one, but he can't find any takers. When will you be back?"

My hand covered the phone mouthpiece. "Ricky, are you just about finished?"

"Yup. I'll let you out and close up shop."

"Should be there soon."

"Take all the time you need," Ida said.

Ricky said, "I don't expect anyone will be going anywhere tonight, but meanwhile this generator has enough fuel to keep everything warm and toasty for a long time. Hey, William." The can clanged to the floor of the storage room. Ricky turned off the light and pulled the door closed, checking the knob. "I can give you a ride. Then no one will be out in this mess longer than necessary."

"Sure, Ricky. Thanks."

Maverick jumped into the backseat. Liselle circled her fingers around his collar. He sat very still and let her haul herself next to him. I stared at him and crawled into the front seat. With my cap pulled down over my ears and my fuzzy mittens gripping the steering wheel, I gave it a little too much gas and the SUV roared to life. I gave a contrite shrug and backed out of the garage. Ricky followed in her dilapidated truck. We turned one way, and she went the other.

The wind had relented and although the big puffy flakes swirled, I could see our path more clearly. We travelled a parallel route to Liselle's home so we wouldn't impede any repairs or service being done on the downed line. But that didn't stop a big black truck from careening through an intersection in front of us. With all my senses tuned to high alert, I repeatedly tapped the brakes and rolled to a stop. I caught my breath, and Liselle pounded on the door.

"It's just not fair," she said. "Patrick wasn't perfect— not by a long shot, but he was a good provider. I don't know what I'll do now. Our larger natural diamonds are gone, and the value of what I have remaining is less than half. I don't know if I'm up to running the store by myself."

Maverick scratched the same panel Liselle had struck.

"Maverick, sit." He sat but continued to paw at the door. I checked my rearview mirror and inched forward. "Helen and William both act like they know what they're doing. Won't they stay and help?"

"Maybe. But I can't imagine them working for me. Can you?" I heard a thump. "Sheesh. Now my car is falling apart."

Maverick barked, once, and Liselle shouted, "Stop the car."

I came to a standstill at the side of the road under a streetlamp with my emergency flasher pulsing. My hands shook. My heart thudded. "What happened? Why did you need me to stop?"

She held out her hand. My jaw dropped.

NINETEEN

A deafening grind rumbled next to us, and snow
engulfed the SUV. Strobing lights from a snowplow
flashed across Liselle's glowering face and vanished down
the street. Nestled in the palm of her mittened hand were
two medium-sized, clear, shining stones.

"After Helen and I sorted the gems, I still had empty
slots in the diamond chest. Do you think you could take me
to the store to check these? So far, all of the substitutions
have an LG inscription." Her intoxicated haze had lifted.
"I can make the comparisons in just a few minutes. It's just
a block out of our way."

Safely ensconced in the hospital and under Pete's care,
I wouldn't worry about Dad. Ida would be fine for a few
extra minutes. The flurries had dwindled to nothing, and

I could follow a newly plowed portion of the road. "I can take you, but we should get back to Ida soon. I don't want to leave her alone in the dark."

We detoured through the quiet streets until we turned onto Main. Downtown was unaffected by the power outage, and the soft white light illuminated the shops. We parked in front of Donaldson's Fine Jewelry. Liselle hopped from the car and jogged around a snow-covered mound to the front. She unlocked the door, and once inside, she was in her element. She stomped across the floor, entered a code on a keypad, and flipped the interior lights on. She marched through the backroom and was swallowed by the basement.

I held Maverick at the top of the stairs, remembering his last trip down and comparing the gaping cavity to the jaws of doom.

"The city workers finally found the break in the water line and repaired it," Liselle called up. "And Henry made sure the pickle pot on the workbench is hooked up correctly with a brand-new cord. Nothing's going to happen."

"Who's Henry and what's a pickle pot?" I asked, as we clomped into the basement one slow step at a time. The room smelled musty and damp, but the standing water was gone, leaving a powdery residue. I shuddered at the cool air an industrial floor fan blew into my face. Liselle had opened the safe and removed the diamond chest. She paged through the envelopes and teased out a few. With a stone secured in the clamp, she turned on a high-powered lamp and rotated the knobs. She inspected the stone and recorded her findings on a card.

"Look for yourself."

I lined up my eye, adjusted the lenses, and peered into the microscope at a clear, brilliant round rock. "It's lovely, but even I can read the inscription." I looked away and, leery of trusting an unknown person to comment on the electrical hookup in this deadly basement, asked again, "Who's Henry?"

She removed the gem and analyzed the second stone with equal scrutiny. She slumped on the stool. "These are two more of the …" She groped for a word. "I guess I can say replacements. The statistics match the info on the glassine packages except for the lab grown part and the inclusions, but what were they doing in my car? Patrick had to know something. I'm so angry with him right now. If he weren't dead, I'd kill him."

I must have looked stunned.

"I didn't mean it." She turned a crank and released the stone. She poured each into an envelope and filed them in the chest. Before I thought of something to say, she deftly changed the subject. "Henry Mullhern's a friend."

"Do you have confidence in this friend's ability to work with electricity?"

She snorted. "Before he became a project manager, he tested for his journeyman electrician's license. Patrick and Henry started the electrician program together, but he stayed with it longer than Patrick," Liselle said. "He's a troubleshooter and can do just about anything."

Maverick paced. He balanced on his hind legs and brushed his muzzle against a white box tucked into the safe.

"That, my furry friend, is Patrick's refrigerator." She replaced the chest. "I suppose there's food in there I'd better get rid of. Do we have another minute?"

My phone buzzed. I held up one finger to indicate she had one minute more. I punched the button as she reached into the safe and opened the small white door. All that remained was a pungent odor that made my eyes water.

Liselle covered her nose. "He loved his stinky cheeses." Maverick circled her legs, and she opened a miniature freezer compartment stacked with ice cube trays.

"Hi, Ida." I shoved my phone between my shoulder and my jaw and attempted to haul Maverick out of Liselle's way with one hand, but he wriggled free, jumped up, and pawed the refrigerator shelf, searching.

"Are you on your way? I found something," Ida said.

"We'll be there in a few minutes." I hit end and wrapped my fingers around Maverick's collar. "Come." He turned. I unwrapped my fingers, and he casually sauntered next to me. I had to remember to use my word cues more often.

Liselle closed up efficiently, and we exited the building. The wind had stopped. Everything was still—the calm before the rest of the storm. She stood immobile. "Isn't it beautiful? Under these lights, the glinting crystals of snow look like billions of tiny diamonds. They'd be worth a fortune." She sighed. "Oh, Patrick."

I held out the SUV keys, but she shook her head. "I shouldn't drive. You go ahead. I'm going to call Chief West and tell her what we've found."

She left a message as I turned the key in the ignition. Nothing happened. I tried again.

"What kind of lousy tune-up did Ricky do?" Liselle growled, lifting her phone to her ear. "Henry, my car won't start."

She listened for a moment and said, "Release the hood." She jumped from the car and waited in front while I searched for the elusive control. After jabbing and pushing and pulling knobs and buttons, the hood popped. Liselle lifted it the rest of the way and propped it open. She leaned over the engine, still on the phone. I could see her hands working, checking connections, turning caps, rubbing the grime away.

I dialed Ida, hoping to tell her we were a little behind, but she didn't answer. I texted. No response. I didn't want to worry, but I wondered what she could be doing.

Liselle slammed the hood and pocketed her phone. She climbed in and said, "Give it a go."

The engine turned over. "What do you think of Henry now?" she said.

"Good job, Henry."

She looked at me guiltily. "If it hadn't worked, he'd have rescued us.

Ida's phone went to voicemail again. I shifted the gear to drive to get as close to Ida as fast as possible with as much care as necessary. I bit the inside of my cheek and expelled my angst over a long exhale, forcing out the words. "Can you please call your house phone? I can't get through to Ida on my cell."

She punched in some numbers. "Do you have a message?" she said cautiously.

"We're on our way. Call us back."

My mouth dried up. First Dad, then Ida.

"What does Henry do?"

She bit her lip and winced. "He's in charge of reconstructing and renovating the street in front of the store. They've been working on it since Christmas. He promised Patrick they'd complete the project in January."

My forehead scrunched. "How could Henry have rescued us?"

"He lives in the apartment over Bella's Boutique."

My first thought had been that Henry had sabotaged the car so he could rescue a damsel in distress. My second thought was that my first thought was dead on.

TWENTY

I gasped, observing the unlit ground floor of the Donaldson home. Liselle's car plowed up the drive, through the hills of snow. She pushed the garage-door opener and pushed again. No power. We glided next to Ida's car. I sprang out the door. Maverick sailed over the front seat to join me at the service entrance. Liselle unlocked it, and we hurried inside.

Behind us, Liselle said, "What's the rush?"

I pounded on the locked door to the house, anxious for Ida to answer. Liselle stepped in front of me with her key poised to open the lock "One second."

When the door opened, Maverick disappeared inside, and I pushed past Liselle. I called out in a panicked voice, "Ida. Where are you? Are you all right?"

"I'm in here." I followed the soft words to the living room. Ida sat in the big puffy chair under a thick woolen afghan, waving a leather-bound book in the diminishing firelight. "You should see this."

I knelt next to her and wrapped my arm around her shoulders. "You had me worried."

"Because the power's out?"

I nodded. "And you didn't answer your phone."

With her free hand she dug deep into her pocket and pulled out her cell phone. She tried to turn it on and held up the face for me to see. Blank. Her phone battery was dead. "Sorry," she said. "Maybe Liselle has a charger." She put her phone on the end table and looked down. "You're dripping onto the carpet."

I tugged off my boots and lined them up on the marble hearth.

"But you have to see these," she said again, flapping the pages of one small book. "They're just your cup of tea." She leaned close and said softly, "I think they're more of Patrick's code."

Liselle said from behind us. "Where did you find that?" She dropped her boots next to mine. "It's Patrick's."

"I'm a curious old bat. I was looking for something to read when I found this one among the vintage hardcovers on the shelf over there, inside the book-jacket of an old edition of *Robert's Rules of Order*." She pointed to the left of the fireplace. "I searched through a few more before the lights went out and found a second one masquerading as Asimov's *I, Robot*."

Liselle poured another glass of wine. Hypnotized by the swirling ruby liquid in her hand and the burning embers, she stood motionless. The wind curled the ashes with a ghostly howl.

Ida stared into the flames as well.

"What are you thinking about, Ida?"

"Just missing Casimer," she said. Although Casimir had been gone for a number of years, she still adored the love of her life. I reached for her hand.

"Ida, you're freezing." I shoved her hand back under the afghan. "Liselle, we need more wood." When she didn't answer, I tugged at her sleeve. "Liselle," I said more loudly.

She spun around, snatched one of the little books, and slid the mesh curtain on the fireplace to the side. "Patrick's journals are full of gibberish I can't read." She aimed to toss it into the lessening fire. "But they should make good fuel."

"Liselle, you can do that, but I may be able to help you decode it if you want."

She threw back the wine and weighed the book in her hand. Sparks hissed when she tossed it onto the remains of the fire. In the blink of an eye, she reached in with a fireplace tong and seized the smoking pages. She hiccupped and let the journal drop onto the end table. "Take it, but I want it to stay private."

The door creaked on the cabinet next to the fireplace which held wood stacked to six feet. Liselle stretched onto her toes and dragged two hefty logs from the top of the pile. She tossed the wood onto the smoldering ashes. In seconds the dry curly white bark of a birch branch ignited, and the flames burst with crackles and pops. She added more logs, and heat flooded the room.

Ida's head lolled to the side with the purr of a light snore. Liselle sat on the floor, feeding the fire. Maverick sat between us.

I opened the book and scanned the first few pages.

"He'd sit in his chair, writing, erasing, and rewriting his

private thoughts, trying to get it right." She took another sip of her wine. "He'd write me a message in his mystery language and when I couldn't read it correctly, he'd laugh and I'd pretend to laugh with him, but I never thought it meant anything. Can you?" she said staring into the flames. "Can you make sense of it?"

Some of the words on the first page were phonetic re-creations. By sounding out the letters, I translated a few messages. "Listen."

Early on, the text contained more real words than invented ones, and I read Patrick's sporadic entries detailing his dream of owning a jewelry store. He wrote about hiring Helen 'Ghocks' and the evolution of the game they played with the sounds of words. The more sophisticated phonic infographics appeared after he met Liselle—after he wrote 'Aye loaf hur.' I love her. The words were sweet and romantic. Liselle sat motionless, the colors of the fire dancing on her face.

Liselle's stoic façade melted, and she wiped the tears trickling down her cheeks. I skipped what followed. 'Seau duzz henrea.' So does Henry?

The room came to life when the electricity returned. The bright lights blinded me for a second, and the television blared. Ida startled awake, and I closed the book. "Sorry." She dabbed at the corners of her mouth. "It was too quiet in the house by myself, so I turned on some noise to keep me company, but I didn't think to turn it off after the power went out. Time to go," she murmured and wriggled to the front of the chair.

"Let me warm up the car first."

She acquiesced and flopped back, nestling into the cushions. I dragged myself from the floor and fumbled for my keys.

"The front door's closer, and there's a shovel." Liselle didn't look at me but continued to stare at the fire. She sounded composed.

I accidentally grabbed Liselle's boot and looked enviously at the fancy insignia on her footwear. I exchanged it for one of my own and squeezed my foot in. After I yanked on my second boot, I donned my coat and jangled the keys. Maverick followed me as I retraced my steps to the front door. "Stay." I gave him the hand signs to sit and wait.

I opened the door and breathed in the clean icy air. With a correct prognostication, the weather would hold for a short time before the snow picked up again. I grabbed the shovel from the stoop and tunneled a narrow path to the car. I thought twice about leaning the shovel against Ida's pristine wheels and dropped it to the ground instead.

The car started, and the fan blasted air I hoped would soon be warmer. I climbed from the car and cleared the snow from the windows and hood. Ida was bundled in her coat ready to leave by the time I reentered Liselle's house.

"Let's get going while the going's good," she said. "Good night, Liselle Anne. If there's anything we can do, we're only a phone call away." She looked thoughtful. "But you'd be luckier if you call Katie's phone."

Liselle handed me the pair of books wrapped in a plastic film. "Please." Her pleading eyes searched mine.

I tucked the package under one arm and led Ida out with the other. Maverick frolicked in the winter wonderland the entire trip to the car. He waited by my door while I settled Ida in the passenger seat and jumped in the driver's door to sit between us. His tongue dangled, and he panted happily as he swung his head from side to side, not willing to miss anything on the short drive.

We wrestled our way through the snow up the walk to my back door and shrugged out of our winter clothes. I set the books on my table and reset the digital clock in my kitchen, adding the missing seventy-two minutes, and followed Ida to her end of the house. Ida checked the thermostat. "It's a little chilly," she called. "Could you start a fire, Katie? And why don't you sleep here tonight?"

I assembled the bedding on the couch and warmed up some hotdish for the two of us. She turned on the television to a vintage episode of *I Love Lucy*. We chuckled at Lucy correcting Ricky's mispronunciation of multiple words ending in 'ough.' There was through, rough, bough, and cough.

My spoon clattered in my dish, and I jumped up. "That's it, Ida. There are so many ways one sound can be spelled, and Patrick Donaldson used as many of them as he could." I reached for one of the journals at the same time my phone rang. I handed Ida the little book and accepted the call.

"Dad?"

"How are my girls?"

"We're fine. But you're supposed to be resting. How are you?"

"Pete and I watched the blizzard rage for a while, but he got called away, and I'm bored. I did, however, overhear the nurses on the floor. They wheeled in a victim of a hit-and-run who's in critical condition. I'm checking to make sure you're safe and sound."

"We are, Dad. We're watching *I Love Lucy* reruns." He didn't need to know we'd also been driving around in the blizzard. "What do you think of that? No smart comeback?"

Alarms sounded. I heard a 'Code Blue' announcement

in the background. I croaked out. "Dad." When he didn't answer, I said more forcefully, "Dad?"

My panic met the noisy exhale of a yawn, and Dad said, "It's not me darlin'. And now I probably won't get any shut eye. They're scrambling all over here. I'd better go. I'll see you tomorrow."

I stared at the phone screen, wishing him home soon.

"It sounded like Harry needed someone to talk to. Is he doing well?"

"I think he is."

Ida fanned the pages of the journal and stopped on the first page. "I can read a few words of what Pat wrote. Would you be so kind as to explain a bit more?"

"I don't have it all, but I think I can muscle it out given enough time. Mr. Donaldson used a variety of spellings for the same phonetic sound. Like Desi trying to read 'ough.' If it were bough, the spelling for the sound could be 'ow' as in cow. Though has an 'ough' that rhymes with the 'ow' in throw but also 'oa' and 'eau.'"

"This is an arduous task, but Pat's not in any hurry."

I yawned and nestled the books among Dad's tomes. "No, but Susie might be."

TWENTY-ONE

The rest of the predicted snow never fell. The plows cleared the roads. Although the heaps of white had grown by inches, school started on time—a fresh beginning. I spent the morning welcoming old and new students, assigning seats and books when necessary, sharing expectations and classroom rules, and working through a short lesson plan in the few remaining minutes of each hour. Luckily, ZaZa kept herself equally busy, and the only interaction we had was a mutual head bob—until I entered the teachers' lounge at lunchtime.

"Katie, over here." Jane waved a hand and pointed to the seat next to ZaZa. To sit elsewhere would have been awkward.

They talked fashion and travel. I didn't have much

to contribute and nibbled on leftover bean casserole. Although I worried about Dad, he was safe, and I itched to unlock the infographics in Donaldson's journals, and weird combinations of letters coalesced into sounds in my head. Maybe it would help Liselle read what few notes she had left and help figure out if Donaldson had exchanged his diamonds and why, or maybe how he died.

"Katie?" ZaZa pursed her lips and frowned. "You didn't hear a word I said."

I gave my head a tiny shake. "I guess I was thinking of—" If it didn't sound important, I'm sure ZaZa would pout. "Dad."

"Your Dad?"

Among other things. I nodded. "He blacked out. It's the second episode in a week, and they kept him overnight in the hospital."

"Is he doing well?" Jane folded her lunch bag, collected her trash, and leaned forward to speak past ZaZa. "When's he coming home?"

"I'm expecting a call any minute with an update."

"Mock trial practice is all I have on my docket today, and we can do it without you. Take care of your dad."

ZaZa's bottom lip stuck out. "Jane, I thought you were going to help me shop for my winter togs?"

Jane and Charles had much the same eyeroll when it came to ZaZa, and I bit my lip to keep from laughing out loud.

"I assure you we'll get everything sorted out later today," said Jane.

ZaZa began enumerating her list of necessary 'togs,' and I zoned out again, catching snippets of conversation from the other tables.

"Smart as a whip. He won the industrial ed competition

as a junior."

"Dumb as a box of rocks. Doesn't know how to apply himself."

"Caught him on camera. Practically looked right at it."

"They've looked everywhere."

"What's everyone talking about, Jane? What did I miss?" I'd interrupted ZaZa. The look on her face could have frozen fireworks.

"Drew said Chief West thinks that Lenny guy might've been working with someone and had a falling out. It might even have been Donaldson. Video footage from the pawn shop downtown has Lenny hocking a ring. William Dix has a habit of frequenting the pawn shop, just like Pat, and the ring turned out to be one from their inventory."

"That certainly sounds suspicious. How did Lenny get the ring?"

"Guess someone will have to ask him."

My phone dinged with three minutes left in the lunch break. I excused myself, reading a text from Dad as I rushed to the math office.

Your FRIEND is keeping me for a few more hours.

That's good Dad. I wouldn't want you to come home too early. Any particular reason?

His response took too long, and I texted Pete.

Dad said he gets to stay for a while?

The three dots of doom took forever to translate into words.

Harry blacked out again this morning. It may have been nothing, but the hospitalist scheduled him for a few more tests. I concur.

What tests?

An EKG and a tilt test. But I'm certain he'll be ready to leave after school.

I texted Dad.

I'll call before I come to pick you up. LOVE YOU. Behave.

I received permission from Mr. Ganka to leave as soon as I finished teaching my last class, so I texted Dad my projected arrival time.

I listened to the voicemail Dad left while I had droned on about integrals and derivatives with my calculus class. Dad had replied he couldn't wait to see me again. He really wanted to get out of there. I couldn't wait to see him either.

We played telephone tag. When Dad didn't pick up, I placed a call to the nurses' station on his floor.

"He's a hoot," the voice said. "He's been chomping at the bit for an hour."

"Please tell him I'm on my way. I'll be there in less than ten minutes."

"We'll get him checked out, Katie. He'll be waiting at the entrance."

I called Ida on the short drive with an update.

"I'll have supper ready," my food maven said.

As I swung through the porte-cochere at the front of the hospital, Dad threw back his head and laughed at something he heard from a man in wrinkly blue-green scrubs. He rose shakily from the wheelchair and latched onto a steadying arm. My car's vents still blew cool air, so I made sure it was in park and left it running before leaping out to join them.

"Why do you need a wheelchair, Dad?" I said, my voice hitching. *What new malady had attacked him?*

I took his one small bag and his other arm and must have looked ridiculous as I gazed into their amused faces.

"Aren't you going to say hi, darlin'?" Dad asked.

The stubble on Pete's chin didn't disguise his pallor. Gray bags hung under his huge brown bloodshot eyes, but they still twinkled. "The wheelchair is required use by all patients being released. Harry's doing well." He winked at me. "Hi, Katie."

"Hi, Pete. Sorry, I didn't recognize you, but I had this galoot to worry about." I plastered a grin on my face. "Long night?"

"Twenty hours." He tugged off a blue cap and untethered a riot of chocolate waves. "Not a bad night, all in all."

"He took care of that patient I told you about—the hit-and-run on the east side, next to Carlson's Hardware. Our friend here probably saved the guy's life." Pete stared at his feet. Dad nudged him lightly. "C'mon. You did great, kid."

"And he saved yours too, Dad," I said. "Thanks, Pete. You look like—"

"I know." A yawn escaped. "I'm finishing up as soon as we get Harry settled in your car."

Pete installed Dad in the passenger seat and handed me a page of instructions. We waved as we pulled away from the curb.

"Do you need anything before we head home?"

Dad's head dropped back against the headrest. "Nope. I have everything I need right here." He patted my arm, and for a second, I thought I'd have to pull over to clear away my tears.

He closed his eyes and said, "The nurses couldn't praise Pete enough. He worked on that patient and wouldn't give up even though they thought it might've been a lost cause."

"How awful."

Dad didn't say anything or move for the rest of our short jaunt, and I snuck sidelong glances at him to make sure he was still breathing.

We took slow methodic steps up the slippery walkway and were greeted by the sound of Maverick's nails scraping the door, occasionally connecting with the knob, and rattling it. I opened the door. Dad smiled at the picture-perfect ebullient canine welcome.

Ida fixed a luscious roasted butternut squash soup for Dad and me. I cleaned up, and she fussed about, straightening his lap quilt, delivering a cup of lemon verbena tea, and adding logs to a roaring fire. "If you need anything, Harry, just call out." She winked, parroting his phrase of days earlier.

"I'm fine, Ida. And you will be the first …" He slowly turned his head and caught my eye. "… or second to know if anything changes. Go."

And just like that she disappeared.

Dad sat with his herbal tea and a book, and I prepared for day two of the semester.

When Maverick lifted his head and slowly uncurled from his spot next to Dad in front of the warm, crackling fire, he stretched and padded to the door adjoining Ida's apartment, standing expectantly.

"I knew it couldn't last," said Dad.

TWENTY-TWO

The knob turned and Maverick sat. I swallowed the smart remark I planned for Ida when Susie stepped through. Ida stood behind her, gave me a commiserative look, and closed the door.

Susie furiously wiped tears from her eyes. "I'm sorry. Hormones."

Dad rose and hugged her. "Congratulations. Now, if you'll excuse me, I've got a good book to finish." He held up a water bottle. "And this to drink as per doctor's orders." He gave me another look I couldn't read and retired to his room. Maverick curled up in Dad's place.

"What can I do for you, Susie?"

"I'm afraid I top Chief West's list of suspects."

"That can't be true. Even I know you wouldn't kill

anyone. She's a good investigator. She'll find the real killer."

"Not this time. She doesn't believe me. I'm not at all sure I would either. I need your help."

Stacking books and papers is a great way to avoid looking someone in the eye. "I don't know how I can help you."

I watched Maverick bound from the chair and sidle next to Susie. He shoved his nose under her hand, closed his eyes, and leaned toward her as she scratched between his ears. He opened his eyes and tilted his head—kryptonite to my resolve. *Traitor.*

"Please. I didn't do anything. You know I wouldn't ask, but I don't know where to turn. Gregory's a wreck." It took me a moment to process Tiny's given name. "I've been put on leave from the hospital, and Pete's busier than ever." She looked at Maverick and raised her voice. "And you owe me."

"Right." I froze in place and anger simmered around my words. "If Maverick hadn't stopped you from barreling into the basement to do what you were trained to do, you might not be here."

"I mean telling you about ZaZa. I was right, wasn't I?"

I swallowed, nodded weakly, and met her gaze. Behind the sulky pucker of her lips, I saw a touch of fear.

She put her hands on her hips, and the Susie I knew came back full force. "Come to think of it, I stopped *you* from going to Donaldson's rescue just like Maverick stopped me."

She had a point. "Have a seat. Can I get you something to drink?"

"Water would be great." She removed her coat and settled on the couch. Maverick followed her and stretched out at her feet, blinking his big brown sappy eyes at me.

I returned with two glasses of water. She took one big gulp after another and set the empty glass on the coffee table.

"Where do I begin? I'm sorry—"

"You already said that."

"Please, let me get this out." She looked at her hands, opening and closing her fists. "I'm sorry I got between you and Pete. I'll claim hormones again, but it was a little of everything. Jealousy is a wicked sister. I laid it on a little thick when I saw you with Dr. Bluestone."

"A little thick?" I gulped the air and crossed my arms like protective armor. My right palm covered my mouth, smothering the invectives I wanted to let fly.

"I told myself I wanted the best for Pete, and you weren't it."

I bristled. Before I could respond she went on.

"When I found out I could be expecting, I wrote Gregory every day for a month and never heard from him. At least I didn't know he responded. I was afraid and I panicked." She lowered her voice. "Next to Gregory, Pete is one of my oldest and dearest friends. He's the only other person I told, and he promised he'd take care of everything. When he asked me to marry him, I figured my prayers had been answered. If Pete hadn't intervened, who knows …" Her eyes met mine. "Pete loves me like a little sister." I didn't respond. "With all that entails."

My jaw dropped. "You mean you never …"

One corner of her mouth went up. "Can't say I didn't give it a thought, but I love Gregory. I've always loved him, and he adores me. Pete contacted Gregory, to make sure he knew what he would be missing, and he came back for me." She blinked away bright tears. "Life would be great except I'm the number one suspect in a murder investigation."

I took out a notebook and pencil. "Why do you think Chief West has you on her list?" I tapped the paper. "Hit me."

She took a deep breath, closed her eyes, rubbed her tummy, and exhaled slowly. When she opened her eyes, they were filled with fierce determination. "First of all, I didn't steal that SUV. I was directed to pick up a vehicle at the hospital garage. It would be parked inside the door with the keys in the ignition, just like Donaldson's. My outreach supervisor sent Chief West a copy of his email with his explicit instructions. I did exactly what I was told." She shook her head. "I had no idea there were gems in its panels. I wonder what would have happened if the police would have found them Thursday when they stopped me. I probably would've been locked up and wouldn't be accused of Donaldson's murder."

"Who told you about the diamonds Liselle found?"

"Ronnie Christianson. He came to the hospital and said he had a few innocent questions to ask me. Let me tell you, they felt anything but innocent. That's why I was put on leave." She sighed.

"I don't know much about diamonds, but Gregory doesn't make things up. If he said the ring was different, it was." Her head angled to one side. Susie, sitting next to Maverick, pleading with a parallel head tilt, doubled the effect of the kryptonite. "You thought they were different too."

"I'm no expert. I just wondered aloud."

"I know someone must have switched the stones, and I confronted Donaldson before I had proof. I checked with the jeweler at the mall. He confirmed the stone in the ring was more square and shallower than the measurements written on the appraisal. I went back to challenge Donaldson with my new evidence. Maybe the other characteristics are subjective, but the numbers are not. Unfortunately, that big mouth Dix guy took my earlier remark out of context and already told Chief West."

My eyebrows lifted. "You were so focused on getting the ring back, you didn't notice Jane and I were shopping for jewelry that day. I heard you say you couldn't be held responsible for what you might do, and it sounded like a threat to me too."

"I didn't mean I'd do *anything*, but I was so angry." She sniffed and wiped her face with the back of her hand. Spidery red lines covered her cheeks.

A little panicky, I asked, "Are you alright? Your face is all red."

"It's telangiectasia. My mom had it when she was pregnant with me. Where was I?" She scratched her head. "Oh, yes. Then William found a ring in the pawn shop."

I didn't respond.

"You don't seem surprised. Did you know about it? It could have been mine."

"The teachers at school talked about the pawn shop and a ring Lenny brought in. They also hinted that Lenny and Donaldson might have been working together. Why does Chief West have you on the top of her list?"

She wiped her eyes and ticked off the answers on her fingers. "Well, let's see. I was mistakenly arrested for stealing Mrs. Donaldson's SUV. Someone at Donaldson's stole my diamond. I threatened Donaldson. You and Maverick found me with the body. I don't have an alibi for the time of death, and because Lenny's in the hospital, she's focusing all her attention on me."

I stopped scribbling. "Lenny's in the hospital?

"He was the victim of a hit-and-run."

I forced my face into a deadpan.

"He'd just left the pawn shop." Her wistful tone caught me off guard. "I heard he might have a great girlfriend and gotten a full-time job. More power to him, but it is totally out of character. He never seemed able to make any commitment before. But he isn't out of the woods yet. Pete stayed with him most of the night to help ensure his well-being."

I cocked my head. "That's awful, but what does that have to do with your guilt or innocence?"

She lowered her eyes. "Gregory and I broke up the summer after he graduated, and Lenny Capsner and I got together. He was nice enough for an old guy but a little too unindustrious for me. Ronnie insinuated Lenny might have had some damaging information, something from our personal history to sabotage my relationship with Gregory, of the blackmail kind." She looked up and her voice hardened. "Chief West has two theories. She suggested I paid off Lenny with my ring. Or Donaldson took my ring, and I had Lenny use his miniscule background in electricity to do away with the thief, and we had a falling out. Either way, I could have run him over to get rid of him. They've even confiscated my car. But that's completely absurd."

"What's Lenny's background in electricity?"

"He won an industrial ed competition his junior year in high school, but he never did anything with it."

Her head dropped forward, and her shoulders shook. Maverick put his head in her lap and her hand grasped his fur as if holding on for dear life.

Susie wiped her eyes and glanced at the questions I'd scratched onto the notepaper. In an increasingly incredulous tone, she read, "When was the Donaldson's

SUV supposed to be delivered to Ricky for its tune-up? How often did William frequent pawn shops and why? Who benefits from Donaldson's murder? Was Lenny run down purposely? Does he know something? Where was Susie when Donaldson was killed?"

"Do you know when Lenny was struck by the car?" I asked.

A mix of anger, confusion, and panic filled Susie's face, and she sputtered.

"I-I'm not sure. I use all my powers of concentration at work. Gregory says I suffer from pregnancy-induced hypoxic encephalopathy." A tiny smile reached her eyes, and I could see so much love there.

"Come again?"

"Baby brain—my brain sometimes acts as if it doesn't get enough air. I walk into a room and ask myself, why am I here? But, if you're curious, I'm sure Pete knows the details. He was working when they brought Lenny in."

"Susie, where were you when Patrick Donaldson was killed?"

"I can't say."

Can't or won't.

"Do you know where Tiny was?"

"Don't go there, Katie. Gregory is the kindest, sweetest, most loving man on the planet, and he wouldn't hurt a flea."

I cleared my throat. "Susie, he's a hunting guide."

She burst into tears.

TWENTY-THREE

Lucky for me, on the first day of classes, I had no homework to correct because two minutes after Susie dried her tears and composed herself enough to drive home, the doorbell rang again.

Tiny looked worse than Pete had after his twenty hours in the emergency room, like he'd been living on fast food, sugar, and caffeine. "Katie, Susie's banking on you." He walked back and forth. He stopped, yanked up his pants, and paced again. "She doesn't think anyone cares. She's scared. So am I."

"I don't know what I can do."

"Do your magic. She's been through so much. Help her." He took a greedy drink of water. "Find out who did these terrible things."

"What has Susie been through?"

"I've said too much." His mouth twitched.

"Tiny? What has Susie been through?" I said more gently. "Maybe it'll help. How will I know what she's been through if you don't tell me? How do you expect me to help her?"

He gritted his teeth. His whiskers shifted back and forth. "The first time we broke up because she was gambling and couldn't stop. She wasn't old enough to go anywhere and placed her bets with Lenny—always picking losers."

"He was her bookie?" *Not good.*

Tiny nodded. "She thought it was funny. I did not. She promised she'd stop but blamed me for her lapses because my job took me away for weeks at a time. But then she found a career she loved, and she had people who cared about her. She had help fighting her gambling obsession. We've had our ups and downs, separated by time and distance, but she's stuck with Gamblers Anonymous for five years. I'm so proud of her."

"If she's doing so well, why are you worried?"

His breathing filled the room. "Since I've been back, she's disappeared a few times and won't tell me where she went. I know she didn't kill anyone." His chin trembled. "Please, Katie. I love her."

"I'll do what I can, but I can't promise anything."

"That's all I ask." His words rushed out. "Thank you."

Tiny left me stewing with many thoughts, but none of them would help Susie. I thought transcribing Donaldson's journals might spark my creativity, but I forgot where I'd put them. I searched my briefcase, my desk, the kitchen counters, finally remembering I'd put them on the bookshelf.

I dusted soot from one cover and opened the journal.

Maybe because my mind was wrestling with other thoughts, when I stared long enough, more of the letter combinations started to make sense, and I performed an internal fist bump for each breakthrough in the painstaking translation of the altered words. I penciled my transcription in the margins and snapped a few photos.

The daunting task gave me a little insight into the narcissist who thought himself brilliant. Donaldson detailed his work with 'Ghocks' since he opened the doors of Donaldson's Fine Jewelry. He admitted using Helen's loyalty and good-natured personality to create the phonics game for her when engraving. The anecdotes described the self-proclaimed clever ways he baffled those around him. Every word in the journal was written to make him look disgustingly superior. My lips puckered as if I'd downed something sour.

The tenor of the text changed after he hired Liselle. He wrote how proud he was of her artistic prowess. Initially, Donaldson had been pleased by the sums paid for Liselle's one-of-a-kind silver creations, but soon his words sounded jealous. He didn't want her work to outshine his. After he married her and put her in her place—his words—the vituperative remarks multiplied. I snapped a photo of some of the more intelligible messages and closed the first journal.

I yawned, and the next thing I knew, the book thudded to the floor. I picked it up, and the embossed leather cover slid askew. The crusty glue residue became dust on my palm as I tried to reposition the book block, but a scrunched-up piece of paper got in the way. I squashed it against the cover and wriggled it loose. The bent corners acted like tiny handles I used to peel the folded page apart.

I flattened the sheet and squinted to read the print, then

performed a little research dance on my phone. I wrinkled my nose and couldn't begin to imagine the trouble I'd be in if I waited on this. Checking the time, I inhaled deeply and punched the keys on my phone.

"This better be good, Katie." came the terse greeting.

"I found a copy of a plane ticket to Vanuatu in one of Pat Donaldson's journals."

"A journal. More gibberish writing, I suppose."

"Yes, but …" I texted a screen shot. "Amanda, the journal contained a first-class ticket for Monday."

I heard rustling. "I'll be right there to pick it up."

"The backyard light will be on."

I flipped the switch, illuminating the entire yard. Maverick tore into the snow as I hustled out to open the gate. I hightailed it back to my warm kitchen, and Maverick continued to plow through the fluffy white stuff with relish. I sighed. If only I could be so carefree. In one brief moment, I lost track of Maverick, and the door flew open. He had perfected the one exercise I wished he'd never learned—he'd stood on his hind legs, drawn down the handle, and pushed. His nails clicked as he pranced into my kitchen like a king. I reached to close the door. The yelp I let loose scared me.

I clutched my chest, eyeing a figure at the top of the stairs. Before I could take a breath, Dad barreled into the kitchen wearing a hot pink t-shirt and black boxers covered in big red hearts, carrying a baseball bat. He snuck around behind me and said to Maverick, "Some watch dog you are."

I covered my lips and smothered a laugh.

"You scared the bejeezus out of me, Katie. And you." He pointed the handle of the bat. "I almost made mincemeat out of you. What are you doing here, Doc?"

"I suppose you're here to encourage me to help Susie." I tilted my head.

He laughed. "I wanted to see how my girlfriend was doing." My stomach did a nosedive to my toes. He cleared his throat. "I may also have heard from Tiny who informed me you were on track to help Susie, and he'd just left." He put both hands out. "I'm here to help."

We turned in unison as headlights bounced down the driveway. Amanda parked her patrol car behind Pete's Ram truck.

"Let's get this party started." Dad wriggled, then looked down at his knobby knees and bare feet. "Never mind. Don't stay up too late. Goodnight, Doc." He turned and hustled to his room. The door clicked softly.

"I hope I'm not breaking up your evening rendezvous." Amanda's throaty chuckle carried through the calm night as she trudged across the yard. Her kinky black hair hung over her shoulder in a fishtail braid. "Evening, Doctor Erickson."

"Evening, Chief West. No rendezvous yet."

She looked him up and down. One eyebrow rose as if to say, 'I wonder how much of that line is true.' Her mischievous eyes didn't miss a thing.

"It's not like that." He looked cute, fumbling for his words.

Amanda's buffed skin shone under the moon. She shoved one hand in a pocket and used the other to draw the collar of her jacket closer.

"Come in. Come in." I backed up from the entry. They hung their coats, and I led the way to the kitchen. Circling the table, Amanda scrutinized the book, the ticket, and the cover. I heated water.

"How did you come by this?" Amanda drew on nitrile gloves.

"Ida and I brought a casserole to Liselle. Ida found this journal hidden inside the cover of *Roberts Rules of Order*. I saved it from becoming fire fuel by promising to translate it for her if possible."

She picked up each piece, examined it, and placed it in an evidence bag. The gloves came off in time for lemon verbena tea and Ida's molasses cookies. "You said *this* journal. Do you have more of these?"

I handed the second one over reluctantly. Taking both books would halt any headway I could make decrypting the coded messages for Liselle. Amanda tugged at the cover and held the book open right side up and upside down. She jiggled the book block, prying the spine from the cover, and returned it to the table.

"If you find a secret compartment in this one, let me know." She secured the evidence bags in a satchel. "We'll follow up on the ticket." A cookie froze on the way to her mouth. "Why wouldn't anyone mention his upcoming trip? It's a big one."

"Maybe he hadn't told anyone?"

"The question is why not? And why Vanuatu?"

"It doesn't have an extradition treaty with the United States." They looked at me incredulously. I shrugged. "I had a little time to kill. I looked it up."

"You believe he was running away." Pete dipped his cookie in his tea and watched Amanda's face. "Do you think he took the natural diamonds? He could have cashed them in and pocketed the difference in value, hoping to escape … something."

"Possibly, but neither the currency nor the diamonds have turned up. We've tried to follow a money trail, but there doesn't seem to be one." Amanda sipped her tea daintily and carefully set the cup on the table.

"Is Capsner a suspect? He pawned a ring."

"They weren't part of the cache of missing stones. He might have been in on a theft, but he was seen on camera at the mall on Saturday after he left Donaldson's. And I'm not sure when he could have pulled off the electrical scheme." She bit into one of Ida's molasses cookies, closed her eyes, and hummed. When she opened them, she said, "The question remains. How does that prove Susie Kelton's guilt?"

Pete's face turned gray.

Amanda bade us good night with a sly smile. Pete stayed to finish his tea, and we examined the first few pages of the second journal, translating some of the passages, and sharing thoughts. Although none of our ideas directed us to the killer, they didn't all lead to Susie either. Pete and I divided up a list of people to talk to until my uncontrollable yawns sent him on his way.

TWENTY-FOUR

When students got antsy, I lectured quickly, assigned homework to support the skill, allowed time to digest the material and ask questions in class, and provided a funny, interesting, or mysterious anecdote of a brilliant mathematician. I did the same when *I* felt antsy.

"Einstein maintained an incredible ability to simplify the complex. As an eminent professor at Princeton, he received invitations to gatherings, and he tended to decline because if he accepted, he was invariably asked to explain, in a few words, his theory of relativity. Once in a while, business required he make himself available to patrons with funds."

I opened and read from my ancient copy of *In Mathematical Circles*. "Einstein said he was reminded of a walk he one day had with his blind friend. The day was hot and he turned to the blind friend and said, 'I wish I had a glass of milk.' 'Glass,' replied the blind friend, 'I know what that is. But what do you mean by milk?' 'Why, milk is a white fluid,' explained Einstein. 'Now fluid, I know what that is,' said the blind man. 'But what is white?' 'Oh, white is the color of a swan's feathers.' 'Feathers, now I know what they are, but what is a swan?' 'A swan is a bird with a crooked neck.' 'Neck, I know what that is, but what do you mean by crooked?' At this point Einstein said he lost his patience. He seized his blind friend's arm and pulled it straight. 'There, now your arm is straight,' he said. Then he bent the blind friend's arm at the elbow. 'Now it is crooked.' 'Ah,' said the blind friend. 'Now I know what milk is.' And Einstein, at the tea, sat down. Relativity."

I finished reading and closed the book, smiling gaily, and looked up into a roomful of blank faces. Lorelei carefully mouthed one word. "Weird." Although I appreciated the humor in the story, most of them did not. Thankfully, the bell rang and relieved my growing embarrassment. I looked up a new anecdote, just in case: although numbers dictated content, form, and structure to Shakespeare's volumes, among all his dramas, the word 'mathematics' only appears in *The Taming of the Shrew*.

I took my assignment from Pete seriously. I called Liselle during my lunchbreak and arranged to visit at three forty-five. The forensics team had completed their analysis. Amanda had given them the go-ahead to remain open. Liselle, Helen, and William would be there. I planned to meet Ricky at five when her shift ended. In my off moments during the day, I constructed a wheel with spokes to represent the relationships, motives, means, and opportunities of anyone even tangentially involved.

Unfortunately, Susie earned more affirmations than anyone else, and I crumpled my first, second, and third attempts to find a way to tie someone else to the theft or the murder and get her off the hook.

At the end of the day, Jane and I reviewed our team's preparations and answered last-minute questions. "You know you've got this down. You are so ready," she said, catching the eye of each student. "This is going to be one more notch on your belt. Eat a good lunch. The bus leaves at the beginning of fourth period. Be ready to rock and roll." She gathered the students in a circle, and we put our hands together in the middle. "One. Two. Three. EsqChoir." We cheered and raised our fists.

My mind wandered, wheeling through the busy streets. I maneuvered my car into the short misshapen parking space in front of Donaldson's as best I could, and I didn't care the front end stuck out. I sat and gathered my thoughts until jolted when Liselle tapped on my window.

"Have you finished translating his nonsense?"

"No, but I was hoping we could toss around some ideas. Maybe one of you noticed something different about Pat over the last few days. Are William and Helen here?"

"William just stepped out. He'll be back shortly."

Liselle led me through the door to a circle of chairs behind the workbench; we could talk, and they could monitor the front door for customers—just in case someone should decide to brave the weather, the construction, or the circumstances surrounding Donaldson's death.

The silent treatment tactic worked for our mock trial attorney-coach, Dorene Dvorak. I thought I'd give it a whirl. Helen slouched in the chair and bit her thumbnail until the words tumbled forth. "I can't think of a reason why anyone would want Pat dead."

"Do you think it has something to do with the lab grown replacements?" Liselle asked. "Someone significantly decreased the value of our four hundred twenty-thousand-dollar inventory through the substitutions and there aren't too many ways the inventory could have been replaced."

Helen's eyes darted from the cash register to Liselle to me. "Patrick, of course, William, you, and I all have keys and access." She crossed and uncrossed her ankles. "I know I didn't take anything. We had workmen downstairs dealing with the water, but I've never known Pat to leave his precious diamonds unprotected. He opened the safe in the morning and removed the displays to install in the showcases. Then he closed it and reopened it as needed or at the end of the day to resecure the displays and only removed the chest containing the loose stones when a customer requested something special or if he had a new addition." She cocked her head. "The alarm system had been acting up. That's why he hooked it up to a generator. He was being extra careful. I don't know why Pat would pay for the protection and then switch the stones."

"Could anyone open the safe? Or was the combination known only to Pat?"

"Patrick felt it was his responsibility to open the safe as long as he was in the store." Maverick padded to Liselle's side, and she scratched behind his ears. "If he wasn't here, he'd give one of us the combination so we could open the safe, but he'd change the combination immediately afterwards."

"Did he give one of you the combination recently?"

Liselle and Helen exchanged a look. "His memory wasn't perfect. Helen discovered long ago he jotted the combination on the underside of one of the shelves for safekeeping so we always could find it. Would you like to see the safe?"

I blew out a small burst of air. "Please.

Maverick nudged Liselle. She scribbled on a work envelope and handed it to Helen who stood and said, resignedly, "This way."

I stood on the bottom step and wrinkled my nose at the stale smell of the basement, shivering in the cool damp air, noting the dusty white scum on the floor.

"It's safe. After Liselle's friend hooked everything up, Chief West had her people inspect the connections and check out the generator's use." She waved me over and flashed the numbers on the work envelope. Even if I didn't know the one-inch-high digits written in black marker made up a combination code, the dashes helped. "May I try?"

"Go ahead. There's not much in it worth stealing. Liselle found the directions and has already changed the combination once. If we stay open, she's getting a whole new security system anyway."

On my second pass, I increased the number of spins on the dial between the digits. It clicked. I pulled the heavy door open and reclosed it. "Not wholly secure." I spun the dial and tugged on the safe door. Satisfied, I turned around. The grit beneath my shoes crackled in the empty room, feeling like sugar crystals. "Helen?"

"Over here."

I followed the rueful voice around a set of shelves through a narrow passageway, brushing aside slimy cobwebs, to a malodorous, dimly lit chamber housing a mildew covered chair, and a rickety end table with an overflowing ashtray, reeking of stale cigarette smoke. "What is this dismal place?" I said, taking a deep breath through my sleeve.

Helen pointed to a door on the far side. "That opens to the generator room." She pointed to the letter combinations written on the walls.

"Phonic Infographics. Is this a key?"

"He kept track of some of it here." Helen shrugged. "To be honest, his engraving work orders were easy. You've seen how it works. If you read the combinations of sounds out loud a few times, you can come up with a good approximation of a translation. I rarely got it wrong. Pat checked my solutions, and we'd get a good chuckle." She turned a gold band on her finger. "At least in the days before he became so snappy and distracted." She looked up. "His instructions for the newer jobs were more obscure."

I took photos and, in the flash, noticed the shadow of a recessed decorative rectangular wooden panel on the wall. "What's that?"

Helen ran her hand along the depression. "Pat once told me the basement was part of one giant maze below the shops on the block, connected for safety reasons. This is probably the gateway, but the panel has been shut as long as I've been here. I've no idea what's behind it."

"Did Chief West see this place? Does she know about the maze?"

"I don't know. I'd forgotten about the passageway until now. The police were in here though, and Officer Christianson found no evidence he needed to preserve."

Helen sneezed. "Allergies," she said, and sneezed again.

"Do you know how to open the panel?"

She yanked on the drawer handle of the end table and, the third time, it flew open. The contents crashed to the floor. She sorted through the miscellany and freed three tarnished bronze skeleton keys, holding them up in triumph and pressing them into my palm with an encouraging nod.

I turned to the panel and scanned the decorative grating for an aperture, running my fingers along the crisscrossing components and found a camouflaged hollow. The first key fit into the depression but didn't turn. The second key was too large. The third was the charm. It fit and turned, and the panel squawked as it swung about six inches and stopped. I rammed my shoulder against the wood and heard a rasping sound as the panel attempted to dislodge whatever obstructed the entrance.

Helen met my gaze, and her eyes grew. With her help, we opened the panel another six inches. "I'm going to see where this goes." She nodded vigorously. I turned on my phone flashlight and squeezed through. Helen made no attempt to follow. The panel swung back into place.

TWENTY-FIVE

I navigated the crowded space through straight rows of boxes stacked on pallets labeled in neat script, 'Bella's Boutique.'

"Bella." I called over a whirring industrial drying fan. Identical empty plastic tubs lined the storage shelves, and I followed the zigzagging path to the staircase. "Bella?" I grabbed the ornate newel post, circled around the bottom step, and glanced up.

A pale stricken face appeared at the top of the stairs. Bella gripped a cellphone in her hand. "Katie? What are you doing down there?" Her face relaxed. The hand holding the phone dropped to her side. She fumbled for her pocket.

I mounted three steps. "Did you know the basements on the block are connected?"

She tilted her elfin face in confusion and then recognition. "I think I once heard our landlord say something about a warren of gateways to use in case of fire or as a safety backdoor. I've never even thought to look for it. Is that how you got in my basement?"

I nodded and held up the key. "Do you have one of these?"

Her head followed her eyes to a wicker basket on top of a vintage wooden filing cabinet. She dug through the contents, finally raising a matching key. "I always wondered what this was for. Can you show me?"

I directed her to the panel entry for Donaldson's. Helen waved shyly when Bella peeked in. "Is there a similar rectangle someplace else down here?"

Bella nodded and led me under the stairs. "When Susie Kelton worked for me, she helped me organize my storage room."

"Susie worked here?" *More bad news.*

"Yes. She labeled all the totes and alphabetized the contents for me. It's not quite the same anymore, but I try. She built a custom trellis to hang our necklaces, bracelets, chains, beads, and baubles, and hide that ugly panel."

We removed the lattice work, and she handed me the key. "Any idea what might be on the other side?" I asked, slotting it into position.

"I never opened it." She screwed up her face, perplexed. "I believe there are eight businesses on our block, and this faces the street."

I turned the key. The hatch opened into a cubicle. A steel grate covered the spotless window shedding bars of light on the dusty three-by-three-foot egress and a third panel access. I exhaled and punched in a number on my phone.

"What's up now, Katie?"

"Amanda, the basements on Donaldson's block are all connected."

She inhaled and exhaled slowly, sounding like air being released from a balloon. "We're doing our job, Katie. I'm looking at the blueprint for the block of buildings now. You absolutely cannot be investigating. How did *you* come across the network?" Amanda's disapproval was palpable.

"Helen showed me the basement room with the infographics key on the wall, and …" I skipped the mention of how easy it was to open the safe. What could I say so I wouldn't get in trouble. "We found the passageway. Bella's key also opens to the entry on the street."

Paper rustled. "That's not on our plan. Rodgers is on his way."

The phone felt heavy in my hand. I thanked Bella and rejoined Helen, passing her the key.

We made our way back upstairs and walked in on Liselle handing a package to a customer. "Thanks. Have a great day." The patron turned and strolled toward the door, eyeing the beautiful jewelry. With the instincts of a successful salesperson, Liselle jumped at the opportunity. "While you're here, let me show you something I think suits you." She gracefully sidled next to a showcase and within minutes the customer had tried on a necklace, oohed and aahed, paid for it, and strode out the door, grinning.

She turned on us with a scowl. "Where have you been?"

"Katie opened the maze panel." Liselle's face gave away nothing. "The business basements on the block are connected."

"Officer Rodgers is coming to take a look." I said, and Liselle rolled her eyes.

The phone rang, and Liselle rose to answer. Helen and

I sat quietly.

"Thanks for returning my call. Our new credit cards haven't arrived, and I wanted to know when I could expect them." She paced back and forth, into and out of the back room. "My husband reported them stolen or lost. How do I get the replacements then? … I see … I'm afraid that's impossible … No. Nothing." She replaced the receiver. Her head drooped.

"Liselle? Is there anything wrong?"

She shook her hair and threw her shoulders back. "Just a little misunderstanding. I'll take care of it."

"Is it something to do with Pat?"

"He paid off our credit cards and canceled them." Her eyes filled with shiny tears. "He's the only one who can get them reissued. And we know that's not going to happen."

If I wanted to get some answers, I should probably ask my questions before Officer Rodgers showed up. Amanda had already expressed her displeasure, and I didn't want to get in her way. "What do you know about Vanuatu?"

Helen frowned. "What is it? I've never heard it before."

Liselle rubbed her forehead. "I haven't heard that in a long time. Vanuatu's an island country in the Pacific Ocean. In our early days, Patrick talked about going there. He had great aspirations." She sniffed.

Carefully, I asked, "Do you think he might have exchanged the diamonds, and used the difference between the lab grown and the natural stones to buy a ticket and set himself up on the island? You can buy citizenship."

"He never said anything to me." Liselle moaned and sat up straighter. "Evidently, he hasn't said much of anything important to me lately. Maybe his leaving is why he cancelled our credit cards. He said it was because he'd lost his, but now I think it was because he was going away without me."

"Did you think he'd leave you?"

Liselle didn't answer right away. "I hoped I was wrong. I suspected a girlfriend, but I love the store. I thought he did too. Why would he leave and allow it to fail?" She shook her head sadly, in disbelief. "I didn't know a whole lot, did I? Who was going with him?"

"I don't know if there was anyone. I only found one ticket, and I was obliged to give it and the journal to Chief West."

Liselle's brows came together, digesting that bit of information.

"Do you have someone special other than Patrick?"

Her eyes flew open, and she stuttered, "N-n-n-o."

I scrutinized her face. If she hadn't known about the replacements, and Liselle killed Donaldson after he exchanged the stones, she lost the greater portion of their value. She would've done better with a divorce settlement. If she were a consummate actress, and she did know about the stones, she might have killed him in a fit of anger.

The door dinged. Officer Rodgers entered. He nodded at each of us. Without a word, Helen escorted him to the basement and returned alone.

"Is it okay if I read what I might have gleaned from the first journal?"

Their eyes met.

"Absolutely."

"Sure."

I pulled up the photos I took of the journal entries and read a bit from the beginning. Helen said, "Sounds like Pat from the early years."

"It is. But that's all I have from that one.

I wrestled Donaldson's later journal out of my unwieldy

bag. Helen and Liselle looked at me expectantly. "I'll try and use the alphabet in the basement and translate more of this one later, but I think I have the first dozen or so pages."

"I've decoded his messages for all this time, and they've gotten more convoluted lately, more cryptic," Helen said. "Would you like me to take a look at the journal?"

"No," Liselle and I almost shouted together.

"Some of the messages may be very private, Helen. I hope you understand." Liselle bowed her head.

"Listen to this," I said. "'Looks like flash is back to his old tricks.' Any idea who he was writing about?"

Liselle squirmed. "Patrick gave a nickname like that to Lenny Capsner because he won the industrial ed competition in high school. Do you think Lenny took the stones?"

"William frequented the pawn shop and traced one of our rings to Capsner," said Helen.

I shrugged and continued, reading the line about Helen's loyalty and her feelings for Donaldson. Liselle jerked her head. Helen cringed with discomfort. "I never felt that way about him. Liselle, you have to believe me. It was purely platonic. I love working here and had fun playing his game, but I hoped …" She stopped herself from saying anything more.

Liselle wouldn't let Helen's comment end that way. "What? What did you hope?"

"I'm sorry, Liselle."

Liselle rose and walked back and forth, wringing her hands. "What, Helen?"

The tension electrified the room. I cast my eyes down, flipped to the last pages of the journal, and snapped a few photos, pretending to be busy, but shrinking under the intense strain between the two women. I slid the journal back into my bag for more decryption later.

Helen took her time. "Before you came along, Pat said if he ever needed a partner, I'd be his first choice." Liselle gasped. "Business partner—believe me, nothing more. I always hoped I could buy in, but that's never going to happen. There's not much left to buy into. I'll help you get the store up and running if you want, but …" She hesitated. "I'm moving on."

Helen rose and stood behind her chair. "I am sorry." She grabbed her coat, pulled a stocking cap over her smoky brown waves, and headed toward the door. "I'm going home early today."

Liselle's eyes glazed over, shellshocked.

"Do you want me back tomorrow?"

Returning slowly from her stupor, Liselle nodded and whispered, "Please."

Helen dashed through the exit and bumped into William. He jerked a white takeout bag from Sip and Savor above his head and out of her way. "Excuse me?"

He smirked at Liselle. "Did you fire her too?"

"What do you mean?" I asked.

"Pat fired Helen only to hire her back within the hour, so she ignored his tirades."

"Did he fire her often?"

"He fired her on Saturday morning right after you left."

TWENTY-SIX

Maverick rode shotgun and never interrupted. He was my best hope to talk through what little I knew, disentangling and sorting the bits and pieces of clues to solve Susie's dilemma. We arrived at the hospital maintenance garage with fifteen minutes left on the clock. I parked, and we jogged down the street.

"Anyone could have used the basement connection to access Donaldson's. That's good, but that means Susie could've used it too. Do you think William is a little too solicitous of Liselle? He basically offered himself up on a funeral pyre if only she'd keep him on as an employee. I think the word Drew would use to describe him is unctuous. I couldn't get a good take on his motives: love or money or love of money. He must understand the implications of having lab grown diamonds. Maybe he wants to partner-up with Liselle. And then there's Helen. She's sharp as a tack and has figured out she has a lot to offer but maybe doesn't see the possibility of growth given the shrunken value of the business assets. And where are the diamonds? Have they been sold? No one's been on a spending spree, at least as far as I could see. Not even Donaldson."

We jogged back.

"If Liselle isn't discombobulated, she's a very good actress. But that doesn't mean she didn't kill her husband. And then there's her friend Henry. I wonder how friendly they really are. My money is on Lenny though. With what we know, he's been a bookie, maybe a gambler, and Amanda already has him down for pawning stolen goods and probably stealing from the jewelry stores in the mall. He knows a little about electricity, and maybe Donaldson caught him in the act. Or maybe the death was an accident after all."

I didn't have time to flip my arguments. At one minute after five, the long steel slats disappeared at the top as the huge commercial door rolled up and Fredericka Lattimore waved us in. She swiped the tip of her red aristocratic nose and said, "What can I do for you?"

"Could we talk, Ms. Lattimore?"

"Everybody calls me Ricky."

"Ricky, I'm trying to figure out what might have led to Pat Donaldson's death."

She froze. "Why do you want to talk to me?"

"I'm talking to anyone who knew him, trying to understand him. You grew up in town, right?"

She nodded. "And I got to know many people a little bit, but I didn't know Pat, Mr. Donaldson, much better than anyone else. He wasn't anyone special. I hardly knew him. I only met him at the auction. And the deal to tune-up the car wasn't even my idea. I had to do that. It was part of the contract when he bought the SUV. I'm just a mechanic. What could I possibly tell you?"

I tried to keep my mouth from dropping open. So many words. So little information. "Just your observations." Maverick snuggled in under her left hand, waiting for a scratch. Ricky complied and looked over her shoulder at a large man at the back of the garage. "Mullhern," she called. "Make sure you top off the generator. You never know what'll be going on tomorrow." I followed her into her office. She brushed a pile of wrinkled and tattered *Scientific American* and *Popular Mechanics* magazines to the floor. "Have a seat."

She removed her cap, wiped her brow, and began straightening piles and arranging office supplies on a messy desk. I recognized the ploy. She plopped into the leather chair, and it squeaked when she rocked. "What do you want to know?"

"Have you worked here long?"

"Fourteen years." She snorted. "Don't look so surprised. I started when I was fifteen—sweeping the floors, taking out the trash, general maintenance, that sort of thing. My dad managed the place." She gazed into the garage. "It was one way I could spend extra time with him and earn some spending money. He figured out I was good with tools and let me putter around until I could get some training."

"Sounds like you had a great relationship with your dad."

"Not always, but yeah. I learned from the best. He knew the ins and outs of every engine anyone put in front of him. He set up the entire system we use."

"Are you good with engines too?"

"I'd like to think so. The hospital trusts me to supervise the safeguarding and service of our fleet, and it's vital for our outreach program the SUVs operate in all kinds of weather. We can't have our medical teams stuck halfway between here and the backwaters of Minnesota. Not good for patients, goodwill, or the bottom line."

"Has Mr. Donaldson purchased a vehicle from your auction before or was this his first?"

"I can't be expected to remember everyone who ever purchased a used vehicle from us. I'd have to check our records because obviously I don't know, but I think this was his first."

"How long has Henry worked here?"

"Mullhern? He's a sub—on temporary light duty with the city works department. I work this weekend, and he's helping out, substituting for one of our guys who claims he's snowed in. Why?"

"I thought he looked familiar." I pulled Donaldson's book out of my bag and Ricky blinked as though she needed to flush dust from her eye. "Have you seen this before?"

She cleared her throat. "I don't think so. What is it?"

"It's Pat Donaldson's journal." I opened to a page I'd marked. "Would you take a look at this passage?" I pointed to words I'd underlined in red pencil.

'Phredairoccahz kweight a dowel. Loaf ove mai leighgh.'

She looked up, uncomprehending, and relaxed.

"I think it reads, 'Fredericka is quite a doll. Love of my life.' Why would he write that?"

She didn't say a word but sat up tall and leaned forward. She picked at a paperclip and dragged it from under the stack of papers. Her cheek twitched. We both recognized the small dark blue booklet secured to pages of an itinerary.

I couldn't help myself. "Are you taking a trip?"

She turned white and sputtered. "I don't know what you're talking about."

"When I go to the trouble of getting out my passport, I plan to use it, and I was curious. Going to Vanuatu?"

"Van-a-what-u?" She flinched back and raised her chin.

"Pat Donaldson had a one-way ticket to Vanuatu."

She glared at me and shook her head of curls, then peeked at her wrist. "Sorry. You'll have to excuse me. I have an appointment." She stood and rocked back on her heels.

Maverick and I headed toward the door. "I'm sure Chief West can help you. What happened, Ricky?"

"You need to leave now."

Her eyes shifted erratically, avoiding us. The roller door growled open, and the minute we crossed the threshold, the door rumbled back into position.

Maverick barked.

"I thought that was pretty weird too," I said, allowing him to jump into my car first. "The passport should have been a dead giveaway, but the country name surprised her. What if Fredericka was Pat's new love interest? He'd bring her the stones, she would help him, and they would escape to … I don't know … Mexico, but in reality, he planned to go alone to Vanuatu, and she didn't know. Or did she find out? But then where are the stones or the money? And I really can't say anything to Amanda yet. She told me not to investigate."

Maverick circled the back seat, stopped, and flicked his tail, locking eyes on the industrial door rising again. A large man hurriedly ducked under it. He exited, jogged to the end of the driveway, and turned toward us. I cast a quick glance at Maverick. "Stay."

I jumped from my car and called. "Hey, Henry. Thanks for helping Liselle and me the other night. It was frightfully cold. Emergency crews were pretty busy. We could've been stuck for hours."

Henry squinted and tilted his head. "I don't think I know you. I'm pretty good with faces."

I approached with my hand outstretched. "Katie Wilk." Henry took my hand and rubbernecked around me to see what caused the muffled barking. I turned and rolled my eyes. Maverick stood on the front seat with his paws on the dash and his nose to the windshield, yelping. He stepped down, paced, and his paws landed on the steering wheel where he laid on the horn.

Henry laughed. "Yours?"

My face felt hot. "Sorry," I said, taking long strides to reach the car and open the door. Maverick leapt from the front seat, paraded down the walk, and sat in front of Henry, his tail sweeping the concrete.

"Good boy," Henry said. He grunted as he dropped to one knee.

"Are you all right?" I leaned forward, ready for a rescue.

"Stiff. I spent too much time on my back this week." Maverick raised a paw to shake. "Great dog." Henry winked.

"Yes, he is. And he keeps me on the straight and narrow."

Henry stopped his brisk petting and examined Maverick's face. "You're the one."

"Excuse me?"

"This is the pup who found Pat, isn't it? I can tell by the intelligent brown eyes, the shiny black coat, and the affability. Liselle described him perfectly." He waited a beat. "And she told me your name." Maverick rolled onto his back in the snow, and Henry scratched his belly for a second before saying, "Get up, pup. It's too cold for that."

"How long have you known Liselle and Pat?"

Maverick sat, and Henry ran his gloved hand down the sleek back, from top to tail. "Pat and me, we go way back. We started in trade school together, but he quit after the first semester. He was a salesman through and through and could've sold sawdust to a lumbermill. Liselle? I've always liked her. She was good for him. But once they married, he shut her away like some breakable treasure in a chest." His eyes gazed into the distance.

"Do you know Lenny Capsner?"

Henry's hand stopped, and Maverick twisted to get the petting going again. "I used to know him quite well, but he's always been trouble for me. I've moved on."

I filed those odd words for later and moved onto a safer topic. "How did you know what was wrong with Liselle's SUV?"

He shook himself back to the present. "I know the hospital vehicles, and they have a recurring company-reset you need to wait out. If that didn't work, I told her she could call back, and I'd be along to see what I could do to help."

I felt like a puppet on a string. My back went rigid, and my chin rose. "You didn't tell her to wiggle the connections under the hood."

He snickered and shook his head. "That wouldn't do much good."

He struggled to rise, and I reached out a hand. He pushed off the ground. I supported his elbow. "I had emergency surgery Friday, and my wobbly knees are telling me to take it easy." He controlled his breathing. "I'm good. Thanks."

TWENTY-SEVEN

Susie's request for help still hounded me. One sure way to get answers to my nagging questions was to ask the source. I drove to the hospital.

"I'd like to visit Lenny Capsner. May I get his room number?"

The greeter at the desk shook her head. "Sorry. I'm not at liberty to share that information."

"Oh, okay. Thanks." I walked off in the direction of the gift shop where I bought a bunch of flowers in a narrow glass vase and a get-well card. I'd make one attempt to see if I could find Lenny's room, and then I'd let it go.

I strode past the nurses' station on the surgical floor with my head up and eyes forward as if I knew the room number I intended to visit. The medical personnel glanced my way and back down at whatever important work they had in front of them and ignored me. I rounded a corner and, had he looked to his right, Ronnie Christianson would have spotted me, but an alarm sounded, and the call light blinked off and on. He jerked his head around the doorway and drew his weapon, disappearing inside as two nurses tore down the hall, pushing a cart. The room swallowed them as well. I took two steps forward with trepidation when Dr. Pete Erickson blew by me.

I backed into an alcove and my feet stayed rooted to the floor, waiting for the sounds of pandemonium to subside. When the nurses wheeled the cart back through the hall, I crept forward and peeked in the room. Ronnie had holstered his gun, and handcuffs dangled in front of him. He glowered. Pete checked the connections on the IV and turned knobs on a monitor. When he leaned over the patient, I saw Susie standing with her hands behind her back as Ronnie read her rights.

Susie said forcefully, "There was something wrong with the monitor. He was in distress. I couldn't leave him. What would you have done?"

I didn't wait for the answer but retreated the way I'd come and sought the emergency room receptionist. I pocketed the card, arranged the flowers on her desk, and requested a word with Dr. Erickson, constructing my alibi.

Minutes later, the receptionist said, "Dr. Erickson will see you now," and waved me through the open door, leading to his office.

He sat behind his huge desk, his chin resting on the back of his hand, staring at the computer screen. I knocked softly. He beckoned me with a rapid two-finger wave of his left hand not looking up. I stopped in front of his desk and watched for a minute or so.

When he finally glanced at me, the scowl fell away, and a smile stretched across his face. "To what do I owe this pleasurable visit?"

"Would you believe I just came to say hi?"

"Not really, no." He chuckled. "The description of a visitor one of our nurses lost track of upstairs fits you to a tee."

I could've kept the flowers for myself. "Well," I dragged out the word, idling for time. "After my talk with Susie last night, I had some questions for Lenny Capsner," I confessed. "But he's unavailable."

"Very," he said. He crossed his arms. "I'll call you later. We can chat."

I melted looking into his thoughtful dark brown eyes, and the dimple only added to my capitulation. I took a deep refreshing breath, smiled, and said, "I look forward to it."

An hour later, when I saw Pete's name on the screen, I picked up with not so much as a hello.

"You're not going to believe this," I said when Pete answered. "Donaldson had a very jaded approach to everything. I have more possible solutions to his PI—"

"His what?"

"Phonic Infographics, but what I transcribed so far in his journal is filled with self-inflated recollections of Liselle, Helen, William, Ricky, Henry, and even Lenny Capsner, and I think Lenny's the linchpin. If we're going to get Susie off, we've got to determine what he did with the diamonds. Did you talk to him?"

"Katie, Lenny never regained consciousness. He's dead." I couldn't breathe. "Did you hear what I said?"

"I thought …" I slumped in my seat. "He was my best lead."

"I have an ambulance pulling in. I've got to go, but I'll see you later." He clicked off.

I sat at my kitchen table contemplating what to do next—search for another likely suspect, talk to Amanda, find Tiny, offer condolences to Lenny's girlfriend, check the pawn shop, pray for a miracle—and decided to pray while undertaking one task at a time. Maverick and I jumped into my Focus. The car idled with a rumble as I planned my next move.

I'd start by offering condolences. The families of younger children were mostly unknown to me, and I didn't know Lenny's girlfriend's name, but I did know her daughter was a gymnast. I swiped through the fabulous photos and read the grand praise for her coaches. According to the webpage, the club closed at eight and classes were held every day except Sunday which was reserved for competitions. I plugged in the address and my GPS took me through a car-lined street to a huge metal structure—The Columbia Gymnastics Club—a place to begin.

I was working out how I would ask for the information when the front door opened and disgorged a gaggle of tiny giggling girls. I recognized the redhead from Lenny's lapel pin skipping toward a short, wiry woman with identical flaming red curls, talking to other caretakers rounding up their charges.

I clipped on Maverick's leash and pretended to set out on our afternoon constitutional. We neared the group as the redheads broke away. "Excuse me," I said. "I saw your daughter's balance beam routine at the meet on Sunday. She's terrific."

The mother flashed a smile. "Thanks." She regarded Maverick and gave me the once over. "I know you. You live on Maple Street." I might've looked startled. "My older daughter babysits Emma. We'd know this handsome dog anywhere. Maverick visits all the time with Ida. I'm Sadie. This is Maddie." She reached into her huge satchel, pulled out a button, and pinned it to my lapel. "Here. It's good PR."

"Hi, Maddie. Pleased to meet you." I tilted the button, and she struck the pose in the photo. Maddie giggled as Maverick tickled her cheek, trying to get close enough to lick her face. "Maverick, sit." He sat for snuggles. "Sadie, I'm really sorry about Lenny." Sadie stared blankly at me. "I heard he passed away."

"Who's Lenny?"

I blurted, "Your boyfriend."

The women within earshot took a step back. One took the hand of a little girl, separated from the rest, and dragged the youngster down the street. Anger flitted across Sadie's face followed by bewilderment. "I'll have you know I'm happily married to a wonderful provider."

Even though the temperature neared freezing, beads of sweat collected at the small of my back, and I pulled at my collar to cool down. "I'm sorry, but I thought—"

She let out a dry laugh. "Whatever gave you the idea I even knew this guy, Lenny? You're the third person today to mention him, and if my daughter didn't love your dog, I'd take great offense."

I recalled exactly why I came to believe she might know him. "Lenny wore a lapel button with Maddie's photo on it, like this one." I touched my new acquisition. "My friend and I were at the jewelry store on Saturday, and he was looking at engagement rings. We commented on the pin, and he told us the child in the photo wasn't his yet, but he hoped she might be in the future. I apologize for the misunderstanding."

Sadie shuddered. "If that isn't just creepy. I guess I'm not going to be too broken up over his death. I can't help you, but thanks for clearing up the confusion for me."

I watched them go and wondered why Lenny had lied and what else he'd lied about. I dialed Jane's number, hoping to pick her brain. She didn't answer.

Maverick hung his head over the front seat, drooling on my shoulder. He licked my ear, and I giggled. "Well, my friend. That was a bust. But why would Lenny wear a pin of a child he had no business wearing? That is just creepy. Let's hit the pawn shop on our way home. Maybe we'll get a little luckier."

I had my choice of parking spaces, but as we jogged up to the glass door, I heard a click, and a hand flipped the Closed sign. I grabbed the handle and pulled, hoping I was wrong. I wasn't. The church bell tower hadn't chimed the hour, so I tapped on the door, pointing to the sign next to the sign: Dogs welcome, people tolerated. It read 9:00 — 6:00." A man with bushy eyebrows and a sour expression peered at us through glasses enlarging his eyes twofold and shook his head. I held up one finger, smiled, and carefully mouthed 'one minute.' His frown deepened, but he opened the door.

"What do you want?"

"One minute of your time." We squeezed through the narrow opening.

"Give ya ten bucks for 'im," he said with a snarl. His hand reached toward my leash.

I recoiled and tugged Maverick closer. "He's not why I'm here."

"Why are you here then? I'm closing up. I don't have time for lookie-loos." He turned and walked behind the cash register.

"What can you tell me about Lenny Capsner?"

"I already told the cops I didn't see the car hit him. I heard the screech of brakes. By the time I got out there, Lenny was sprawled in the middle of the street. I did think it unusual for a car to be able to race down this street, with all the construction, but maybe Lenny stepped out and surprised the driver."

"I'm here to ask about something else. He pawned a ring last week that might have belonged to a friend of mine." I hoped my nose wouldn't grow, giving the miniscule white lie.

He seemed to relax. "My best and worst customer, Lenny-boy. Solo, he brought in more goods than anyone, and most often never reclaimed it." He dug in a drawer. "Here it is," he said and slammed a three-inch file onto the countertop. His voice reminded me of the cartoon character, Snidely Whiplash, from one of Dad's famous oldies, Dudley Do-Right of the Mounties. I imagined the black top hat, the twirling of the black handlebar moustache, the heh-heh-heh, and shuddered. "What can I tell you in the twenty-three seconds you have left?"

"Did he pawn jewelry often?" A nod. "And you never questioned its provenance?" His eyes narrowed. I gulped.

Maverick sat and begged. Luckily for me, the man complied with a scratch. "Everybody has something to hock. Sometimes those items are bartered, not necessarily stolen if that's what you're hinting at. All on the up and up. Fifteen seconds."

I swallowed hard again. "What can you tell me about the man?"

"Guy meant well, had big dreams, couldn't pull himself together for any length of time, had a huuuggee gambling addiction, and assisted others with theirs."

"Was he still a bookie?"

"I'd say so—in a big way."

"How would someone go about placing a bet with him?"

"Not here, I assure you. And he didn't go in for all the online shenanigans. He didn't leave much of a digital trail. He liked the old-fashioned way. Face to face. Remember those old movies where the characters searched for the red carnation on the lapel to connect with an unknown person? That'd be Lenny. Those who wanted to throw their money away always found him."

"Why did you consider him your worst customer?"

"The last ticket was redeemed by the chief of police. Not his best move." He eyed the clock and furrowed his brow. "You asked, *was* he still a bookie."

"I'm sorry. I shouldn't say more."

The scowl melted. "Ah, Lenny."

TWENTY-EIGHT

The day of the mock trial meet crept up on me. I checked off names as team members boarded the bus. I could unlock doors, order transportation, take roll, and schedule mock trial meets, but our attorney-coach, Dorene Dvorak, was a master in the art of law. Her methodology surpassed my expectations. Listening in on her teachable moments, even I understood the meaning of *voir dire,* when to make an objection, how to introduce rules of evidence, where to place our exhibits for the greatest impact, and how to use silence to elicit information—very effective in any setting. She loved working with kids. Because of her integrity, intelligence, and strong personality, she was a consummate role model for at least ten attorneys-in-the-making. However, real law topped high school trials every time. She also knew if she spent too much time with our team, they'd drive her nuts, so she traveled separately.

The students used the first rowdy fifteen minutes of our bus ride to grumble about homework or applaud getting out of school early. Once the captive audience settled into their seats, Lorelei and Carlee used the time to oversee the team's review of the individual assignments, enumerate the salient points of their arguments, and focus on presentation.

Jane and I took our role as support personnel seriously. The tubs we carried contained water, snacks, pins, scissors, pens, ties, shoe polish, stain remover, a steamer, bobby pins, coins, anything we'd ever forgotten, or thought we might need. We practiced the art of encouragement. Her noisy chants and my two-fingered whistle-cheers rivaled any challenger coterie.

So far, the arrangement worked.

While they prepared for another successful meet, Jane and I observed their interactions from our seats at the front of the bus, but we couldn't talk of anything other than Susie's arrest.

"How can Chief West believe Susie capable of murder?" Jane said.

I ticked off the motive, means, and opportunity on my fingers. "Donaldson accused her of stealing his wife's SUV. Susie wanted her ring back. She knows about generators. And Chief West couldn't verify Susie's alibi for the time of the murder. To compound her problems, she has a history with Lenny, she doesn't have an alibi for the time of his hit-and-run, and she was found at his bedside when he coded."

"You don't believe she could do it, do you?"

"No, but I don't know what we can do to help her."

She studied my face. "You shouldn't get in the middle

of this one."

A siren ringtone blared from Jane's phone cutting off my retort, and a recording of Drew's voice said, "Your boyfriend is calling. Answer the phone if you are able." Her face softened, and when she accepted the call, I mentally blocked her syrupy voice.

I took a deep breath. Jane was right. What could I do? But Susie had also been right, and I couldn't help speculating about other possible suspects.

William Dix, Helen Fox, and Liselle Donaldson knew their way around the jewelry store. Helen had years of employment under her belt, and Dix had a solid year. Why would either want their boss dead now? Helen cried a little too much when she heard about Donaldson's death. Maybe they had more than just an employer-employee relationship. What did Donaldson think of his employees? Did William lose a ring on Saturday, did Lenny take it, or did someone give it to him? I suppose the Donaldsons could have been happier, but was murder Liselle's only way out? Who was Henry? He knew the ins and out of electricity. What did Lenny mean to Susie? Where was Susie and, for that matter, where was Tiny at the time of Donaldson's murder? My head pounded, attempting to unravel the knotted web of connections.

Brock plopped into the seat next to me and whisked his walnut-colored hair out of his brown eyes. "Ms. Wilk, Lorelei doesn't think these boots will help me put my best foot forward." He shoved his feet into the aisle. "They're just out of the box, but she doesn't believe an attorney would be caught dead wearing them. What do you think?"

He pulled up his pant legs and flaunted his boots. I could see the reflection of sunlight on the polished brown footwear. "If we were in the state playoffs, I'd say she's right, but we aren't there yet, so I think …" I took a closer look. "Brock, what is that symbol?"

His brow furrowed, and he followed my gaze. "That's the electric safety symbol. These are the same brand as Mr. Simonson's protective gear. He said they are the most comfortable waterproof footwear he's ever owned, and I was due to get some new boots. So are they okay to wear today as the defense attorney? Otherwise, I can play a different part."

My mind raced. The lightning bolt inside a triangle was the same symbol Liselle had on her boots. "Lorelei's right—"

His face fell. "As always."

"But they'll be okay today."

"Great." He bounced cheerily to the rear of the bus, and my mind bounced around the issue of electricity. It didn't necessarily mean Liselle had a need for dielectric gear, but she couldn't be ruled out. I started a list in my head of suspects with means. Liselle, Henry, and Lenny may have had a little knowledge of electricity. William, Helen, and Liselle had keys to unlock the store, and there was a generator on the premises. Susie had working knowledge of generators. And so did Ricky, but there could have been others. Anyone could have gained access.

William had been pretty quick to offer up an alibi for Liselle. Maybe they were an item. Helen said she'd been shopping at the time of the death, but she'd had a misunderstanding with Donaldson Saturday morning. After reporting the theft of the diamond ring, William wasn't too happy to be thrown to the law enforcement wolves. I had no idea where Henry and Ricky were on Saturday, but I could ask around, quietly. As I cataloged the motives, our bus pulled into the parking lot, and in the rush to monitor an orderly exit from the bus, I put my thoughts on hold.

Jane's eyes shimmered. "Do you think you can survive the bus ride home without me? Drew is on his way through and asked if I could ride home with him after the meet."

"I don't see why not." The shimmering eyes began to glow.

Dorene waited inside the front door. Dressed in a black skirt and jacket, white blouse, and stacked heels, she drew the kids like a magnet. The first thing we did was to gather in a circle and intone, "EsqChoir. EsqChoir. EsqChoir." We followed her to our assigned room, looking like a long line of baby ducklings. Dorene set to work. She noted points of interest on the scoring rubric and gave final instructions. Psyched by a last-minute pep talk and ready to win, she wished them *bonne chance*.

Jane spent the next two hours covering the defense cases, and I observed our plaintiff's team. We met back in the room and compared notes while we waited for the posting of results and Drew's call, whichever came first.

Jane bent her head to mine. "Our presentation certainly lacked the finesse and luster of our last meet. It was a little painful to watch today. Dorene harped about not providing any extra information, but this time it felt void of excitement and emotion."

"And the plaintiff team acted like cardboard cutouts. I wonder what's going on."

Galen accompanied our group when he wasn't wrestling, and his flamboyant antics usually eased the tension, but he had practice today and couldn't attend. The uncommon quiet was unsettling. Lorelei paced. Brock sat on the floor, with his knees pulled up, and his head drooped forward, feigning sleep. Carlee pulled papers out of her backpack and appeared to be concentrating on homework. A few of the students grabbed a bottle of water or a snack, but there was minimal interaction among the kids.

Dorene marched in. "If I can have your attention." She scanned the room and, when all eyes were focused on her, said, "You almost had me rooting for the other teams today. What's going on?"

The kids looked from one to another and fidgeted. Kindra took a deep breath and said, "Everyone's entitled to one off day."

"I agree. But I'm an attorney—"

"With superpowers," Jane said. Her phone pinged. She read the screen, grabbed her coat, and said, "Listen to your coach." The only face with a smile sailed out of the room.

Some students rummaged in their carryalls, and some took slurps of water or bites of a snack, avoiding eye contact, as if Dorene could read their minds if they looked at her directly. "I know when someone is keeping the truth from me. It's one of my *ex cathedra* essential assets." Her eyes scoured the room.

The loudspeaker crackled and broke the quiet before the silent treatment she employed reached maximum effect. "Results have been calculated. If teams would please report to the auditorium, we'll begin the awards ceremony in ten minutes."

"I'm going to find out what's going on, but until that time, this team will perform with its usual grace. If you win, which I believe is doubtful, you will be considerate and commend the losers. But even more importantly, when you lose, you will be courteous and congratulate the winners."

Our team filed out wordlessly, but the death march back to the room epitomized the agony of defeat. Third out of four wasn't bad, and Dorene addressed the sullen faces carefully. "Thank you for being polite and affable to the first and second place teams. And for being so genial and respectful to the team from Park Rapids."

"It was easy because it was true. That case could have gone either way. We could've gotten fourth place as easily as third today," Carlee said matter-of-factly.

"It's time to smile," said Dorene. "There's always another trial. Poetry, you know."

I heard a knock. Everyone stopped moving. Lorelei stepped to the door and flung it open. "Oh, it's you," she said grumpily.

Brock had followed her and flinched.

ZaZa swept into the room. "*Mon Dieu.* Because I had to teach until the end of the day …" She gave me a withering look. "I only witnessed the last defensive trial." Her superior smirk dropped back into place. "You were marvelous, but you would've won if you'd have used my proven strategy."

Dorene strode confidently across the room and stood in front of ZaZa. Since I'd never seen her grin from ear to ear, the look was terrifying. "Who the …" She stopped herself, bowed her head, and raised it again. "Who are you?"

"I am Katie's assistant. Who are you?"

Both ZaZa and Dorene turned to me. Lorelei raised her chin, took Brock's arm, and stood next to me. Then Carlee joined the front, followed by Kindra, and one-by-one the other students did the same.

"What did you tell them, ZaZa? What is your proven strategy?" I squinted.

"I told them." She stammered. "I told them to use every asset they possess to shake up the opposition. A languid glance at the right moment or a sly smile can undo the best intentions, and coming from these confident adolescents, the opposition would be putty in their hands." She smiled with conviction.

I shook my head to clear my ears.

Kindra said, "At practice Sunday, we rehearsed one of our killer tactics—our come-hither looks. I think I've got mine down." Kindra tilted her head, turned her shoulders, bent a knee, pouted her lips, and batted her eyelashes.

I was appalled. What had I subjected my kids to?

Dorene clasped her hands in front of her, clenched her jaw, and clamped her lips.

"*Ma belle chérie*, it would have worked," said ZaZa like a proud mama. "You loved the idea."

Kindra slid back into her own skin. "Yeah. No. Most of us decided it was a dumb idea and probably bordered on an ethical violation of some kind or another."

"Not all of you thought it was a dumb idea?" ZaZa's head pivoted in Brock's direction.

"It was a really dumb idea, and I'm sorry I ever considered it. I forgot what it takes to be a team."

"So did we." Carlee nodded. "Sorry we jumped all over you, Brock."

"It could've worked," ZaZa said, sulking.

"That may be, but you stay away from my team," Dorene said, menacingly.

"Katie asked me to help," ZaZa whined.

My voice rose. "You volunteered to Open. The. Doors."

"You," Dorene growled. She pointed at ZaZa. "Out." She pointed to the door.

"Katie?"

"Go home, ZaZa."

Her heels clacked as she scurried from the room. My kids applauded.

"I finally understand John Dickinson's quote, 'United we stand, divided we fall.' At least our loss wasn't due to my boots."

Carlee gave Brock a supportive, sisterly hug. The rift between the two camps reconciled, and Lorelei beamed the entire ride home. I felt like I'd let them down until Brock and Lorelei took the seat next to me.

"It wasn't your fault. We thought she was doing what you asked her to do, but she doesn't know any better," said Lorelei. "Look at her. She has so much going for her, and she's still not happy."

I teared up. "How is there so much wisdom among ones so young?"

Brock's head bobbed. "She wants a place where she can belong, but I think she'd be better off with a different extracurricular activity."

"You mean like baseball," said Lorelei.

His eyes grew round. He would pitch for the Columbia Cougars come spring. I could see he didn't want to have any more problems with Lorelei. When he caught on to her teasing, he roared with laughter. "We'll beat them next time, Ms. Wilk," he said, and they picked their way back to their seats.

I pondered the wise words of my students and scooted around on my seat. "Hey gang, next run-through on Sunday at two. We need a hiatus."

No one moved. I thought I'd made an error. The kids looked at each other and broke into raucous approval. I settled into my seat and texted Dad and Ida with the results of the day. A message came back. I had company.

TWENTY-NINE

I drove past a well-worn emerald-green Lincoln parked on Maple Street and took a moment to wonder who it belonged to. Ida and Dad were home, so I wasn't too afraid of anyone trying to do away with me.

I had second thoughts, however, when no one greeted me. Even if Dad and Ida were playing hosts, Maverick usually met me with a sloppy kiss. I stepped gingerly through my kitchen, fingers on the emergency button on my phone, through the adjoining door into Ida's kitchen, and on to her living room. The four of them sat primly, but silently, around Ida's coffee table, sipping from bone china cups and nibbling cookies. Maverick lifted his head from his spot on the rug, gave a quiet woof, meaning something like, "Fix this," and collapsed on Helen's feet.

"Hi, Helen." Dad and Ida hustled to their feet. "You don't have to hurry away on my account."

Dad said, "Goodnight, Helen," turned and left.

Ida said, "Take your time, girls." Maverick woofed again. "And Maverick." *How did he know?* Ida slowly dragged herself up the stairs.

"You're here to see me, Helen?"

"Yes. I …" She picked up her cup in a rush. A small amount of liquid sloshed over the rim and onto her shirt front. She grabbed a napkin and dabbed furiously, way more than necessary. Her hands halted and dropped to her lap, shredding the napkin into micro pieces as she twisted it. "I didn't kill him. I didn't take the diamonds. I admired him. Pat Donaldson was a crackerjack salesman. Mother's Day gifts came with a free corsage we made in the store. He was lucky too, buying low and selling high. He made some great deals on old jewelry as well—he'd buy vintage settings, reset, and sell like new. He was a shrewd businessman. We provided engagement photos if a couple bought their engagement ring here. Until recently, I thought we were doing quite well, but Valentine's Day sales will make or break the store this year, notwithstanding the loss of the natural diamonds." She picked at the tiny white flecks dotting her clothes, the couch, the rug, and Maverick's back.

"We can still sell the lab grown gems. They're real diamonds in every sense of the word, but they're man-made. Customers can get more bang for their buck. They're considered more environmentally friendly, so there is a demand. I just wish I knew what happened to our original inventory and the tremendous difference in value."

"You don't think Donaldson took the diamonds?"

"Looking back, I think he was going to take the

diamonds and leave, retire to that island with Ricky Lattimore."

I tried not to react.

"She'd been coming into the store too often to merely take care of some little problem with that SUV. She and Pat would invariably run out for coffee or lunch. And then I found out her uncle's a fence, or at least that's what William said, so Pat had means to get his money. He took the SUV for its six-month maintenance call on Thursday. But I think he might've planned to deliver the stones to the fence when the SUV disappeared. That's why he was all bent out of shape when it accidentally ended up on its way to Ortonville. He must have checked the stones when the police returned the SUV—I would have— and discovered the switch. In his hurry, maybe Pat didn't know he'd left some of the stones."

"What about Ricky? She might have known about the stones, but she was surprised Donaldson only had one ticket to Vanuatu."

Helen pursed her lips. "He dazzled Ricky. She was more to Pat than a mechanic, but I don't know if he was ever willing to share with anyone."

"You've been thinking about this. Why are you telling me, Helen? Why not Chief West?"

"I have no proof. Liselle is a gifted artist. Pat married her and got her out of the way, so he'd be the best. I feel sorry for her. I'll help her get through February, and then I should probably move on." Helen looked up with a sense of purpose in her eyes. "I love the store. I want it to make it, and I don't know what I can do to help. But I think Pat was as surprised as everyone else by the substitutions."

"Do you have any idea where the stones might be now?"

"With that maze beneath the shops, the thief could be anyone. Buy one lab grown, sell one natural, buy four or more lab grown and so on. It wouldn't have taken long."

"Who do you think killed Donaldson?"

"Not me, I assure you. Either the person who stole the natural diamonds or that Kelton girl, of course."

THIRTY

On Friday, the fire department elected to hold a drill during first period. I peeked in at ZaZa's students sitting rigidly at their desks while she awaited a message from beyond. She had no idea what was going on. I stuck my head in the door and even though she wouldn't acknowledge me, she and her students filed out when I ordered, "Follow me."

I avoided her for the rest of the day. A confrontation wouldn't have done anyone any good; she and I stayed in our respective rooms. I didn't see her again until the final bell rang. She stomped past me without a glance.

I draped my coat over my arm and picked up my briefcase, edging toward the exit when Jane appeared.

"Have you seen ZaZa?" she asked.

"She left as soon as the final bell rang." I turned off the lights. "Do you have any plans for the weekend?"

Jane unleashed her words. "Katie, how could you embarrass ZaZa like that? She just helped out when asked."

Words froze on my tongue. *Where did that come from?*

"What did she ever do to you?"

I stood stupefied, my mouth hanging open. She took one look at me, shook her head, and pushed through the door. I forced my feet to move and followed her. "Jane," I called, but she'd disappeared.

My slot in the main office usually held one or two pieces of mail by the end of the day, but this time, I unpacked a full cubicle, sorting through ten thank yous from my students and identical envelopes for Dorene, a note from Mr. Simonson, an invitation to another mock trial contest, a manilla envelope, a notice for an upcoming math conference, and a message from Mrs. McEntee. I found her sorting stacks of printed material in the workroom.

"Mrs. McEntee, what can I do for you?"

She continued collating pages and stapling the collection while she spoke. "ZaZa said you wouldn't help her find the supplies she needed for her class, and she's tired of asking you. It's making her job ever so much more difficult." She stopped and gawped at me. "And mine. What's going on?"

I didn't have an answer.

"She seems not to hear well or pay attention. I've heard her ask Mr. Ganka the same question I just answered on numerous occasions. He's oblivious, but she's taking advantage of her newness, making duplicate inquiries, and it's taking up too much time and too many resources. She's only been here four days." To calm the edginess in her voice, she took two deep breaths. "I know you, Katie. I trust you. I thought you should know. I can't be expected to give her special treatment or grant her individual privileges just because she's your friend. Her expectations aren't realistic. I think she has the credentials, but maybe not a teacher's mentality. In her application, she wrote you really wanted an old friend on staff and so she'd consider taking the job if certain conditions were met, but that wasn't true, was it?" She must've seen the answer in my wide eyes. She turned back to her work and mumbled. "She doesn't seem like a very good friend."

Relieved ZaZa was now seen as a regular person, I said, "I can neither explain nor excuse what she's doing. Honestly, she seems to be taking advantage of our friendship. I thought it was just me, so I've been staying out of her way, but I'll see what I can do. I'll talk to her—set some boundaries. If she encounters enough resistance, maybe she'll start rethinking her requests. Send her my way."

"Thanks, Katie."

I texted, deleted, and texted again on my way to my car. **My dear friend, Talk to Dorene**.

I sat in my car, waiting for Jane's response, my eyes locked on my phone screen. When she didn't answer, I hoped she couldn't respond rather than wouldn't. I headed home to walk my dog.

When my phone buzzed, I expected Jane and answered without looking at the screen.

"I put up the bail, and she disappeared again."

"Tiny? Who's disappeared? Susie? Where was she? Where are you?"

"I'm at her apartment. She's supposed to be here. What do I do?"

"Who have you already talked to? I don't want to waste time duplicating tasks."

"I called the hospital—she's not allowed in. I called

Pete—he's too busy. Now I'm calling you. I'm worried."

"I'll check Donaldson's. You stay there in case she returns."

"Don't tell the chief yet, Katie. Just find her, please."

That would've been my next call, but he was right. If I called Amanda, she could haul Susie in again and throw away the key.

Maverick's stride is longer than mine, and we flew past the Sip and Savor onto Main Street. We didn't stop until we were thwarted by the Road Closed signs. Skirting the orange and white barriers, we steered clear of the heavy machines blocking the street, working on filling the gaping hole, and edged up to Donaldson's.

William jumped up first when we entered and immediately dropped back onto his workbench. Liselle appeared from the back room. Gray circled her eyes and the corners of her mouth turned down. "Katie, what can we do for you?"

Although he'd been in before, I thought I should ask. "Is it okay for Maverick to come in?"

Liselle heaved a sigh and grinned. "Sure. That'll make four visitors today. Did you have a purchase in mind or just more talk?"

William made a funny noise, sucking air through his teeth, ignoring us.

"A question."

"Come on back. We can talk while I work." She led the way to the basement. The fan continued to whirr, and there was only a hint of the fusty smell. Shiny tools gleamed from small piles on the desktop. She picked up an apron and tucked the chair under the workbench. The safe stood open with identical totes of neatly stacked supplies.

Maverick tugged the leash from my hand, jumping at the little fridge in the safe. I grabbed for the leash and hung on. "Maverick. There's nothing there for you." He continued to paw at the safe door. That stinky cheese smell lingered an awfully long time.

"What did you need, Katie?"

"Has Susie Kelton been here?"

Liselle's poker face slipped, but she said with conviction, "No. Why would she?" *Would Liselle lie?*

"She's out on bail. Her fiancé can't find her. He's worried. So am I. I thought maybe she came to get an update about her ring."

"Nothing yet. It didn't show up among Patrick's belongings or in the store's loose stone inventory. It wasn't pawned, at least in Columbia, and Lenny didn't have it."

I paused before saying, "Tiny said Susie's been disappearing."

"Sorry. Haven't seen her."

"If she gets caught in the wrong place, she may give up the opportunity to be out of jail."

"I'll keep an eye out. Is that all?"

"For now, I guess. Thanks." She hung the apron on a hook and looked longingly at the torch.

I said, "I can see my way out," and clambered up the stairs.

As I exited the back room, the bell dinged and Helen stepped in, shaking snowflakes from her hair.

"Diamonds are falling from the sky again," she said with a bright smile.

THIRTY-ONE

The tang of sizzling Szechuan shrimp punctuated with piquant garlic and green onion tickled my nose. Dad had poured warm Sake in tiny ceramic cups and sat patiently, chopsticks poised at the ready. I fumbled for the correct grip and practiced bringing the chopsticks' tips together to simulate picking up a tender morsel of Ida's fabulous food. She delivered the large steaming dish with a side of sticky rice, and said, "What do you have to say now? You've been quiet for too long."

Between scrumptious bites, I talked about Susie's engagement, the loss of her ring, and her arrest. Before I could tell them about her disappearance, a knock interrupted my story. Jane stood outside on the top step, bundled in her quilted coat, hunched against the wind.

"I'm sorry," she said. "I spoke to Dorene, but I shouldn't have had to speak to anyone. I just got caught up in ZaZa's stories, and I believed her when she said you wanted to be a lady in the worst way and—"

"She told you I went after Charles? She's convincing. No apology necessary. The kids think she believes her own tripe. Come on in and have some dinner." She shook her head until I used my most alluring voice. "It's Ida's astonishing Asian."

"Okay. I've decided to give ZaZa two more weeks in my apartment—I don't think I can handle her mess any longer anyway, nor her tales. She said … never mind. Then I have to—"

"Stay and help us figure out how Donaldson died and what happened to his natural diamonds," I said. We sat, and I wondered what preposterous story ZaZa had told Jane. I gave up on the chopsticks and reverted to the use of a fork. "Remember, while we shopped for possible Valentine's gifts, we heard Susie threaten Donaldson." Jane nodded. I felt my face redden remembering Pete call me his girlfriend in front of Amanda. I stammered as I continued. "Lenny Capsner was there looking at engagement rings."

"The button he wears has the cutest little gymnast. He's so proud of her."

I turned to Ida. "The pin spotlighted Maddie. I talked to her mother Wednesday."

Ida pursed her lips. "Emma's friend, Maddie?"

"Yes. Maddie's mom, Sadie, said she'd never met Lenny, and I was the third person to bring him up." I got up from the table and retrieved the button.

"What a sweet photo," Ida said at the same moment Jane reared back from the table.

"Sadie was creeped out that some guy she didn't know

had a button with her daughter's photo on it. Lenny lied to us."

"Let's grill him," Jane said, shaking her chopstick at me. "He has to have a really good reason to wear that button and not be thought of as some sort of pervert."

I cleared my throat and said, "Lenny Capsner's dead."

"Then what do we do?"

"You have to figure out who killed Donaldson," said Ida. "I've known Susie for a long time. She's selfish, at times irascible, a pain in the neck, but she's also protective, hard-working, intelligent, and our friend. She isn't a murderer."

"I'll call Pete. We were going to get together—"

Jane looked at her watch. "He's out with …" She closed her eyes and groaned. Her eyes snapped opened, and she said, "You three had plans for tonight." She pulled an envelope from her pocket with my name on it. "I was just going to leave this apology because you were supposed to be out with ZaZa and Pete. ZaZa said you were working out your differences."

I almost felt steam spewing from my ears.

"Do you want to join them?"

"No." *I trusted him, didn't I?* "I know Susie didn't kill Donaldson. We have work to do." Ida cleared the table, and Dad provided notepaper and pencils, just like he did for my high school study groups. They never went as well as I hoped; most of my friends treated every get-together as a party. But Jane, Ida, Dad, and I were on a mission. Dad replaced the wine glasses with mugs and kept the coffee pot brewing, and Ida dished out cookies.

"Maverick stopped Susie from entering the basement and possibly being electrocuted." I closed my eyes, picturing them at the bottom of the stairs, trying to determine what didn't fit. When I opened them, I surprised myself. "Her shoes weren't wet. Even if she had used the business basement connecting gateways, she'd have stepped in the water." I rubbed my forehead. "I just don't see how she could've done it."

Maverick barked and pawed the door right before we heard a knock. I answered.

"Are you going to invite me in?" I stuck my head out into the night and looked both ways for a person in hiding. "You promised you'd always give me a heads up, so I passed on the dinner plans." Pete smiled. I tugged him inside. He stomped snow from his boots and hung his jacket. He pulled out a chair and said, "What did I miss?"

I filled him in on what we'd discussed so far.

"And Helen said—"

Jane said hurriedly, "But what if Pat tried to sell the stones as natural diamonds and someone found out? Was Susie's diamond a natural diamond? Tiny's grandmother wouldn't have had a lab grown diamond, would she?"

"But Helen thinks—"

"I wouldn't think so," Pete said, intently. He gazed into the dark liquid in his cup. "I researched their development and although scientists created the first synthetic diamond in 1954, it took decades to refine the process and make the stones commercially available and economical to grow. They are identical to mined diamonds in chemical composition, Mohs hardness, physical properties, and optical appearance.

"But—" I began again.

"If he didn't say they were natural, and no one asked, he wouldn't have committed fraud."

Pete shook his head. "That would be a question for the courts. He had to intend to deceive the purchaser for gain. He had not renewed his insurance, and the policy would have lapsed by the end of the month, so he wouldn't make anything from a false claim there."

"He did what?" I said and Helen's conjecture blew out of my head. "Why would he do that unless he didn't want to be accused of something?"

"He had that ticket to Vanuatu. I think he was prepared to leave." Pete supplied an answer to the curious looks. "But something came up and spoiled his plans."

I remembered what I'd been trying to say. "Helen thinks Pat planned to leave with the natural diamonds. They were his after all. He could do anything he wanted with them. She also thinks he stashed the diamonds in the SUV to take to his girlfriend and a fence when Susie accidentally borrowed it. When it was returned, he carefully checked them and found they'd been replaced." I pulled out the journal. "I've been slowly transcribing the meanderings of his supercilious mind—he wrote in phonic riddles."

"Why the colored tabs?"

"The blue references Helen. William's yellow. Liselle is red, and green tabs mark notes about Ricky. He called both of them the 'love of his life.'" Pete slid his chair away from the table, came around behind me, and peered over my shoulder. I fanned the pages to disperse the intoxicating scent of his cologne. "The white ones denote comments regarding Henry, purple—Lenny, and the clear are unaffiliated. I still have three-fourths of this journal left, but there's already a change in the tone of his notes, and I'm going cross-eyed reading the strange spellings."

"Show me," said Jane.

"Here he says, 'It looks like Flash is up to his old tricks.' Lenny was a bookie. Flash might have been Donaldson's nickname for Lenny."

Jane nodded. She bent over the book and used my

notes to read the letters phonetically. Pete and I listened, wrote what we heard, and compared our interpretations. She read the same passage with a different sound using the same letters, and we corrected our transcriptions.

"This is going to take forever," Jane said. The smile almost reached her eyes.

"It's much faster together," I said.

Maverick barked. We heard a piercing, pulsating beep. Dad and Ida exchanged confused looks. Dad opened the door adjoining the two apartments and black smoke billowed out. Pete looked around and grabbed the fire extinguisher off my wall. I clipped a leash on Maverick, and Jane called 911. Maverick yanked me after Pete as he ran through to Ida's kitchen. He threw open the oven door and shot white foam over whatever was burning. Maverick barked again and dragged me back toward our apartment.

Dad had wisely closed the door between apartments to keep the smoke and fumes contained, but he stood coughing. Ida filled a glass of water for him. Jane and I opened Ida's windows, and the temperature dropped so fast, Ida distributed afghans and quilts to each of us. The fire department arrived, checked her apartment, and removed a foam-soaked, blackened, wadded up dish towel from the oven. They gave the all-clear.

"Ida, you're sleeping in our apartment tonight. No argument. The second bedroom upstairs came partially furnished, remember? We'll all sleep better knowing you're safe. I don't smell much smoke, and there's no water damage so you should be able to get back in tomorrow," I said. "Grab what you need, and I'll make up the daybed."

Jane wiped out the oven. The extinguisher residue cleaned up easily; it hadn't been a large fire. Pete turned on Ida's kitchen fans and closed all the windows but one. He left the window above the kitchen sink open an inch and by the time Ida returned, nearly all trace of the fire had vaporized.

We paraded into our half of the beautiful old Queen Anne home, and Dad firmly closed the door between our apartments, but it was the unusual sound of the lock click that unnerved me. The door was always open.

Ida dropped her plastic bag on the floor and slid into a chair at my kitchen table. Her head fell forward. "I can't imagine how that happened. I've never left my oven on unattended before. And what's worse, I wasn't prepared. Tomorrow I'm going to make my irreplaceables accessible, ready to grab in an emergency." She yawned.

"You're so spent you're going to bed. Upstairs. Now."

She looked up, and tears pooled in her eyes. "Thank you all."

Dad said, "I'm leaving my door open. If you need anything, just call out."

I carried the bag, and Maverick dogged her steps, but Ida waved him away. "Not tonight, big boy." She plodded into the room and dropped onto the edge of the bed, staring into space. Her head dropped back and rested on the pillow. I lifted her feet, laying them gently on the bed, and covered her with a quilt. She grabbed my hand. "Katie, I'm losing it."

I squeezed back reassuringly and tucked her in. "I doubt that very much. Goodnight, Ida." I turned off the light, tiptoed out, and went back downstairs.

Pete waited at the door with his coat on. "Has she left the oven on before?"

"Never. She is very conscientious. I can't imagine her forgetting."

He draped his arm around my shoulder and kissed the top of my head. "I should go."

"Could you drop me at home?" said Jane.

"You've got it. Goodnight, Harry."

I stacked the dishes in the dishwasher, and Dad started it. He pinched the bridge of his nose. I gave him a hug and a tiny shove toward his room, but he stopped and said, "Katie, where's that book of weird words?"

THIRTY-TWO

I texted Pete and Jane and asked if either had borrowed the journal. Their immediate responses confirmed what, deep down, I already knew. Someone had started the fire intentionally to divert our attention.

Amanda answered after the first jingle. I briefed her on the fire as a ruse to get us out of our apartment in order to steal Donaldson's second journal and my notes.

"The journals didn't look important, but there must be something there," said Amanda. "Were you able to make sense of any of it?"

"My notes on the first few pages disappeared with the journal, but Donaldson generated lots of comments about the people he knew. The tone of the writings started to change; he sounded more arrogant. I did discover if I read the words aloud to someone, what I saw wasn't always the same as what they heard, and I think, if we ever find the journal, we'll be better able to figure it out."

"Come to the station tomorrow. We'll talk. Be careful, Katie." With that she was gone.

My phone pinged before I set it down.

Won't say where she's been, but she's back.

I stared at the phone in my hand and took a deep breath. *Poor Tiny.*

I collected a pen and paper and wrote what I could remember. The photos of the last few pages in the journal I had taken on my phone yielded as yet unintelligible drivel. As Helen noted, Donaldson's messages had become more difficult to interpret, and I'd need another ear or two to sound out the words. I set that aside.

I jotted headings for two columns: murder, robbery. I yawned and dragged my lids open while again cataloging motives, means, and opportunities for and against my scant list of suspects.

The relationship between Liselle and Pat had seen better days. She was a frustrated artisan, denied a chance to demonstrate her creativity, and with her husband gone, she'd be able to run the store the way she wanted. For some reason, he'd cancelled their credit cards. She'd have to run the store without Donaldson's keen sense of salesmanship and without the natural diamonds. She had keys to the store and could've stolen the gems, but where were they now? And why were there two gems behind the panel in her SUV? Her dielectric boots, and her understanding of how the store's generator operated and the power it produced proved she had at least a working knowledge of electricity. She'd heard of Vanuatu but seemed surprised by Pat's purchase of a single ticket. But it was to her advantage that she and William had an alibi for the time of Patrick's death.

Helen had wanted to partner with Donaldson before the loss of the stones. She understood most of Pat's Phonic Infographics. Maybe she understood more than she was meant to. Pat thought he had her wrapped around his finger, but that didn't seem to be the case. She also had a set of keys and did not have a strong alibi for the time of death. It's tough to pinpoint a shopper in a crowd. A new thought occurred to me. Helen could've taken the diamonds to use in her new undertaking, and when she was found out, killed him. And maybe she knew about the gateway among the shops all along. She may have made her disclosure to throw me off track.

What did I know about William? He was good looking in a rugged sort of way, but terribly smarmy. He had keys and knew about the generator. He might've known about the gateway. He held Liselle in high regard, promising to join forces now that Donaldson was gone. Maybe he liked her too much and got rid of the competition, but he had an alibi too.

What wasn't merely circumstantial had me grasping at straws.

Lenny died before giving up his secrets. He was caught on camera pawning a diamond ring about the time Donaldson was electrocuted, so he had an alibi for the time of death. He could be involved as a partner. If he was Flash, what was he up to? Lenny could have exchanged the stones, but he would have had to buy the initial lab grown replacements, and he didn't look like he was made of money. However, if he scored big on a bet recently, maybe he had enough to cover a purchase. What would have happened if Pat had confronted him? Lenny knew a little about electricity—enough to win a high school competition.

I couldn't figure out how and when the stones had been exchanged. I yawned again, and I squinted.

The ticket to Vanuatu nudged me to look at Fredericka. She protested too much when I asked her about Donaldson, his new used SUV, and his journal. I wrote 'love interest.' Were Ricky and Pat partners? If he didn't know they were substitutes, could he have given Ricky the gems to fence, and she killed him in a fit of anger when she found out they weren't what she'd expected. Had she feigned surprise when I asked her about the exotic island country? With her passport at the ready, my assumption she was preparing for a trip had to be right on, but maybe Donaldson wasn't taking her with him, and if she found out, she certainly knew the ins and outs of electricity well enough to rig the wires. The gateway beneath the stores had been there forever. She may have known about the passageway.

Or could Pat have taken the stones prior?

Henry was an enigma. He knew both Donaldsons but had a soft spot for Liselle. His emergency surgery Friday could be easily verified and took him out of contention as murderer. Having earned a journeyman status, however, his understanding of electricity was beyond the average man. He knew Lenny too. Maybe he had something to do with Lenny's demise. And what if Donaldson finally confronted him about Liselle? He seemed to care for her.

I hated to write her name. With trembling fingers, I printed 'Susie' and too many bullet points below. Donaldson wrongly accused her of stealing his wife's SUV, and she'd been arrested. She argued with him. He was the last one to have seen the ring when Tiny brought it in for cleaning. In the past, Susie had placed bets with Lenny, and Tiny was afraid she'd slipped and was wagering again. Amanda thought a losing bet may have necessitated the pawning of her ring. Or Lenny knew Susie's deepest, darkest secrets and was demanding blackmail payments. Susie didn't have alibis for Donaldson's death, Lenny's hit-and-run, or his subsequent turn for the worse in the hospital. She had taken the obligatory course on generator maintenance, so she could've understood the logistics necessary to do away with Donaldson.

To top it off, given the maze opened to the outside, anyone could have entered Donaldson's basement, but would they? And how many individuals knew about the Donaldson's safe combination under the shelf?

I kept coming back to who could have exchanged the gems. Everyone but Susie had a connection to Donaldson's before Friday. How long had the gems been gone? Where were they now? Maybe there wasn't a connection between Pat's death and the loss of the natural diamonds. He could have orchestrated the exchange of the stones and planned to escape to Vanuatu with or without company, who may or may not have been Fredericka Lattimore. However, Donaldson didn't commit suicide—or did he, or was it really an accident, plain and simple?

When those muddled thoughts jumbled, I almost crumpled my notes. I surrendered to my tired mind, rested my head on my crossed arms, and closed my eyes for a moment, only to wake five hours later when Maverick's wicked tail-wag smacked my knee, and he burrowed under my arm to lick my face, reminding me his kibble was due.

THIRTY-THREE

"At least I'm not losing my mind." Ida brightened considerably when I told her we suspected the fire was a diversion. She fixed a fabulous breakfast, after which Maverick and I took our morning constitutional.

I felt a little like I was losing *my* mind. My head swam with the confusing observations I'd collected. Susie seemed to check the most boxes in Donaldson's death and emerged as the most likely suspect, but I knew Amanda was mistaken, and I theorized what holes I needed to make in her argument.

Maverick pranced under the bright blue sky, encouraging me to wander onto the path near the frozen slough, traipsing over deer and bird prints stamped into the snow. A squirrel darted in front of us, and I should've known something wasn't right when Maverick didn't even give a hint he wanted to chase it.

A voice called from behind me. "Hey, wait up."

I turned. A short squat man with coarse gray stubble all over his head jogged up the path. Maverick sat. The hair on the nape of his neck bristled. I clutched the leash, shortening it by inches, and unwisely wrapped it around the fingers of my left hand. "Sit, Maverick." I felt a rumble grow deep in his throat. "Can I help you?"

"I hope so. You the new player? I've been looking for you for over a week. What's the spread on the Wild/Stars and the Wild/Blackhawks games? I got a parlay to make up for my bad bet last week."

"I don't know what you're talking about."

"Don't gimme that. I tried to catch you yesterday and lost you by the hardware store. I ain't gonna do that today. I know what's what." He reached into his jacket and Maverick reacted with a vehemence he saved for kidnappers and murderers, yanking the leash, and painfully squeezing my fingers. The fireplug of a man raised his hands and took three giant steps back. "Hey missy, that ain't no way to do business."

My hackles raised with Maverick's. "Don't call me missy," I yelled over Maverick's overprotective barking. "What business do you think I'm in?" I fumbled for the bag at my waist and undid the tie. Reaching into the pouch, I withdrew two of Maverick's favorite homemade dried sweet potato treats. "Good boy," I said quietly. "Sit."

Maverick's nipping and yipping and barking stopped while he scarfed down the treats, long enough for me to hear the man say, "I wanna place a bet."

"I don't take bets."

"But you're wearing the …" His eyes grew as he

recognized his error. He backed away. "Never mind. But you might—"

Maverick's tirade returned full force.

The man pointed to his left lapel, then turned and fled. Mirrored on my left lapel was Maddie's button. It seemed Lenny used the button as a signal, indicating he was open for business—money business. Sadie probably had a similar encounter.

Two treats later, I tipped my forehead to meet his. "Good boy, Maverick."

And then I thought, Amanda won't be happy.

We returned home, and Dad overheard the message I left for her. "Let's take a ride," he said. "I think I'd like you to accompany me to look at something for Elizabeth. And …" He held up his hand as I started to speak. "Let's hit up that jewelry store you've been frequenting. I think they could use an infusion of Wilk funds."

Dad and I didn't spend much time together away from home, and I jumped at the chance. We pulled up in front of Donaldson's, and before I got out of the car, I patted my pockets for my phone. I smacked my forehead, remembering it sitting squarely in the center of the kitchen table. *Surely,* we *wouldn't be gone long enough for me to need it.*

Liselle and William both popped up when the door dinged, but William sat back down after moaning, "Oh, it's you again."

Liselle walked up to my dad. "Katie, you didn't tell me you had such a handsome brother." A saleswoman at heart.

Dad smiled good-naturedly and reached out to shake her hand. "You must have left your spectacles at home, dear girl. I'm Harry Wilk, Katie's extremely handsome and patient father. I'm here to find a Valentine's gift for my ex-wife."

I almost forgot to breathe, but Liselle contained her surprise as if men bought Valentine's gifts for their exes every day. Dad had no need to explain to her. *We* might exchange words later.

She asked questions about the jewelry Elizabeth already owned and her attire, what her job entailed and what special occasion events she might attend. I modeled rings, bracelets, and earrings, but something with less romantic entanglement caught his eye—a slim silver business card holder. While Liselle engraved an E in elegant script, we perused the showcases and the variety of lovely gift items on the glass shelves against the wall I'd failed to notice on my previous visits.

"Would you like this gift-wrapped?" She handed him a 'Thinking of You' enclosure card.

Dad methodically turned the card in his hand, flipping it end over end. His eyes glazed, lost in the past, but when he smiled at Liselle, his face lit the room. "Yes. Please. And can you engrave a second one with an I?"

He returned the signed cards. She boxed the gifts, precisely folding shiny silver paper at the corners, tucking in the overlapping pieces, securing the ends with tape, and attaching bright duo-colored bows on top. She added a sprig of tiny white flowers to one. "Just like the color of a rose, yellow can mean friendship and white can mean fresh start. I hope this is to your liking. The E engraving was done on the gift in the box with the baby's breath."

Dad nodded and handed over his credit card. Liselle stared at it, holding it as if it might explode. She ran it through her machine and returned his receipt with the presents in a white paper bag. "Thank you," he said. "I think these are going to be just right."

From Donaldson's we drove straight to the mailing

company, bought a carton, fitted the gift, and shipped it off to Elizabeth's new home base in California.

"I know things haven't gone the way you'd hoped, but this is a sweet gift, Dad. I'm sure she'll like it. And you never know what might happen."

He stared out the window, then turned to look at me and patted my hand. "Elizabeth and I haven't discussed finalizing our current arrangement, but I want you to know I won't stay indefinitely and be a burden—"

"You are *not* a burden. You are welcome to stay forever. I love having you with me, Dad." Tears welled up in my eyes and I quickly brushed them away.

"That Liselle's a nice girl. Hey, darlin', can we make another stop?"

I sniffed. "Of course. Where to?"

I followed turn by turn instructions and as realization dawned, my spirits soared. I idled the Focus on the street, blinded by the sunlight reflecting off the vehicle parked in front of Dad's mechanic's shop. "It's finished?"

The corner of Dad's mouth inched its way up. "Elmer finished Thursday and look at him. He's so proud of his work, his buttons are ready to pop off his shirt."

I pulled the keys from the ignition and caressed the dash of the old beater I'd come to rely on. Dad and I casually, with my heart banging in my ears, sauntered to the office. Signing on all the dotted lines and peeling off the necessary bills for a cash payment, Dad was once again the proud owner of a gleaming cream-colored 1957 Ford Fairlane 500 Crown Victoria, his pride and joy, besides me, of course. I anticipated removing my things, swapping keys, and we'd be off, but there was more to it.

Because his car was so old and hadn't met the standards required of automobile use for decades, we could only drive to and from the service station, in rallies, car shows, at fairs, and parades, but certainly not for daily jaunts to work, school, church, and shopping. We'd be allowed to purchase classic license plates only if we provided proof of a primary vehicle, so in addition, Dad began to haggle on the purchase price of my Ford Focus.

"But Dad ..." I couldn't protest too much. It wasn't a pretty car, but I wouldn't worry about the faded blue finish when parked outside in all kinds of weather, and it had withstood a Minnesota winter without stranding me yet.

He bartered among the finest and finagled a good deal on new tires and a block heater with the promise of a yearly tune-up on the Crown Vic and an occasional tour with Dad.

"Although a gorgeous ride, the Crown Vic isn't practical or economical," Elmer said.

"Both cars are in your name, darlin'. Given my medical history, my insurance rates would skyrocket, but I'll help you keep up with it. We'll come back for the Focus, but right now, could we just cruise home?"

I tugged on the gleaming chrome handle and slid onto the soft baby-blue-and-white leather seats. For Maverick to ride, we'd have to get a canvas cover for pets. My hands circled the narrow grip of the oversized steering wheel. The unblemished dash shimmered from behind. The key turned, and the engine bellowed to life. I removed the parking brake, manhandled the gearshift into drive, and pressed gently down on the gas pedal, easing the car with the weightiness of a tank into the nonexistent traffic. Gliding well below the speed limit, I took the long way to Maple Street.

Dad closed his eyes. His head dropped back onto the seat as he repeated a ditty I'd often heard as a child, "Get a little gas, and a little bit of oil. Get a little spark from a little bitty coil. Get a piece of tin and a two-inch board. Put it all together and you've got a little Ford."

I parked the vintage wheels, and we made our way into the apartment. I ran into Ida already bundled in her coat.

"I'll be back in a jiffy, Harry." She snapped her fingers. "Let's get a move on. Your father and I are signed up for the Grand Slam."

"What's the Grand Slam?" I grabbed my phone from the table, hustling to catch up.

"It's the semi-annual bridge tournament at the Community Center. Everybody who's anybody is going to be there."

I stopped so quickly, I stumbled on the pattern in the rug. "He doesn't know how to play bridge." She looked over her shoulder and continued on to the garage. I scurried to catch up. "Does he?"

Before she opened the car door, she stretched to her full height, adding tippy toes, and said, "It's been a while for both of us, but we reviewed the rules last night, and we're up for all takers."

I slid in next to her. "Is it an all-day event? Are spectators allowed?"

"Double elimination. We can have our groupies attend the finals tomorrow." She gave me a quick sidelong glance. "You can come then."

I learned more about my dad every day. It seemed he could do just about anything. And having had such a great time picking up his car and mine left me ill-prepared for the mountain of text messages and voicemails I found awaiting me. I listened to the latest.

Liselle said, "Katie, your dad left his credit card at the store. Could you stop by and pick it up?"

Ida prattled on about their last-minute preparation for the afternoon and dropped me at Elmer's. I collected my keys and thanked him for his great workmanship. "When my dad is happy, so am I," I assured him.

I picked up the Focus and listened to the voicemails from Amanda becoming more and more insistent. I parked and read through the "call me" text messages from Amanda, Pete, Susie, and an unknown number.

Henry Mullhern waved as he stepped away from the entry. "She's doing all right. Thanks for coming so soon." He scrutinized my face. "She didn't tell you, did she?" I squinted at him. "Forget I said anything."

Helen stopped polishing the teapot for a second and greeted me with a wan smile. Liselle jumped up from behind the workbench, reaching out with Dad's credit card. "Sorry. I thought I'd wound the receipt around it. I hope coming back downtown didn't inconvenience you." Her hand shook. The glassy look in her eyes and her pale face brought to mind a junkie in withdrawal.

I took hold of the card and whispered, "Are you feeling okay?"

Helen set the teapot back in its niche and walked to Liselle. "You don't have to do this alone, you know. Tell her. She'll understand."

THIRTY-FOUR

"Follow me, please."

I'd made too many trips to this basement. I trudged slowly to the stairs and sank into the depths. Liselle sagged into the chair in front of the work bench where her husband had died.

"Tell me what?"

Liselle focused on her shoes and mumbled. I could barely make out the words. "Did you say you're an addict?"

She lifted her head. "I can't stop gambling. I palmed your dad's credit card to use for a little cash. Just a little. He'd never even notice it, but …" Her chin dropped back to her chest. "I just couldn't."

Inside, I seethed. This woman would've taken advantage of my dad. "What stopped you?" My tone was harsh, but I wasn't in a generous frame of mind.

"As much as I wanted to gamble, I didn't really want to use your dad's card. I like him. So, I called my sponsor. He's talked me off the ledge many times and made me see the error of my ways. I don't know what I'd do without him."

"Henry Mullhern is your sponsor?" *That's why he was so cryptic.*

She swallowed hard and nodded vigorously. "I don't know where I'd be without him. Patrick didn't understand. He had no faults and couldn't abide them in others."

Given a second, I could think of one or five faults Donaldson had exhibited to me and to others. "On Saturday, your husband told you he'd replaced your credit cards because he couldn't find them, but he'd cancelled them. That was how he planned to curb your addiction." She looked at me in disbelief. "You needed money and thought you'd scam my dad? You're not going to win any points with me.

"The clincher is you became so enraged with Pat cutting off your resources, you killed him. One of the final infographics encoded in the journal said something about no longer letting her suck him dry. You are her."

"I didn't kill him." The strength of her voice startled both of us. She hung her head.

"What happened then?"

"I loved … love working with silver. It's static, tough, and resilient, but under fire, it's alive." Her hands moved, mimicking a bud blooming. "I can almost see which way the precious metal wants to go, what it wants to make of itself. Patrick gave me a chance to try my hand at the art of silversmithing when I was seventeen. I learned so much from him. And I was in love."

"But not with Patrick."

She shook her head. "He was a good man. He provided all the tools and materials and let me create wonderful art until we married. Then he took that opportunity away. He gave me jewelry, trips, fancy clothes, a nice house—things I hadn't even dreamed of, but he didn't want me here anymore." He didn't want to play second fiddle, I thought uncharitably. "So, I channeled my creativity in another direction, and at first, I was good at that too."

"You found Lenny." She dropped her head in her hand, and embarrassment rolled over her. She had motives to kill both Donaldson and Lenny and I took a step back, but she had an alibi at the time of both deaths.

I didn't have the heart to leave her wallowing in shame. "Tell me about this set up." There were tools and gizmos, appliances, machines, and thingamabobs all over the desk.

She wiped her tear-streaked face. "Would you really like to know what I do?" I nodded. Her eyes cleared, and she swiveled in the chair. "Let me show you what I mean."

She cut a paper pattern to fit around my wrist, and she placed it on a flat silver-colored sheet, outlining it with a felt tip pen. She cut away the excess and stood, looking inches taller than when we came down. "The belt sander rounds the edges and straightens the sides." With protective eyewear in place, the machine buzzed with life, and the sander ate away the silver until the black markings disappeared. She stepped to a two-sided machine and held the piece next to a grinder. "This will help smooth and polish the piece." Her fingers moved steadily over the edges, checking the smoothness of the rims. Satisfied, she secured the piece to a small anvil and handed me a hammer with a patterned head. "Pummel away."

I tapped lightly. She snatched the tool from my hand and gave the metal ten loud, substantial thwacks before handing the hammer back. "This is a great way to take out your aggression. Do you have anything you'd like to change but can't?"

A few things came to mind, and I followed her lead. How satisfying. The more hearty whacks I put in, the prettier the pattern on the metal. Liselle's eyes met mine, a kindred spirit of sorts, and I understood how much she enjoyed the entire process. When I'd adequately covered the piece in dents, she took it back to the grinder. "Fine tuning," she said. After a positive inspection, she lifted a swatch of leather from a box and a slender wooden wedge. "Shim," she said. A loud hum filled the room when she activated a machine rotating soft polishing wheels on both ends. "Buffer," she added, and handed the dull rectangle to me.

I wrapped the silver in the leather and secured the bracelet to the shim. I held the pieces up to the fluffy head and witnessed the speed at which it shined the bracelet.

Liselle handed me a rawhide mallet and demonstrated how to shape the silver. "Pound it around the mandrel, a bit on each side. And while you do that, I'm going to use some leftover silver snippets and make a ball for ornamentation." When I caught the flame of the acetylene torch out of the corner of my eye, I stopped walloping and watched intently. In moments, the silver pieces turned red against the cavity, curled inside a charcoal block, and slid gracefully into a sphere. She removed it with copper tongs, but as she reached for the cover of a crock pot-like apparatus, she froze.

"What's wrong?" A little anxious to see where we'd go with this, I didn't want her to stop.

"It was plugging an appliance like this which caused—"

"I'm so sorry." The hammer dropped from my hand.

"You don't have to do this."

She lifted the lid, and the ball sizzled when she dropped it in. "Yes, I do. The pickle pot cleans the oxidation, and we'll be well on our way to finishing your piece. And this pot is new."

She picked up the hammer and deftly finished shaping my bracelet around the metal arm.

Arranging the pieces in front of her, just as Kindra had when the kids constructed the K.E.G., she pointed at each. "Third hand tweezers," she explained and cinched the bracelet inside. She brushed on a white film. "Flux," she said before I could ask. "And this is solder." She placed tiny silver pieces on the end of the bracelet, set the silver ball, and checked her creation. She lit the torch and waved the flame within the circle of the bracelet and above. Nothing happened until all at once the ball was set. She dipped the bracelet in the pickle pot and when she brought it out, I sighed. It was gorgeous, and I had a hand in its creation.

"All I have to do is burnish the inside and polish it up, and it's finished. Can you come back in thirty minutes?"

"It's for me?"

The grin was contagious.

My watch read twenty past twelve and I gasped. "I've got to go. I'm sorry I took up so much time. I didn't hear the church bell chime, or I'd have been out of your hair already."

"The chimes have been off for two weeks. Henry said they accidentally cut the line."

THIRTY-FIVE

Amanda answered after the first ring. "Where've you been?"

"I stopped by Donaldson's to pick up my dad's credit card, and Liselle helped me make a silver bracelet."

"Why do these things keep happening to you, Katie?" Amanda huffed. "What's with the guy this morning?"

"He thought I was a bookie because I wore Maddie's button. The pawn broker told me Capsner liked old movies, especially those in which strangers recognized each other by the flower they had with them. You know, 'Wear a red carnation so I know it's you.' I think Lenny used the photo button of Maddie as a signal, enabling wagerers to find him in a public place and word got around. What do you think?"

"Possibly. I talked to another woman yesterday who had a similar occurrence." I wondered if Sadie had reported her encounters. "I'd like to use the button to investigate your hypothesis. Bring it with you when you come in to make your statement about the fire. Please."

"Could I have it back when you've completed your sting operation? Maddie's a friend of my neighbor, Emma."

Amanda snorted. "And you still believe the fire was intentional?"

"I haven't been able to locate the journal, and we last saw it on my kitchen table. The back door was unlocked."

"See you in fifteen minutes."

Before two o'clock, I'd walked, eaten breakfast, helped buy and mail a gift to Elizabeth, purchased a car, made a bracelet, tried Pete's number four times, spoken to Amanda, and handed over Maddie's button. But I hadn't been able to change Amanda's mind; she still believed Susie had flipped the switch, sending the electricity through Donaldson.

Dad's car was parked in my garage stall, but he had removed the snow from the cement slab at the end of the drive for me. When I got out of my car—my car, how wonderful it sounded—I heard muffled barking. Maverick kicked up a fuss when he saw someone he loved, but this time he announced a relative stranger on the stoop. I stutter-stepped when I recognized the spikey heels and the pink coat topped by a wavy dark updo. What could she possibly want now?

She pounded on the door. "I know you're in there, Katie. I can hear your dog.

ZaZa nearly tumbled off the stoop when I called from behind, "What happened to your boots?"

She swung around, clutching her chest, and said, "You frightened me."

I ignored her.

"They made my feet sweat." She lifted her chin. "I sent them back," she said curtly.

My eyebrows shot up. "I hear you've been telling everyone I'm not very accommodating. I'd like to make amends. What do you need?" Her mouth hung open. Apparently, she wasn't expecting brutal honesty. She blustered. "I only have my course work texts at home, and we don't teach the same thing. What else can I help you with?"

She grasped the railing and descended the icy steps. "You're sabotaging my life here and setting your friends against me, letting me flounder when I need help the most."

I looked down at the ground to hide my grin. No way was I taking credit for my friends' wisdom. "I'm doing nothing of the sort. You used our friendship to get this job and have tried to undermine me at every turn." I stepped around her and opened the door. Out popped my nuzzly fuzzy greeter. "My friends, students, and coworkers have seen through your pretense, ZaZa." *At least some of them.* "They won't be listening to anything you tell them anymore without wondering if you're spinning a tale. You've lied. If I didn't know you left the job of your dreams and were looking for a new position, why would I have asked you to apply here?" She started to interrupt. I hurried on. "Mrs. McEntee told me, and I do trust her. You put my students at risk with your antics, and Dorene, our head coach, rightfully asked you to butt out." Her face turned red. "You told untruths to my friends. In spite of all that, and with many reservations, I'll offer my assistance. Then you won't have reason to blame me or bother someone else."

"I don't bother anyone."

I aimed for the doorway. If she didn't follow me, so

much the better. She did. *Drat.*

"Cocoa?" I tossed my jacket on the rack.

"Wine." She slid her feet out of her stilettos.

"Cocoa is offered."

"Cocoa," she sighed and hung her coat.

I poured half and half in a pan and turned the heat on low. I stirred in cocoa powder, added a dash of vanilla, sprinkled sugar, just like I'd watched Dad do a million and one times, and while I tipped the saltshaker, ZaZa said, "Why do you hate me?"

The conversation had taken a turn I hadn't expected. "I don't hate you, ZaZa. After my dad, I've known you longer than anyone else in Columbia. We had some great times." Charles' grinning face came immediately to mind.

She reached out to pet Maverick, and he turned away from her. He dropped his head on his paws and looked up at me with almost an apology.

"No one likes me," she whined.

"Liking you is the least of your worries. I can't speak for anyone else, but I don't like what you're doing. You're saying things that aren't true and doing things behind my back, and maybe doing the same to others." She shook her head vehemently. "I can't trust you."

"Talk about trust. You took Charles away from me," she said in a whisper.

I looked directly at her. "I'm sorry you were hurt. Neither Charles nor I realized until it was too late. We fell in love. But trying to get back at me won't change anything. Were you in love with him?"

She shrugged.

"Or were you in love with being in love."

"We'll never know, will we?"

Lorelei and Brock were right. She didn't know how

much she had going for her. "You were, are a great mathematician, but teaching is an art," I turned back to the stove and spoke over my shoulder. "A countryman of yours said, 'The whole art of teaching is only the art of awakening the natural curiosity of young minds for the purpose of satisfying it afterwards.'"

As if I was making it up, she asked, "Who said that?"

"Anatole France." I stirred the cocoa. "Maybe teaching isn't your thing."

"You've transitioned to teaching well. I can do at least as well as you.

"Don't try to be someone you're not. Be yourself."

She took a huge breath. "You are right." She smiled sweetly. Her eyes glinted. "Katie. Remember, *en amour comme à la guerre, tous les coups sont permis.*"

"French is a beautiful language. What did you say?"

"Unimportant," she said as she squeezed her feet into her heels.

"Do you need anything?"

"I'm good." She sashayed to the door, made a wild grab for her coat, and stumbled to the floor. As she sat on the rug, she picked up the heel of her right shoe, and she began to weep. Sobbing for a pair of shoes? Maverick went in for a slobbery smooch. She shoved him away.

"We'll get it fixed. You shouldn't be hiking out there in your Jimmy Choo's anyway." She looked at me, incredulous. "I do know designer labels, and I'm still not wearing them, not on a teacher's salary."

"What about your barony, Lady Katherine?"

Mention of the title stopped me cold. It came down to that. "In name only, ZaZa."

She scoffed, trying to fit the heel to the sole.

"I can take them to my shoemaker. You can borrow a

pair of my boots. At least for tonight?"

"Your feet are so much larger than mine," she said, with an air of superiority.

"True enough, but I have heavy socks to help fill the gap and keep you toasty."

"Why haven't you thrown me out?"

"ZaZa, we've had many of the same experiences, and if you decide to stay in Columbia, we may have more. Be the ZaZa I met in school." I didn't know if that would be possible any longer.

She sniffled. "I'll borrow the boots."

"What happened to your old job?"

I poured the hot cocoa into mugs and grabbed a bag of marshmallows.

"I was tired of the politics in government. I needed a new start."

"I'll be right back." I ran upstairs and chose the ugliest pair of socks I owned. I returned and found ZaZa slurping the last dregs of her cocoa, delicately swiping a white marshmallow moustache with the back of her hand. She took the socks and wriggled her Cinderella feet into the age-old scuffed boots. "Thanks," she said begrudgingly.

"No problem." I took a sip and immediately spat it back in the mug. My salt addition had been a touch heavy handed.

ZaZa snorted and vacated the premises.

I chuckled. We wouldn't be friends, but we had memories we couldn't forget.

THIRTY-SIX

Seconds later, Maverick barked, and I reopened the door, expecting to see ZaZa. Instead, Lorelei's hand hung in the air, poised to rap. She grinned, and her five cohorts, standing at the bottom of the stairs, sent up a greeting. I widened the gap, and my students marched in, dropping into chairs around the table.

"We researched electronic geocaches—"

"*She* researched electronic geocaches; we went along with it," Carlee said, her mouth in a serious line but her eyes laughing.

"Yes. Well. Crew3545 placed the cache within the last three months, and it hasn't been found yet. Not for lack of trying, though. There is a long list of DNFs."

Patricia signed a question, and Kindra was quick to

explain. "Do not finds. That means—"

Patricia replied, annoyed, "I know what it means. I didn't see what she said."

"What's the description of the cache?" I pretended to lack enthusiasm, but in reality, Lorelei had hooked me with the word researched. Anything that followed had to be good, and a geocache always tickled my fancy. I couldn't wait to head out.

"It rates a three in difficulty, one point five in terrain, and the size is not given. But it's downtown, and the hint recommends you bring four double A batteries. The attributes indicate it could be found in the snow. Are you game?" asked Carlee.

"I guess I don't have anything better to do." I feigned nonchalance for about a second before my eagerness burst into a huge smile. "I'll ask Ms. Mackey to join us. She loves these things." I left a message on her phone.

I grabbed my coat and shoved my arms into the sleeves. When I dug out my new and, should I say, stylish Mukluks, I had a thought. If we wandered past the shoemaker, I could drop off ZaZa's broken heel and maybe mend a small fence. I zipped the narrow heel in the right pocket on my sleeve and stuck the shoe in the voluminous left pocket.

"Do you have four double A batteries?" asked Brock.

"That's really the only reason you included me, correct?" I deftly covered up the fact I'd already forgotten the need for batteries and said, "Mrs. Clemashevski has them, I'm sure." I knocked and entered, borrowing four batteries from her stash, left an IOU, and cheerfully returned to the kids with Maverick nipping at my heels.

"Can someone show me where we're going?" Four hands flew at me, all clasping a phone opened to the Geocaching website. I backed away to focus on the nearest display. "You lead and we'll follow." I clipped on Maverick's leash. He was as ready to go as I was.

I texted Jane the general vicinity we'd be searching, hoping to meet her there. Two by two, we paraded down Maple, laughing, talking, signing, and skipping. Fortunately, the brilliant sun gently heated the sidewalk and melted the ice crystals, flaunting the best of another Minnesota winter day.

I kept a tight rein on Maverick who had his own idea which way he wanted to go. The leash tightened. My fingers tingled.

I think the kids had forgotten I was with them, and their honest, unguarded conversations revealed a slightly more humorous and less reverent side to their nature.

"Pure sodium." Carlee said and Kindra giggled. "That's what Ms. Mackey said about Mr. Kidd."

"What does that mean?" asked Patricia. "Is it a compliment?"

"Of the best kind," Kindra signed. "The chemical symbol for sodium is NA. Get it?"

"No." Patricia said. Unwilling to concede she might not understand, she urged Kindra to share more.

"N stands for nice." Kindra waited. "Now do you get it?"

Patricia shook her head although the titters of everyone else led me to believe the meaning should be obvious.

"The A stands for a special part of Mr. Kidd's anatomy. The part he sits on."

Patricia's mouth hung open. *Wait until Drew heard that tidbit.*

Following our compasses, we strode past the shoe store which had closed at noon. I missed picking up my bracelet at Donaldson's by minutes.

We followed the GPS directions into a city park. The units pinged our nearness to the cache, and my charges scattered. Brock dropped to the ground, rolling under a piece of playground equipment. Galen climbed the ladder to the slides, running his hands over, under, and around the surfaces. Carlee, Lorelei, and Kindra each searched an apparatus, but Patricia meandered to the bank of electrical boxes, pushing and pulling the pieces to determine if any were temporary.

We were just about to give up when Jane trudged through the snow, re-invigorating our search with a shout, "You can't give up now. I just got here."

The kids refreshed the app on their devices. The compasses pointed in the same direction, noting an identical distance. We tried again. This time, Galen took a good look at a birdhouse, and chuckled. "No bird can call this house a home. The entry is painted on."

We converged on a box built to look like a quaint cabin atop a four-by-four-inch post. By knocking, Brock discovered a two-by-four-inch piece of metal halfway up the five-and-a-half-foot high pillar, but he couldn't get it to budge. Brock and Galen poked and prodded, jiggling the miniature flower boxes under the fake windows, tugging at the roof, tapping the black circle, and wiggling the screws and rods.

One of the rods moved beneath Galen's searching fingers, and a window box slid off short glides, revealing a battery holder mounted on the wall. He slotted the four double A batteries. Brock followed the directions inked above the batteries and wrapped the wires. Carlee flipped the switch to 'discover,' and we heard a whirring. The metal piece was a door of sorts and as it rose, a bright red bison tube attached to a cord presented itself from a hollowed-out cavity as if descending on an elevator. When it struck the bottom, the switch flipped to a neutral position. Patricia opened the tube and pulled out a paper log and flash drive with FTF—first to find— written on the side. She handed the flash drive to me. Kindra signed the log and returned it. Lorelei reversed the switch to 'hide,' and the cord drew the tube back inside the four-by-four post, closing the metal door.

The switch held the power. I repeated the words to imprint in my memory, but with the kids' swirling words and happy faces after the successful find, I didn't retain them with as much clarity as I needed.

We replaced everything so that it looked the way we'd found it.

We stood silent for a moment until Jane said, "That's got to be my favorite yet. Let's celebrate. I'll pick up cupcakes from the bakery, and Katie can make hot cocoa."

My stomach clenched at the thought of my most recent cocoa fiasco, and I said, "How about hot Dr. Pepper with lemon instead?"

"Deal!"

The return walk was made with more intention and took less time. We waited for Jane, and I poured Dr. Pepper in a saucepan and sliced lemons. While it heated, I plugged in the flash drive, hoping my computer wouldn't seize up with some transitory virus.

The flash drive contained a congratulatory Word document, explicit instructions, and the code for a gift card to purchase supplies to make our own fake birdhouse geocache.

"I'm certain Mr. Simonson would help. He asked when we were coming back," said Galen.

My students polished off the cupcakes and the Dr.

Pepper, and when they bade us farewell, reality came crashing down.

Jane noticed the change in my demeanor. "What's wrong?"

"I feel guilty. While we were out playing, Susie and Tiny have been worrying about their future, and I haven't come any closer to figuring out who killed Donaldson."

"You're not supposed to be figuring out who killed Donaldson. Leave that to Amanda."

I chewed on my lip and added, "I had a talk with ZaZa today. She thinks I hate her."

"Well." Jane let that comment hang in the air.

I scrunched my face and tried to pull up the French words ZaZa shared with me. "What does '*on amor come a la gare too lay coo son permi mean*'?"

She blinked. And blinked again.

"My French is horrible. I could have all the words wrong, but I think that's what she said."

Her left eyebrow rose, and she said, "All's fair in love and war."

I shouldn't have been surprised. My vigilance had just begun again.

THIRTY-SEVEN

Jane went home to do laundry and cringed, mentioning the extra cleaning she needed to do; ZaZa wasn't ready to add neatness to her routine. Pete's call schedule had him working. Dad texted their three winning bridge scores so far. Neither played with much regularity, but they knew the rules and wanted to get back into it. They were already more successful than I'd anticipated. Maverick and I had finished our walk. I'd checked off more than everything on my to-do list, and I couldn't wait to pick up my bracelet at the next opportunity.

I had time. It had been too long. The cardboard cartons called to me. Hot Dr. Pepper swirled in the mug I set on the table in the office bedroom, and I sat on the floor, working up the courage to look inside.

The final box opened to the last photo I'd packed, a professional black-and-white head shot of Charles in his movie star pose, head tilted resting on his fist, dreamy eyes caught shimmering and following my every move, enigmatic smile playing on his lips. I could almost hear him say, "What are we waiting for?"

One by one I removed the mementos, photos, and notebooks from the cardboard box, a grin plastered on my lips as I realized how lucky I'd been to have had Charles in my life. The rest of the precious photos were few in number, and not good quality, but each told part of our story. I snickered, realizing ZaZa posed in half of them. Had I been paying attention, I might've noticed the tenderness with which she looked at Charles. My grin softened, and electricity traveled up my arms when my fingers traced the red ribbon tied around the love letters Charles had written. I didn't need to open them; I'd memorized all five. Maverick licked the hot tears from my cheeks.

I ruffled the hairs on the top of his head. "You would have liked him, my furry friend. Your mother certainly did. He and Pete are very much alike."

Maverick lifted his head and cocked it.

"No. They don't look anything alike, but I may have gotten another chance with a wonderful man." I sighed. "Keep me on the straight and narrow path so I don't blow it, okay?"

I carefully repacked my keepsakes and decided to gnaw on a nagging morsel of Susie's problem. Ricky and Henry had to work the weekend, and I might be able to catch one or both of them in. Ricky had a good reason to be angry with Patrick, and there was no love lost between him and Henry. A little probing couldn't hurt.

Maverick danced around my feet, accompanying me

to *my car*, and plowed into the passenger seat, sitting and panting expectantly, before I finished opening the door. "What a dog." I didn't even mind the snowy pawprints on the seat.

We cruised the back streets to the hospital garage and splashed through puddles of melted snow glinting on clear roads in the crisp moonlight, fashioning a vivid tableau. The snow sparkled with a blue tinge under the streetlights and defined stark black trunks. Craggy branches reached up into the clear starry sky.

Ricky probably wouldn't want to talk to me, but I hoped Henry could help me straighten out a few of my thoughts. I glided to a stop in front of the huge door, parked under the harsh lights in the driveway and took a big breath. I grabbed Maverick's leash. "Everyone loves you. You're like a master key. Maybe they'll admit us."

I stepped up to the service door, pounded three times, waited a beat, and pounded again. I glanced down at Maverick who gave no indication we should return to the car. A pair of watery eyes peeked out the small rectangular window, and the door creaked open six inches, revealing Henry's unhappy face.

"What do you want?"

"I'd like to talk to you and Ricky. Is she here?"

"She'll be in shortly." Henry opened the door fully, allowed us to enter, and settled the door back in place. He eyed me warily and waited.

A wave of awkwardness washed over me. "I have a few more questions."

"Of course, you do," Henry growled. Maverick glanced up at me. "Ricky has been looking over her shoulder all weekend. What did you say to her?"

"I'm hoping to find out who killed Pat. You knew him

better than most. Don't you wonder?"

His shoulders drooped a little. "When we first met, I thought he was a great guy. He insisted on making a success of everything he did, and we partnered up. He raised my expectation of myself, but he never could stand to be second best. When he didn't think he'd be the number one electrician, he pulled out of the program, but, boy, could he sell. He bought the store, and every year showed a huge profit. We'd get together and celebrate after inventory in January.

"He loved going to work. Helen's a good salesperson too, but she'd rather do things—solder, engrave, wrap, change batteries, repairs. They fit well. He'd already started that puzzle game and she enjoyed playing it. With all the positive vibes, it became *the* place to go for jewelry, the place to be, and soon he needed help. He hired Liselle right out of high school. She kept taking classes, getting better and better, and the number of custom jewelry commissions skyrocketed. I think their admiration for one another grew to love. But he also resented her."

"She was becoming a fine artisan. Ida told me she did amazing work with silver."

Henry nodded. "After they married, he made her time at the store tedious. Unfortunately, I think it became a chore for him too, and he suggested she'd enjoy staying home more."

"He took her out of the equation?"

"But boredom brings with it its own set of vices." He looked deep into the palms of his hands. "I think you need to hear the rest from her."

"What about you?"

"What about me?"

"You've known them for more than a dozen years.

What do you think happened? Who do you think might have wanted Pat dead?"

"Put me on your list."

I sucked in a breath.

"You asked who might have *wanted* him dead. I didn't kill him. I couldn't. I was in the hospital, recovering from emergency surgery for a ruptured appendix. I was in bed for three days, just long enough for me to blow my cool and demand to be released from the hospital hoosegow. I hate being cooped up. I had a job to complete downtown. The broken lines are mended, the power restored, and we're ready to fill the gaping hole on Main Street."

"What will happen to Liselle?"

"She's resilient. She'll bounce back, and Donaldson's will return to its former glory."

"Do you think Pat took the diamonds?"

Henry looked as if I'd just hit him with a question in Zulu.

"Liselle and Helen have checked the loose stones in the inventory. All the larger stones have been replaced with almost identical lab grown diamonds. Do you think Pat would switch the stones, pocket the difference, and hightail it to Vanuatu?"

"That's the second time you've brought up that godforsaken island. What does it have to do with Pat?" The ice-cold voice belonged to Ricky Lattimore, stalking through the row of white SUVs, one measured step at a time. "Thanks for your help, Henry. I've got this. You can leave now." Her laser-sharp eyes bore into me. "Isn't it enough he's gone? Why can't you leave it alone? You're ruining everything."

Henry pulled a white linen handkerchief from his back pants pocket and rubbed the front grill on the SUV nearest him. He continued the polishing act until he reached the door handle.

"Ricky, you look angry," I said, noticing the straightedge she held in her right hand.

"I am angry. I finally had a future mapped out and you …" She pointed her chin at me. "You're taking even the memory away." Her forefinger ran up and down the back of the blade.

"That wasn't my intention. I'm trying to figure out who might've killed Pat."

"The nurse did it. She kept accusing him of stealing her ring, but she stole the SUV." Tears filled her eyes. "He's dead now, and nothing will bring him back." Her shoulders quavered.

"Tell me about Pat, Ricky."

Her voice was almost imperceptible. "We were going away together. He took the diamonds and stuffed them behind the panel in the door, and all I had to do was remove the stones, his stones, from the SUV, and we'd trade them in and be set for life. He left the vehicle for me to service and remove the stones, but she took it."

"Susie took it. Is that what you mean?"

"Of course, that's what I mean. When I called Pat to ask why he hadn't come to the garage yet, he got so mad. I've never heard anyone so angry. At first, he blamed me and was afraid to report it missing, but then he thought, he'd have a scapegoat to blame if he needed it. When he got the SUV back, the diamonds were still behind the panel, and he said we'd just try again on Friday. But he checked one of the diamonds, and it was wrong. He was livid. He said she'd swapped every one of them."

"Ricky, how would Susie have known about the diamonds and had the time or wherewithal to exchange them?"

"I don't know. But she took our whole future. Pat was going to teach her a lesson. He was going to keep her ring."

"Ricky, did you kill Pat?"

"No," she cried. "I loved him."

"But he was going to Vanuatu without you, wasn't he?"

She sobbed. When her shoulders stopped quaking, she said, "He planned to take the diamonds and leave me behind. In my heart I knew it would never last, but a girl can dream, can't she?" She raised the blade.

Before I could move, Henry grabbed Ricky's arm, sending the metal clanging and skittering across the cement. He wrapped her in an embrace, and they collapsed to the floor, Ricky a blubbering heap. I secured the blade in Henry's handkerchief. He looked up with sorrow-filled eyes. "She needs more help than we can give her."

I placed a call to 911.

THIRTY-EIGHT

Henry sat forward in the passenger seat, gripping the dash, chewing on his bottom lip all the way to the hospital. We watched as the EMTs ushered Ricky into the ER. Pete met her, gently sliding her into a wheelchair, speaking softly but with concern etched on his features. He caught my eye, nodded once, and disappeared into the inner sanctum.

It only took a few minutes for Henry to finish his report with the officers who accompanied the ambulance, and I gave him a ride back to the garage. "She didn't know," he said defiantly as we drove the quiet streets. "She had no idea they weren't going away together, no reason to want him dead." He spat. "And according to her, Pat didn't know the natural diamonds had been exchanged."

I couldn't bring myself to agree outwardly, but Henry was right. Ricky didn't know. She loved Pat and wouldn't have killed him.

"I'm not family, but she gave them permission to keep me apprised of her condition. I'm going to make sure she gets the best care." Henry shook his head. "You think you know someone, but I didn't know the real Pat. He took advantage of her. He may have loved her, but he loved himself more."

"Dr. Erickson will see she gets the help she needs."

His head wagged from side to side. "If Pat didn't swap the stones, who did?" He turned to look at me. "And who do you think killed him?"

"Helen, Liselle, William, and Lenny all had motive and means and perhaps opportunity. You said you had a reason to see him gone, but no opportunity. Are there others who might have had a reason?"

Henry turned his head to the right to observe the endless winter white.

"What's wrong? What are you thinking? Is it about someone you sponsored for Gamblers Anonymous?"

His head came up rapidly. "I can't believe she'd kill anyone or steal anything. She's sweet and kind—"

"And you're in love with her. Liselle told me you talked her through her distress on more than one occasion."

"But I let her down last weekend. She needed me, and I was unable to take her call."

"She was in crisis, and you couldn't take her call because you were under the knife. That's not on you." I pulled up to the service door, shifted to Park, and faced Henry.

"Liselle was ready to quit, but her husband, if you can call him that, cut off the funds she needed to finally pay off Lenny, to break his hold over her. Lenny threatened to go to Pat. She really didn't want that. Pat didn't need more ammunition to goad and ridicule her. She was trying to stop gambling. But maybe Lenny went to Pat anyway." He examined the upturned hands in his lap, as if they'd betrayed him. "I only read the messages and saw the missed calls after I left the hospital. I contacted her. Liselle said she'd taken care of it, but she wouldn't tell me how. I asked if she'd found someone to help her, and she wouldn't answer. I could feel her discomfort in revealing the name of a person who might have helped her because that would jeopardize their anonymity."

"Or maybe Liselle killed Patrick hoping to control the funds in her future."

"No," Henry said adamantly.

"You have to consider her a possible suspect."

"I have to do no such thing. And if you continue looking at Ricky or Liselle as suspects, don't bother to come back to see me." Henry hopped out and slammed the door. Maverick whimpered like he'd lost a good friend, and perhaps he had.

The clock on the dash read 7:26. My phone pinged with a text.

Still in it, darlin'. One more round of bridge tonight. Wish us luck.

Can we come watch you play?

Not tonight! Quarter-, semi-, and finals tomorrow. Better action.

But what if, by some circumstance, you don't win tonight, I thought contrarily. Maverick and I meandered home by way of downtown. The construction crew had reduced the mound of snow and filled in the hole. The festive red and white and pink decorations reminded me Valentine's Day was just around the corner, but my daydreaming lasted only until Maverick barked.

Donaldson's bright lights cast yellow trapezoids on the street in front of us. If someone were working, maybe I could pick up my bracelet, so I parked.

Maverick jumped back and forth, and I could almost hear him say, 'friend, friend.' "I suppose you can come. It'll only take a moment, and if they don't want you this time, they'll tell me. Right?"

He bounded from the car so quickly I didn't have time to grab my gloves or phone. He jerked me along behind on his leash. *Who was walking whom?*

I rapped on the glass. When no one answered, I rapped again. A strange feeling of *déjà vu* flooded my chest and I found it difficult to take a deep breath. I secured Maverick's leash, lest he decide to race inside without me, and tentatively pulled on the cold silver handle. The door squawked as it opened.

"Hello," my raspy voice called. I cleared my throat. "Anybody here?"

Maverick continued to yank me between the showcases glittering under the vivid illumination toward the backroom and the top of the stairs.

"Liselle? William? Helen?"

Maverick took up a position at the top of the steps and howled, songlike, but howled, nonetheless.

An unsteady voice rose from the depths. "Maverick, is that you-hoo?"

"Helen? Can we come downstairs?"

"Katie Wilk, c'mon down," she sang, sounding a bit like she'd been imbibing. "I'm just cleaning up."

For safety's sake, my safety, I let the leash flap behind Maverick as he galloped down the steps and I trudged behind, my perfunctory steps thumping on the wooden planks, wondering why she decided to clean on a Saturday evening.

Maverick leaned into Helen's hand as she rustled his ears and muttered, "Good boy, good boy." She looked up. "You scared the dickens out of me. What are you doing here, Katie?"

"I saw all the lights on—"

"It's a bit creepy without them, let me tell you." She reached onto a nearby shelf, seizing a can and sloshing golden liquid over the rim and onto the floor. "Oopsie." She slurped the top of the can.

"I thought I might be able to pick up the bracelet Liselle helped me make today." Heat blew from the vents in the ceiling, and I unbuttoned my jacket.

"Want some?" She held out what remained of a six-pack from a local brewery, and I shook my head. Helen turned back to the desk and rifled through the white envelopes lined up in a small metal tray. She dumped the contents onto the desk, carefully read the lines on the front, and returned them one by one. "Nothing here, and I don't know where else she would've put it."

"What are you doing here tonight, Helen?"

She swung the can to and fro like a pendulum. "Pat left the basement in complete disarray."

I scanned the room. Identical boxes fit tightly together like bricks on the tidy shelves. Shiny black plastic bags lined the empty trash receptacles. Under the scent of malt, chlorine perfumed the air. She followed my disbelieving eyes as they wandered to the pristine workbench top, devoid of tools.

"I'll need what I brought with me when I start my new job." She pouted. "I found my things and only took what belongs to me. I didn't take anything else, but I straightened out the place."

The contents rattled as she opened a drawer and pulled out one of several small flat toolboxes. She slid the catch and revealed tiny screwdrivers filling every slot in graduated sizes. "These belong to Liselle." She ran her index finger over the smallest instrument. "She does fine work, and she'll need them if she stays open." She replaced the box. "I even disconnected that evil power switch until they figure out who killed Pat." Her eyes misted. She guzzled the rest of the contents.

"Where are you off to?"

She hiccupped and meticulously positioned the can on the shelf, manhandled a broom, and swept together a small mound of debris. "I'm still evaluating the possibilities."

"You haven't accepted another job yet?" She swept more vigorously. "What's with all the white stuff? It looks like it came from a beach." Helen shrugged, reached for a dustpan, and stumbled.

"Let me help." I put out my hand and collected the dustpan, and she finished brushing the floor. Curiosity got the better of me. I touched the tip of my thumb to the white residue. I did think twice, but tasted it anyway.

THIRTY-NINE

Mr. Simonson had said salt increased conductivity of electricity. In my mind, with the lack of fingerprints and the flipped switch, the salt was one more element, solidifying premeditation in Donaldson's death. I tasted again to make sure.

"Helen, who do you think killed Pat?"

"I don't know. He could be a real pain in the neck. If you let him get to you, he could cut you to the core."

"Did he do that to you?"

She thought for a minute before answering. "He was unpredictable. If you played his game, he'd be pleasant."

"That's why you played the infographics, isn't it?"

"Partly. I'm going to miss him. When he was content and unchallenged, he was a brilliant vender and could sell anything. Cream to a milk cow. Black paint to a crow. You name it. The more he sold, the more satisfied he became, and we all made out better." She clasped her hand over her mouth and hiccupped. "Excuse me. But if something wasn't going the way he wanted, and I interpreted too many of the infographics without asking for help, or sold too much more than he did, he'd find a reason to fire me." My eyes must've given away my astonishment. "He'd hire me back within the hour," she giggled.

Every time? Maybe the last time was the very last time.

"I guess he planned on being the best thief too, if he was leaving with the diamonds, but it didn't work out that way."

Sweat beaded on my back. *Was I in a creepy basement with a crazy murderer who'd been cleaning up the scene of her crime?* My knees turned to jelly. I needed to talk to Amanda. I reached for my phone and patted my jacket and my pants pockets.

"What are you looking for?" She gulped what remained of her drink.

"I guess I left my phone in my car. It's about time for me to check in with Dad. He gets worried when I'm not home." I inched my way toward the steps.

"I saw him at the Community Center playing bridge with Ida."

Caught. "Was that today? I forgot. Were you there as an observer or contender?" Dad hadn't wanted me to watch, I thought sourly, and I eased closer to the way out.

"I love bridge, and I watch any chance I get. It's cerebral. Ida and your dad know how to finesse a strong finish even when their cards don't support their crazy bids." She wobbled. "I'm all through here. I'll walk out with you."

She waited for Maverick and me to climb the stairs and turned off the lights behind us.

"Thanks for keeping me company." She slurred her words.

"No problem."

We sat in my car until my heart beat its regular rhythm. If she wanted to get rid of me, she could have, so maybe Helen wasn't the killer, or maybe she was a really fine actress.

"Let's go home, Mav."

My mind turned somersaults, wracking my brain with the clues to Donaldson's murder. Neither Ricky nor Henry killed him. Helen could have, but would she? We crept down Maple Street and jolted to a stop in front of Ida's lovely residence, confused. Every window was lit.

I rubbernecked to peek in the windows as we crawled down the driveway and behind the house but couldn't see so much as a flaming red hair. I parked on the cement pad, and Maverick and I jogged to my entry. Kool & the Gang's *Celebration* blasted when I opened the door, and Maverick danced into the kitchen, seeming to step to the music, right up to Ida as she raised her arms above her head and spun on her toes. Dad leaned against the counter, clapping hands and wagging his head from side to side, beaming the grin of the victor.

Miming to turn down the volume had its desired effect. At the end of the song, Ida collapsed onto a cracked vinyl chair, fanning her flushed face. She plucked a silver business card holder from the torn bits of wrapping paper and shook it at me, grinning. Dad brought three tall glasses of water to the table.

"We made the quarterfinals." Dad smiled so big his eyes became tiny slits above his cheeks.

"I figured as much," I said.

"We thought we'd celebrate tonight because tomorrow

we'll have stiffer competition, and we wanted to have our party on a high note. What did you do today?"

With too many things to enumerate, I said, "Same old, same old."

Dad caught my lips curl up, and his left eyebrow rose. "What's that about?"

"I unpacked my last moving box and found some precious photos of Charles and even some of ZaZa. It bridged the gap to so many good memories."

Ida raised her index finger. "I have some older annuals I'm donating to the historical center, but maybe I'll take another look through them too." She sprang from her seat and scurried through our adjoining door, her newly colored red curls bouncing in her wake. She returned moments later, balancing a column of books resembling the Leaning Tower of Pisa. I nabbed the top half, and the imbalance nearly toppled her. She staggered, and the bottom half of the pile thumped to a halt in front of Dad.

"Do we know anyone?" he asked, picking up the top copy and reading the spine— *Cougar Compendium.*

Ida sorted through the mound and smiled when she located a particular book. Her finger ran down the list of names in the index, and she fanned the pages, alighting on one. As she tossed the open book in front of Dad, she pointed at a photo and said, "There." She crossed her arms over her tummy with a *harrumph.*

I peered over Dad's shoulder, and we both laughed aloud. The photo featured the stern face of Pete Erickson and the caption below read, 'Holding the hand of his Homecoming date—the anatomy class skeleton.'

Our search turned up sports snaps, photo finishes, candids, club memberships, and a freshman class headshot of Pete abounding with curly dark hair, a forbidding grimace, and shining impish eyes. We flipped the pages back and forth and located the vintage picture of Ida among the staff and teased her mercilessly. I sobered when I found a photo of Lenny Capsner, accepting a foot-high award from the industrial ed department, flanked by two bespectacled students displaying palm-sized trophies. He was so young and pleased with himself. I set the annual to one side for a longer look later.

By the time we closed the first, Ida had tagged pages in two more annuals. One of the pages displayed gorgeous silver jewelry modeled by the artist, none other than a bubbly Liselle Anne. Another highlighted a formally dressed couple I hardly recognized—a skinny, junior Gregory Teasdale wore a light gray tux, and his sun-bronzed sophomore date Susie Kelton wore a forest green dress and cradled a single white calla lily.

Ida pawed through the rest of her annuals, swiping pages, laughing or tearing up, and lined them up in chronologic order.

"Time flies." Ida said and collected half her treasure trove of bygone images. "If we want to be fresh tomorrow, Harry, we'd best be off to the Land of Nod. I'll be back for the other half—"

"Or I can deliver them to you now," Dad said, yawning.

One yawn begets another, and soon we all admitted to our need for unencumbered peaceful repose.

"What do you have planned for tomorrow, darlin'?"

"After church," I began, knowing I'd be expected to attend and pray for their victory. "I've got something to pick up from Donaldson's, and mock trial rehearses at two."

"What time do you begin tomorrow?"
Ida said, "Finals are at four. Be there."
"Or be—" she cut me off with that look.

FORTY

Ida, Dad, and I attended early Mass, enjoying the message in the succinct homily, the fabulous music, the bell choir, our student vocalists, and Ida's light and airy homemade donuts served with coffee in the parish hall after Mass. The lively discussion on our way home revolved around the high quality of our latest service, and Ida offered up a prayer for a successful afternoon of cards.

Dad had a cup of the best coffee in the world. I wished them luck, and they were on their way.

In the intervening hours, I could get into a lot of trouble if I didn't carefully organize my time. I reviewed my jumbled notes, checked my gradebook, tossed the postcard describing an upcoming conference, penciled in a possible mock trial meet, finally read the thank yous from our mock trial students hoping there weren't any surprises, and examined the manilla envelope.

At first, I thought it was empty—nothing inside. I held it open and shook it and a ring that looked an awful lot like Susie's spilled into my hand. I turned the envelope back and forth looking for the identity of the sender, any indication from whence it came, but there was nothing.

I called Amanda.

"Chief West," she said brusquely.

"You didn't look at the caller ID, did you?"

After a beat, while I was certain she checked the ID, she said, "What do you want now, Katie?"

I took a deep breath. "I received an envelope last week. I just opened it."

"Yes." Her patience had worn very thin with me.

"There is a ring inside, and I think it belongs to Gregory Teasdale." There. I said it, but I didn't hear any retort. "Chief?"

"Who's it from?"

"I don't know. It arrived in my school mailbox. There's no stamp, no return address, nothing written on it anywhere."

"Bring it in, Katie. I'll have Mr. Teasdale come in to identify it. I suppose your fingerprints are all over it."

"Yes, but—"

"And no one else was there to see you open this envelope?"

"No, no one." I thought I might as well lay it all out. "Did you know there was salt on the floor at Donaldson's. I tasted it."

"You what? You're getting to be a regular pain …"

"Sorry."

"So am I, Katie. It's already been a long day. Come to

the station and tell me about the salt. Let's hope we can get some evidence from the ring or envelope and close this case."

I packed the ring in a tissue and slid it back into the envelope, then placed the envelope in a plastic bag to prevent further contamination, though there couldn't be much more. I'd dragged it around in my briefcase for days. But one could hope. Stepping out, I lifted my face to let the warmth of the sun wash over it, and I was glad I hauled Maverick with me. It had been a long winter.

Amanda collected the plastic bag without a word and left me standing open-mouthed in the entryway. She never let me teach her about salt water and electricity.

I had nothing to do before practice but pick up my bracelet, so I drove the short distance to Donaldson's. It was scheduled to open in seven minutes. We jumped out of the car and made a loop around the corner, through the parking lot, back to Main Street, past other downtown establishments in time to see William turning the key.

"Is Liselle coming in today, William?" I called.

"Yes, but what are you doing here? I don't think …" As he eyed Maverick, I recognized him from Ida's annuals. He'd been one of the runners-up to Lenny in the high school industrial education competition. He looked a bit different, and I understood why he changed his name.

Liselle's voice sang out from behind us. "Hey, you good looking guy," she said, a little breathless from jogging across the street. The budding smile slipped from William's lips when she continued with, "What a good doggie. Good to see you, Katie. You've come for your bracelet, I'll bet. She's a regular artiste, William. We might have to hire her." His eyes darkened.

"Come on in." She pirouetted and skipped happily

through the store. "I'll get out the displays, William."

"I can do it, Liselle."

"No, that's all right. I have to get back into the swing of things. Your bracelet is on my desk, Katie. Wait until you see the finished product." She rubbed her hands together in anticipation.

Maverick led, so he couldn't trip either one of us, and Liselle waxed eloquently about the job we'd done. But when she landed on the bottom step, she gasped.

"What's wrong?"

"Someone's been here. I've been robbed." She turned around to race up the stairs.

"Wait," I said as I touched her arm. "Helen was here last night. She wanted to leave everything in tip top shape." I rushed to the workbench and pulled on the drawer. I held up several small toolboxes, fanning them like cards. "She said she wanted to collect her tools, but she organized yours, so you'd be ready to take over."

Her eyes flooded with tears. "Why didn't she tell me? How'd you know?"

"I was driving by last night and all the lights were on…"

Liselle snickered. "That's Helen, afraid of her own shadow."

"She'd been drinking a bit, but she had good intentions."

"The best." Liselle wiped the tip of her nose. "I don't know what I'm going to do without her."

Liselle spun the dial on the safe lock, and the door swung open. She removed two trays and carried them upstairs. "I'll get William started and then show you your work of art."

Liselle disappeared upstairs, and Maverick jumped at the contents of the safe. "Stop that." I said in a hushed tone. "Leave it."

But he didn't. He danced out of my reach and back, pawing at the interior of the safe, dodging in and out. Finally, he released the latch on the fridge door and nudged the freezer compartment open. "Oh, that horrible cheese smell, is that it?" Before I could close the door, Maverick caught the edge of an old-fashioned stainless steel ice cube tray with one of his nails, and it clattered to the floor, cracked cubes scattering right and left. I stooped to scoop them up, but one caught my eye. On the floor, between the halves of frozen water, I picked up four smaller pieces of ice.

Maverick rumbled. I whirled to the sound of steps behind me. William stood on the bottom stair with one finger to his lips. Maverick barked at the gun in his other hand, and I wrapped my arm around my dog, my lifeline.

FORTY-ONE

William Dix, aka Ray Proflasczco, whispered harsh words. "Don't say anything or you're dead. Keep him quiet." He called up the stairs. "Liselle, why don't you get us some coffee from Sip and Savor. Katie will help me set out the displays."

"What if someone steps in?"

"We'll be right up."

"I'll be back in a jiff. William, I know you love their donuts. Katie, do you partake?"

He waggled the end of the gun. "Sure," I yelled. "I'll take two." My voice sounded shaky to my ears, but William didn't seem to notice.

The exit bell dinged.

"Why didn't you just let it go? You're too nosy." *Where*

have I heard that before? "I had it all worked out. I'd help Liselle get it together, pretending to buy diamonds out of the funds I've saved up to buy a store of my own, and she'd finally see me for the gentleman jeweler I am."

Like that'd ever happen.

William's face turned purple, and he growled at me.

Had I said that out loud?

Maverick snarled. I scratched between his ears, murmuring, "Shh, it's okay." William stepped to the sink, and I noticed the exclamation point on his boots. He kicked a pipe loose and turned on the water. It gushed and within seconds lapped at my feet.

"Toss me the leash." I hesitated. "Now. I don't have all day."

I coiled, ready to spring and threw it so he had to bend over to pick up the end, but he was lightning quick. He knotted it around the bottom leg of the metal shelving, shortening the leash, dragging Maverick away from me, and cinching it tight. Maverick howled. William pointed the gun. "Shut him up."

I didn't want to find out if he knew how to shoot. "Quiet, Maverick," I said gently. He listened, looking at me with sad eyes, not understanding. "How did you do it?"

He secured the knot on Maverick's restraint. "When I started a year ago, I was trying to set a gorgeous stone, but it flew out of my tweezers. We looked forever, and I expected to be fired on the spot, but Pat was in a good mood. Said everyone was entitled to one mistake, the stone was insured. I could keep my job, but I couldn't let it happen again. I eventually found the stone and sold it on the side for quite a bundle which I parlayed into six lab grown diamonds. I was going to quit while I was ahead, but it was so easy. Pat never checked. He would sell his stones, and I set them. I pocketed the natural diamonds. Then I saw the way he treated his wife. He was an ogre. I've known Liselle Anne forever." He got a dreamy look.

"Why did you kill him?"

"At first, he thought Kelton stole his diamonds, and he was going to make her pay." Even as the water gushed around his feet, and William paced, the distorted safety symbol on his shoes was visible. "Then Lenny came to get money Liselle Anne owed. Kelton complained too vehemently to have stolen his stones, and Pat put two and two together. He hadn't recognized me until then. He hadn't really looked."

"Lenny remembered you too. That's why he didn't reach out and shake your hand."

William squinted his brooding eyes. Maverick yapped and pulled at the leash but couldn't get loose. "Lenny heard Kelton complain. He knew her. Said she was a good egg and wanted me to fix it for her. I knew where Pat kept it, so I gave Lenny the ring. Her ring."

And he gave it to me. "But you and Liselle have alibis."

William sniggered. "She didn't need the alibi. I did."

My forehead bunched. "You lied about the church bell chiming so we'd think you were where you could hear it."

William snickered and went on. "Liselle didn't want anyone to know she was talking to her sponsor."

I shook my head. "Henry Mullhern was hospitalized …" Puzzle pieces fell into place. "Liselle called her sponsor. Although he didn't answer his phone, someone else did and neither one wanted to out the other. Liselle mentioned the person she talked to would never spill the beans."

"That was Kelton. She answered the phone, and while she talked Liselle Anne off the gambling edge,

Helen left for lunch, and Pat confronted me. He gave me an ultimatum. Helen came back from lunch, fixed the engraving, and he sent her out for celebratory snacks while I rigged the basement. I called him down and told him the bag of stones had fallen behind his desk and well, you know the rest. Your fatal reenactment to test your theory will be so sad."

I stepped back from the rising water. "Two of the last notations encoded in Donaldson's journal were 'Watch phreauphlapstkeau.' 'Flash is up to his old tricks.' I only had Liselle's word that Patrick meant Lenny, but you're Flash, Ray Proflasczco."

"How do you know my name?" He sloshed through the water, taking menacing steps my way.

"I recognized you from a *Cougar Compendium*. You've done a second-rate job on your disguise. Pat was taunting you—your second-place finish."

William's eyes flared. "I should have been first. I was the only one who knew salt water conducted electricity better than tap."

"He never appreciated seconds, did he? But what happened to Lenny?"

"Lenny knew too much. I couldn't risk having him talk to anybody. I couldn't get up enough speed when I hit him, but then I rigged the electronics on his drip. He would've slipped away." His fingers mimed a bird flitting away. "But Kelton stepped in and caught it. I bided my time and pulled the plug just long enough."

His voice hardened. "On your knees," he ordered. "I want you soaking in water."

Maverick yanked hard. The entire wall of shelving groaned and a book looking a lot like Patrick's journal fell from the shelf. William grabbed it and slid it into his back pocket. "Yeah, I smoked out the old broad and stole it. Helen unknowingly gave me a play by play, and I thought he might have written everything down in that book." He sneered. "Turns out I was wrong."

William stepped toward the staircase. I prayed with all my heart and soul Helen, even in her inebriated state, knew her electric Ps and Qs and had disconnected the demonic switch, and Maverick remembered our latest cue.

"Say goodnight, Gracie," William taunted, his voice a sinister grating sound.

I cued Maverick out of William's sightline. He flipped the switch, and at the same time I raised my pointer. I stiffened at the visceral image of a victim of electrocution, grunted as one might, and toppled forward into the water as the lights went out. The splash next to me sounded like Maverick played dead and dropped at the same time.

The entry chimed from above. William stamped on my leg and onto the steps, climbing up two at a time. I counted a fast five seconds, raised my head, grabbed my pained thigh, and came nose to nose with a grinning retriever.

Saints be praised. Maverick hopped to standing. I unclipped his leash.

I put my forefinger to my lips and whispered, "We've got to get out of here, Maverick." I patted my pockets and gave up when I saw my phone lying in the water, but I did see the ice cube tray and thought, why not? The diamond studded popsicles lined my jacket pockets and clinked as we headed to the storage room with the infographics lining the walls. The drawer bucked and jerked as I pulled until I could wedge my fingers in and drag out the three keys. My hands shook as I attempted to fit each. None worked.

I concentrated and tried again. The second key opened the panel door to the warren of safety tunnels.

Maverick's paws clung to the edge. "Go, go," I urged. He resisted, second guessing the gloom, and I lifted his backside to shove him through the opening. Before I could clamber after him, I saw a gyrating beam of light and heard wailing from behind us. William had returned. I'd never get through in time.

"Find help," I cued. He waved his tail and flew through Bella's storeroom. I hurriedly closed and locked the panel. The key jammed. I sagged against the door.

Creeping along the wall, I listened for the sound of William's feet slapping through the water across the cold cement floor or a beam of light dancing on the wall. I frantically searched for a weapon, something, despairing as my eyes adjusted to the blackness, finding an empty cavernous nothing. I knocked into the brick wall and a sharp pain bit into my upper arm. I dug in my pocket and pulled out ZaZa's stiletto.

Gripping the inches-long heel, dagger-like, gave me the promising illusion of survival. I kept my respiration light and strained my ears to find him. If he were moving, I wasn't hearing him. Light shifted past the opening. I raised the slender spike and hoped it was worth the price.

William crossed the threshold with his eye on the key in the lock. The heel came down hard and fast. He grunted. The gun and light clanked to the floor. I raced around the corner, headed for freedom, but he grabbed my foot and pulled me down. I rolled over and kicked at his face—a Jane-trick I never thought I'd use.

He let loose long enough for me to crawl to the stairs, stand, and make my getaway. My speed ratcheted up a notch when I shot a look in his direction and saw him searching for the gun.

I barreled through the empty store to the front door.

It wouldn't budge. I checked behind me for William and all around for something to break the glass, fixating on a three-rung metal ladder. I grabbed the feet and swung the top cap against the door. It juddered in my hands. I struck again. The reverberations in my arms rocked my teeth. Three strikes and I would be out, I thought, listening to William crash up the stairs. I raised the ladder again and came face to face with a terrified Liselle. Her key rattled in the lock. Maverick pawed the door. I dropped the ladder. A short prayer urged haste.

FORTY-TWO

The door banged open. At the same time, I heard a crack behind me. Liselle hauled me onto the sidewalk and next door into Bella's, Maverick cantering at her side.

"Lock the door, Bella," I panted. "Why did you come back, Liselle?"

"Kindra said you'd never ever eat a donut not made by Ida. I wanted to find out what was going on and ran into Maverick—off leash. What happened?" Liselle said, confused and angry.

I ushered us into the shadows.

"Where's William?" Liselle asked again. "Was that a gunshot?"

I caught my breath and said, "William killed Pat."

Liselle let out a snort. "Right." She looked at my face,

pulled out her phone, and punched in some numbers. "Chief, William Dix is holed up in the store, and I think he shot at Katie." She listened for a moment. "I can put her on."

I took the proffered phone. "Amanda? Dix killed Donaldson."

"We're on our way, Katie." Amanda sounded resigned and on the move. "Lock all the entrances and I mean all." Bella heard her insistent order and moved to the back room.

The phone clicked. Only then did I detect the rumble in my dog's throat. Bella returned, roughly nudged by the muzzle of William's gun. He'd used the same passageway through which Maverick escaped. I placed a calming hand on Maverick's head and cued down behind the showcase, out of sight.

"Hello, again." William smirked, and the hairs on my neck stood on end.

Bella's eyes were bright orbs. Liselle's face turned to stone. I stared at the gun which he used to direct us into the back room. "Sorry, Liselle Anne. It's you or me now." When William turned his back, Maverick charged. Taken unaware, William crossed his arms in front of his face, and my dog latched onto the gun arm. The weapon fired. Bella rushed to the front. Liselle and I stormed the killer, each aiming for an appendage. He fell backwards, bucking and screaming, but with Maverick standing on his chest, barking, Liselle gripping his left arm, and me on the right, the weapon crashed to the floor.

A gloved hand picked it up.

"You killed Pat," a small voice said. "You're going to the devil." The gun shook in Fredericka Lattimore's hands, and Liselle and I rolled away from William.

"Ricky, what are you doing?" I said calmly, afraid she might accidentally shoot someone other than William. I hooked Maverick's collar and pulled him to me.

"I came to apologize, but I saw this degenerate grab Pat's journal, and I followed him." Her head tilted to the right, and she took aim down the barrel. "He took Pat's future."

"He did. Don't let him take yours."

Tears cascaded down her cheeks.

"Are you alone?"

"I left Dr. Erickson in the jewelry store looking at rings."

I slowly rose and reached out. The gun twirled around her finger. I stepped close, cradled her shoulders, and secured the gun at the same time Chief West walked in the front door with three officers, weapons drawn.

"It's okay," I said, offering Amanda the offending gun, grip first.

Pete entered on Ronnie Christianson's heels, surveyed the scene, and immediately guided Ricky out of Bella's.

"Never a dull moment," said Amanda. "I'll talk to you later."

Once Liselle and I returned to the store, I dug into my pockets and poured the first handful of dripping diamonds into her hands. Her eyes grew to the size of dinner plates.

The door chimed. Helen stuck her head in and said, "I heard you're looking for good help."

Liselle straightened up and said in a serious voice, "May I see your references?" Seconds later, she laughed so hard, she doubled over. She hugged Helen and said to me. "Let's get your bracelet."

She handed me the gorgeous bangle, and my mouth dropped open. I rotated it in my hand. The silver sparkled.

"Go ahead. Put it on."

I slid the wide silver band onto my wrist. "Thank you."

"No. Thank you."

FORTY-THREE

The wedding happened on short notice. All the more common local reception venues had already been reserved, but Ida pulled a few strings, and the caravan of celebratory honking vehicles escorted the new bride and groom to the Midwest Minnesota History Center.

Jane and I arrived together and volunteered to help Ida with the catering, but she backed us against the wall and out of her way when Lorelei and Kindra showed up with a team of students dressed in white shirts and black pants, ready to serve.

My forehead scrunched, and before I could ask, Lorelei said, "Tuition money."

Kindra smirked. "Concert tickets."

Carlee tied back her long blue-black hair and donned a

white linen apron. "This must be costing a fortune." Her gray eyes took in the elegant place settings, white linen, and glorious floral arrangements.

Ida bustled and, while giving cues to the students, said, "The addition of the *Titanic* exhibit to the history center has provided another venue for large gatherings, but this will be its first wedding, so the board of the history center decided to use this reception as an ad to promote future gatherings."

Jane winked. Ida served as president of that board.

"I think we've got this under control," Ida said. "Enjoy your evening." I started to protest. "I know where you're seated if we need your help. Get out of here."

ZaZa knew no one else, and Susie had seated her at the table with Jane, Drew, Pete, Ida, and me. Rubbing the bare foot, she'd wriggled out of her new stilettos, ZaZa said, "Why didn't Susie just give her alibi? Why didn't she tell the chief where she was?"

Drew explained the rules of HIPAA and patient privacy and applauded Susie's integrity. ZaZa shook her head, disbelieving. Pete and Jane rolled their eyes.

After a tender welcome from Susie's dad, under Ida's astute direction, the kids served the appetizers, salad and breads, potatoes, Brussel sprouts, and tenderloin seamlessly. The scrumptious food garnered effusive compliments to the chef from every single guest at the small gathering. Susie glowed. The grin never left Tiny's face.

Ida finally joined us when Susie and Tiny cut into the Red Velvet Cake to the delight of the guests. As our forks scraped every last crumb from the royal blue-and-gold White Star Line replica plates, Pete took the microphone and rose.

"Good evening. Thanks to Ida for the lovely meal—

" Pete laughed at the expected uproarious applause interrupting his prepared speech. "To the history center for providing the venue and to all of you attending. I've known Gregory since he was seven, and he was just a whiny kid I babysat. Look at him now. He's blushing." The audience hummed appreciatively. "I've worked with Susie and know she's going to keep him on the straight and narrow. Thank you both for finally getting it right." I wouldn't have predicted Susie's mom to whistle and cheer, but I guess she'd come around after Susie accepted Tiny's proposal. "I hope we all learn to laugh hard, take all life has to offer, live with gusto, and love with all we've got." When his eyes met mine, I swallowed hard.

"Let's raise a glass—be it water …" Pete nodded to Susie. "Wine, beer, or the Teasdale Signature cocktail. To Susie and Gregory."

His words continued, but my concentration drifted. Dad read my mind. He took my hand. "One day at a time, darlin'. See what life brings." I had so many great memories and added more every day.

DJs Galen and Brock provided a full range of music. Dad and I danced a polka and a waltz; he and Ida danced a wicked salsa. The dance floor vibrated, and we jiggled and wiggled and shimmied until ten when the groom raised his hand and silenced the tunes. "My bride and I are going to call it a night. We love you all. Thanks for being here with us, and please stay until the music stops at the witching hour."

Susie sought Pete and gave him a special embrace. Tiny stood behind her, looking down at his shoes, drawing circles on the parquet floor. She turned to me and clasped my shoulders. Her eyes drilled into mine for a few seconds, and she dragged me into a hug. "Make him happy," she whispered. "Or else." She released me, and with a quick wave and smile, they disappeared.

Much of the crowd dispersed when the Teasdales left, but the dancing die-hards remained until Brock and Galen wrapped up the night with a few romantic songs for Valentine's Day including John Legend's *All of Me*, the Temptations' *My Girl*, and Suki Waterhouse singing *Valentine*. The dance lessons Pete and I had taken at the beginning of the school year paid off. My head rested on his shoulder, and we swayed.

But when the opening bars of Ed Sheeran's *Perfect* played over the speakers at midnight, Drew dropped to tie his shoe and Pete pulled me from the dance floor. A spotlight hit Jane's blond head, and she raised her hand to shield her eyes from the glaring light. Drew gazed at her so tenderly I gasped. In his hand he held out a glistening ring. I watched my friend through tears of joy. Her quizzical expression fell away, and her hands covered her cheeks before she beamed and nodded. Drew stood, grabbed her, and lifted her above his shoulders, swinging her in a circle. They kissed to seal the deal with passion for all to see.

"Yes, yes," Jane repeated, planting many more tiny smooches on his lips and eyes and cheeks and forehead.

Liselle directed Helen to take photographs of the happy couple, sliding from side to side for the perfect shot. Henry looked on, nodding in approval.

At the end of the song, the house lights came on, and the remaining guests swarmed Jane, wishing her congratulations, and smashing her in a group hug.

Jane held me for a very long time. "It's happening," she cried. "I'm so happy." My cheeks hurt from smiling; I was elated for her. "Will you be my maid of honor?"

My grin got bigger, and my eyes clouded. "I'd be honored."

Drew shook hands with Brock and Galen and passed them an envelope I hoped was full of more 'tuition money.' When Drew was alone, Pete clasped his hand and dragged him into a bear hug, and they exchanged a few words through huge smiles.

Jane and Drew departed, and I realized my ride home had also vanished. I needn't have worried. The boyish, lopsided expression Pete wore led me to believe he'd helped Drew plan the entire event.

"Need a ride?"

"As a matter of fact, I do. Do you know where I can get one?"

He offered his arm and we strolled to the parking lot.

"Pretty gutsy of Drew."

"He was fairly sure of himself."

"Did Drew ask you to stand up for him?"

"Yes. And Jane asked you, so I guess we'll be a couple."

I slipped on the ice, and Pete tensed, catching me before I fell.

"Thanks." We stood face to face next to his truck, under the yellow circle from the parking lot light, breathing the same air, searching. I got lost in his eyes and his lips met mine. A delicious tingle swept from my toes to my nose until the rumble of a distant engine broke the spell. We slowly broke apart, and he gave me a hand up into his cab.

FORTY-FOUR

After Sunday service, exhausted, Ida returned to bed. Dad laughed as I hummed "I Could Have Danced All Night" from *My Fair Lady,* and flounced around the kitchen, pouring two cups of coffee and getting out the ingredients, pretending to make an omelet which turned out to be cheesy blackened scrambled eggs. I set the plates on the table.

"When's Jane's big day?"

I stopped humming. "I don't know." I retrieved cream and sugar, added them to my beverage, and inhaled the fragrance before sipping.

His utensils clattered on the empty plate. "Where will the wedding be held, here or Georgia?"

"I don't know that either."

"What *do* you know?" He sipped his beverage and closed his eyes.

"I know Jane is happy, and I get to stand up in her wedding, wherever it is." I kissed his cheek, gave him a huge hug, and wriggled a happy dance. "And Pete gave me the name of a great physician for you. We can set up an appointment—"

Dad's phone rang, and he silenced me with the raise of his forefinger. He read the screen, and his lips stretched from ear to ear before he punched the answer button. "Hello, Elizabeth," he said cheerily and walked into his room.

I cleaned the kitchen and emptied the contents of my briefcase onto the kitchen table, organizing the week's to-do list. I'd been remiss in checking emails. I opened the one containing my DNA results and heard Ida's doorbell ring. I knew she needed rest. Cooking for the wedding crowd, even with outstanding help, required a lot of work, so I breezed through the connecting door and answered the summons.

"May I help you?" I asked tentatively, peeking through the huge flakes of snow drifting like downy white feathers, obscuring the world just feet into Ida's yard.

The petite, young woman on the top step had a beautiful clear face, bright blue eyes, and mousy-brown flyaway hair, much like my own. She was bundled in a long dark wool coat with a red-and-black swirly-patterned scarf around her neck. She inclined her head, as if to ask a question.

"I'm sorry if you were expecting Ida. She had a long weekend and is taking it easy."

"No," she said, her eyes entreating.

Dad walked through the door between the apartments, his face ashen, his eyes downcast.

The woman looked at my dad and said, "Harry?"

His eyes caught hers and opened wide. She tilted her head and looked at me again. "Hi, sis."

Teasedale Signature Wedding Cocktail

Layer by slowly pouring over the back of a spoon:

Layer 1: 1 oz sweetened condensed milk

Layer 2: 1 oz Liquor 43

Layer 3: 1 ½ oz of a coffee flavored cocktail

  Black Russian

  1 oz vodka

  ½ oz Kahlua

Layer 4: 1 oz amaretto

Layer 5: Milk foam as for a latte

A dusting of chocolate or cinnamon

A curl of lemon peel

After serving and showing off the layered cocktail, stir until well mixed.

* * *

Ida's Baked Bean Hotdish

Brown:

3 pounds of hamburger

½ pound of bacon cut into 2-inch pieces

Pour off grease

Sauté:

1 chopped onion

Add:

1 tsp dry mustard

½ C ketchup

6 T brown sugar

2 T molasses

1 large can of pork and beans

Mix together. Heat in the oven at 350° for 1 hour. Enjoy.

Thank you for taking the time to read *Diamonds, Diesel, & Doom*. If you enjoyed it please tell your friends, and I would be so grateful if you would consider posting a review. Word of mouth is an author's best friend, and very much appreciated.

Thank you,

Mary Seifert

What's coming up next in Katie's life?

Katie Wilk will forgive her dad eventually, but she isn't ready to hear him explain how she'd come to have a sister of whom she'd never heard. When her plans to get away for spring break fall through, she decides she doesn't wear 'green with envy' well and settles for tackling her sky-high to-be-read pile of books until one of her students makes a heartbreaking request.

Choosing any getaway is better than staying home pouting, or is it?

* * *

Get all the books in the
Katie & Maverick Series!

Maverick, Movies, & Murder
Rescues, Rogues, & Renegade
Tinsel, Trials, & Traitors
Santa, Snowflakes, & Strychnine
Fishing, Festivities, & Fatalities
Diamonds, Diesel, & Doom

Get a collection of free recipes from Mary—
Scan the QR code to find out how!

Visit Mary's website: MarySeifertAuthor.com/
Facebook: facebook.com/MarySeifertAuthor
Twitter: twitter.com/mary_seifert
Instagram: instagram.com/maryseifert/
Follow Mary on BookBub and Goodreads too!

Made in the USA
Monee, IL
04 August 2023

40457109R00180